ARCANE TRANSPORTER

COLLISION COURSE

JAMI GRAY

Cover Art: Deranged Doctor Design, www.derangeddoctordesign.com

Publisher: Celtic Moon Press First edition, 2023
ISBN: 978-1-948884-69-3 (ebook) ISBN: 978-1-948884-70-9 (print)

SIGN UP FOR FREE READS FROM JAMI!

Join Jami's newsletter to be the first to hear about new releases, free books, special prices and other nifty events.

Sign up at: https://www.subscribepage.com/jami-gray-books

WHAT READERS SAY...

About Arcane Transporter:
"Taking a refreshing approach to fantasy magic, this fast-paced, economical thriller is told from a highly likable perspective." —Red Adept Editing

About PSY-IV Teams:
"This story is an emotional roller coaster, from betrayal, anger, fear, love..." —InD'tale Magazine

About the Kyn Kronicles:
"...a fantastic paranormal action novel is quite possibly the best book I've read this year. I could not put it down, and had to exercise serious self-control to keep from staying up all night to finish it." — The Romance Reviews

About Fate's Vultures:
"...if you like your characters with a bit more bite, with secrets, with hidden agendas, and all those sorts of things, and your worlds are a far more deadlier place, then this is for you." — Archaeolibrarian

ALSO BY JAMI GRAY

ARCANE WONDERLAND

Last Call

Bitter Spirits

Rune & Tonic

ARCANE TRANSPORTER

Ignition Point (*Prequel Novella*)

Grave Cargo

Risky Goods

Lethal Contents

Collision Course

Blind Spot

Terminal Drift

THE KYN KRONICLES

Shadow's Edge

Shadow's Soul

Shadow's Moon

Shadow's Curse

Shadow's Dream

Shadow's Fall

Tangled in Shadows (*Short Story Collection*)

FATE'S VULTURES

Lying in Ruins

Beg for Mercy

Caught in the Aftermath

Fear the Reaper

PSY-IV TEAMS

Hunted by the Past

Touched by Fate

Marked by Obsession

Fractured by Deceit

Linked by Deception

BOX SETS

PSY-IV Teams Box Set I (Books 1-3)

The Collapse: Fate's Vultures (Books 1-4)

The Kyn Kronicles Box Set (Books 1-6)

Arcane Transporter Box Set I (Books 1-3)

Arcane Transporter Box Set II (Books 4-6)

ACKNOWLEDGMENTS

It was a rough year (and then some) and getting through it would not have been possible without the usual suspects who, as ever, have my endless love and appreciation —

My own personal bevy of Knight-in-slightly-Muddy-Armor and Knights in Training - Ben, Ian, and Brendan

My ride and die crew - Diane, Camille, and Dave

And, as always, my brilliantly wonderful readers who keep coming back for more.

Thank you!

Jami

For all those who come out the other side a little battered and a whole lot wiser...

ONE

"LOOK, work with me. I promise I can make it worth your while."

I tightened my grip on the cage's handle and ignored the easily identifiable East Coast accent that couldn't hide the panic bubbling underneath. Instead, I shoved my sunglasses up to the top of my head and met the hard-eyed gaze of the guard who held open the door. I stepped inside the nondescript building and waited until the guard relocked the door behind me before informing him curtly, "Delivery for Beto."

The guard's gaze dropped to the wire cage in my hand.

The fluffy-tailed chipmunk trapped inside curled its lips and did a fairly impressive snarl. "Whatcha lookin' at, uh?"

The guard's eyebrows rose slightly before he casually turned to lead the way, leaving me and the reason for my frayed temper to follow.

My package decided being ignored wasn't working, so he threw his body against the cage and spit out a colorful stream of curses, some of which made my lips twitch. When one particularly strong hit threatened to rip the handle from my grip, I stopped, lifted the cage to eye level, gave it a particularly hard shake, and glared at the foul-mouthed furball. "Try that again, and I'll tase you." I held the beady-eyed glare and added, "Again."

Inhuman black eyes stared back, an unmistakable mix of fury and fear roiling in the inky depths. Its brown-furred body shivered with barely repressed aggression, and its tail rose behind it like a furry dandelion, every hair standing on end. As an intimidation factor, it was hilariously cute in a deranged kind of way.

Still, it wouldn't be me who blinked first.

A whisker twitched then an ear, and finally, it hissed and looked away. I inclined my head, reined in my triumphant grin, and dropped my arm. I straightened the hem of my shirt and gave my silently amused guide a head tilt, telling him we were now good to go.

After a slow, exasperated head shake, I followed the suit-covered back down the hall to the big boss's office. A perfunctory rap of knuckles against wood garnered a muffled response. With a twist of the knob and flex of muscle, my guide politely pushed open the door then held it as I passed through.

I strode into a sun-washed office done in shades of grand importance. The open blinds filling the large windows were not much of a barrier against the late-afternoon sun or the Phoenix heat. Thankfully, the building's air conditioning rivaled a freezer.

The man behind the ritzy desk pushed back his throne-like leather chair and rose. His attention went to the cage I held, and a pleased smile creased his face. "Ah, you found him."

I stifled my initial sarcastic response—the answer was obvious—and carefully set the cage on the gleaming slate-gray desktop, right next to the oversized crystal ball. The small critter inside froze, its tiny paws clutched in front of its chest, its nose twitching wildly, and its beady eyes locked on the man as he took his time coming around the desk.

When Beto finally made it to my side, he lifted the cage and spoke to the trembling miscreant inside, his tone a silky slide of menace. "Señor Nutter, you missed your appointment."

Tiny paws rose in the universal version of "I come in peace" as excuses fell like rain. "Look, Mr. B, I'm sorry, but there was an unavoidable emergency, and—"

Beto cut off the chipmunk's excuses with nothing more than a raised hand.

Mr. N fell mute.

Beto turned his dark, flat gaze to me.

Repressing a shiver, I kept my expression bland.

"Thank you, Ms. Costas, for being so… prompt in retrieving my property. I do hope he wasn't too much trouble."

The last few hours flashed through my mind—chasing the damn squirrel through a crowded dining patio, a cursing server trying to save someone's lunch as I narrowly dodged a face full of food I hadn't ordered, then rushing into the backstreets strewn with noxious elements I didn't want to think about, until finally cornering the damn fur menace in a lone tree that barely held my weight while Mr. N pummeled me with small objects. I gave the politest answer I could. "As much as expected, sir."

"Well, then I look forward to your final invoice." Beto set the cage on the desk, and Mr. N collapsed into a heart-touching ball of trembling fur. It was an act, of course, but it still tugged on my heartstrings. The valley financier held out his hand. "Pleasure doing business with you."

I took his offering and thought about warning him that his fluffy employee might be a bit more than he'd bargained for, but I figured a magically hexed animal deserved to keep a few secrets, especially when dealing with a bigger, badder predator. "And you, sir."

Business concluded, I inclined my head and followed my earlier guide out of the building.

Only when I was safely inside my precious ride, engine rumbling and air conditioner blowing, did I release a long breath and roll the tension out of my shoulders. "Good luck, Beto," I muttered as I reversed out of my parking spot. "You're going to need it."

Because the Chipmunk Mafia was coming—for him and Mr. Nutter.

▚▚▚▚▚▚▚▚▚▚▚▚▚▚▚▚▚▚▚▚▚▚▚

With my scheduled deliveries for the day complete, I wasn't in a rush to get back to the Guild offices. Not that I was punching anyone's clock but mine, but still… it was closing in on a very busy week. Of course, as an independent contractor, I paid my bills with busy weeks. Between my main client, Sabella Rossi, and my newly acquired account with the Arcane Council, my schedule typically stayed nice and booked. However, Sabella was currently out of the country on what she called a "family tour," which allowed me the leeway to take on new clients.

Beto Montenegro, a bigwig in Phoenix's booming construction scene, was one of those new clients. His name was tied to a mix of developments, some of which skimmed the line of ethics by the barest hair. His behavior might bother me on a personal level, but professionally, as long as my clients paid their bills, it wasn't my place to judge how they filled their coffers. That was a philosophy I'd learned during my time with the Arcane Guild, and it carried over into my entrepreneurial venture when I hung up my shingle a few months back.

Rory Costas, Arcane Transporter, Secure Delivery for Your Arcane Needs.

However, regardless of how he earned his money, I would be adding a special handling fee to Beto's final invoice. I had nothing against magically bound creatures, but chasing down a morally corrupt, churlish, wannabe mafia fur menace then trying to dodge a scurry of miniature goodfellas had not been part of the initial delivery agreement. Beto was unaware that Mr. Nutter had decided to increase his coffers by playing both sides rather than simply doing his job—infiltrate the site of Beto's competitor, identify potential weak points on the construction project, and report back. Instead, Mr. Nutter had gotten caught between an irate construction crew and a swarm of furious chipmunks who didn't take kindly to unwelcome visitors in their territory. The combined threat had Mr. N making pawtracks to the dubious hideout at the nearby outdoor mall. Luckily for me, Beto, trusting soul that he was, had magically tagged his furry spy as insurance.

I was sent to the last-known location to pick up the miscreant, where I made a convincing argument for Mr. Nutter's return with the help of a Taser. After I managed to lock the cage door behind Mr. Nutter, I'd quickly discovered it was my turn to evade the fiercely territorial associates determined to eliminate the treacherous snitch. When I hit the lot where I'd left my Mustang, I ran into an entire scurry sniffing around for my dodgy package. It had taken some judicious misdirection to get into my Mustang undetected. It was only when I looked back and saw two furry bodies perched on a nearby bench, giving my ride an evil eye, that I knew our escape wasn't completely clean. Enduring the twenty-minute ride to hand Mr. Nutter over to Beto also meant listening to Mr. N bounce from high-pitched wheedling to colorful threats and back to wheedling.

It was annoying. It was also no longer my problem.

I turned off Fifteenth Avenue and settled in for a tedious

journey through rush-hour traffic. My phone buzzed in its holder. A text flashed across my screen, but it would have to wait. Phoenix drivers were unpredictable at best, maniacs at worst, and I had no intention of risking my ride for a text message. If it was really important, they would call.

My phone rang. I sighed and hit a button on my steering wheel. "Costas."

"Rory?" My best friend's voice filled the speaker.

"Hey, Lena. What's up?"

"You heading to the Guild or home?"

"Guild." I checked my mirrors and hit my turn signal before switching lanes. "I've got some paperwork that I owe Adele, but I should be home in time for game night."

"Yeah, we're going to have to reschedule," she said. "I just got called out to a job over in Carefree and won't be home until late."

"Okay." I drew out the word since neither one of us was the type to be overly concerned with who was home when since our schedules were unpredictable at best.

"I tried calling Evan, but he's not answering."

"Maybe he's on a job?" Since Lena's snuggle bunny was a high-level electro mage, his services were in hot demand.

"Maybe, but if he's at the office, will you let him know?"

"Can do." I glanced at the clock and made some quick calculations. "I should be there in about twenty."

"Thanks."

"Not a problem." There was a mix of frustration and something else I couldn't pin down in her voice. Normally, I wouldn't have pried, but it wasn't just me who was barely home this week. So I took a second then asked, "You okay?"

"I'm good."

I let the silence share my skepticism. Lena knew me well, because she blew out a breath and added, "I'll be fine. How's that?"

"Something I can help with?"

Her exasperated snort filled my speakers. "Can you erase my name from my family's memory banks?"

"Thought that was a done deal." Lena and I had met years ago when she joined the Arcane Guild at thirteen to escape being the emotional pawn between her mother's powerful Arcane Family and her father's possessive First Nations clan. As a desperate solution, it had worked, for a while. Then it hadn't.

"Yeah, well, ever since the whole Trask and Clarke Family debacle, they've been scratching at the door."

I wanted to tell her to ignore them, but we both knew that wasn't really an option. "Do you want me to talk to Sabella? Maybe she can convince them to back off." My employer, who also happened to be my great-aunt, was an even bigger presence in the Arcane world than Lena's family. Maybe too big since it would be like using a nuclear bomb to swat a fly.

That was why I was unsurprised when Lena said, "I appreciate the offer, but no. I'll take care of it."

"Well, let me know if you change your mind."

My phone buzzed again, indicating another caller. I let it roll to voicemail.

"Deal," she agreed. "So, you going to hook up with Mr. Dark and Broody tonight?"

Thinking her description of my rather-fierce honeybunch, Zev Aslanov, was spot on made my lips twitch. "Not yet, but that may change."

"Right, then if I don't see you tonight, make sure there's coffee in the morning."

My lip twitch turned into a full-on grin. "That, I can do." I knew her job as a Key wasn't exactly sunshine and roses. "Be careful."

"Always." With that, she clicked off.

Stuck behind a dust-covered semi-truck at a red light, I considered my options for my now-free evening. Maybe I could convince Zev to take me out on his motorcycle up through the foothills, maybe find some out-of-the-way place to enjoy a night of food and music. That was, if he made it back into town.

As the Cordova Family Arbiter, his schedule was more unpredictable than mine. I drummed my fingers on the steering wheel as I waited for the light to change, debating whether to send him a text when I got home. Normally, I wouldn't hesitate, but he was working, and an interruption at the wrong time could lead to disaster. As if I were channeling a mental mage, my phone rang, and Royal Blood's "Little Monster" erupted from my speakers. I picked up the call. "Hey, I was just thinking about you."

"Should I be worried?" His dark rumble wrapped around me.

I bit off a snort. "No more than usual."

That earned me a quiet chuckle.

The semi in front of me crept forward, and I followed. "Are you done already?"

"Unfortunately, not even close, which was why I was calling." There was no missing the regret in his voice. "Plus, I was going to leave a message since you didn't pick up."

"I was talking to Lena." *Damn, guess I'm on my own tonight.* I stifled a sigh, because we were both cognizant that our professional responsibilities didn't play well with a social life. "Let me guess—the meeting didn't go well?"

"Actually, it went better than expected, which is why we're now staying overnight. They want to do a celebratory dinner, so we won't be getting in until tomorrow morning."

I'd expected his resignation, but there was an underlying note in his voice I couldn't quite pin down. "But?"

"But they're a little too happy about this." And because he always expected the worst from people, it made him wary.

"You told me nothing came up in the background check."

"Yeah, still…"

I understood his hesitation, but I was also learning that

Zev was sometimes a little too paranoid, a necessary survival skill for the man who was the last resort in dealing with the innate intrigue that infested the Arcane Families. "Any chance of convincing Emilio to bail on the dinner?"

"Tried that. No luck." Someone called his name, likely the man under discussion. Zev said, "Look, babe, I've got to go, but I didn't want you to worry."

That was exactly what I would now do. "I appreciate that, but do me a favor?"

"What?"

"Watch your ass, please."

"Planning on it."

"Good, I'm highly fond of it remaining in one piece."

He chuckled. "So am I."

"Love you, Zev." The words came easier now, but hearing his immediate response squeezed my well-guarded soft spot buried inside.

"Love you, too, Rory. I'll let you know when we hit town tomorrow."

"Sounds good."

With that, he hung up, leaving me alone with a dark tangle of worry.

TWO

I TURNED off Camelback Road and into the parking garage that served the glass-fronted building that housed the Arcane Guild offices, along with various other corporate entities. I strode through the heavily tinted doors and across the glossy tile floor. Since the Guild offices were on the second floor, I ignored the elevators, hit the fire escape stairs, and started up.

A door above me opened, and a deep voice echoed down the stairwell. "So I ended up hog-tying the idiot."

An amused snort was followed by a second male voice. "That's one way to solve an argument."

I didn't recognize the first speaker, but the second one was familiar. I came around the corner and caught sight of the two men heading toward me. The first one was a shaggy-haired bruiser with a bulging duffel bag slung over one beefy shoulder.

The second appeared leaner, but I knew from experience that lean frame was deceiving. Like most combat mages, he was a force to be reckoned with. He caught sight of me and said, "Hey, Rory."

"Hey, Gabe."

Behind him, his companion jerked his chin up in acknowledgement. "Hiya."

"Hi." He seemed familiar, but I couldn't place a name. I waited on the landing for both men to make it by me.

Gabe hit the landing first and stepped aside so his friend could squeeze past. "Heard you're working on contract now. How's that going?" There was genuine curiosity in his voice.

I gave a half-hearted shrug and humble bragged, "It's keeping me busy, but it can be a little intimidating sometimes."

"I heard some of your earlier jobs were a bit of a wild ride." He bumped my shoulder with his. "If you need some sparring time, let me know. I'm happy to partner."

"I might be taking you up on that." And my intent was serious. If the last few months had taught me anything, it was that being able to save my own ass needed to be a top priority.

"Good. You've got my number." With that, he jogged to where Bruiser had stopped about halfway down the last set of stairs. "Have a good night, Rory."

"You too!" I called back as I headed up the last flight. I pushed through the door at the top and stepped into the quiet hall.

The offices of the Western Division of the Arcane Guild took up the entire second floor of the building. I found it interesting that a magical mercenary storehouse shared its home with lawyers and number crunchers in the heart of upscale Phoenix. Then again, I was pretty sure the building's other occupants went out of their way not to cross paths with the motley crew that made up the Guild.

In the lobby, the man of Lena's dreams stood behind a younger, less-put-together version who was typing away madly in front the terminal. He wore his irritation with a thin veneer of patience. "Next time, when you run that ghost program, make sure the cache is included." He leaned in, the overhead lights glinting off the flecks of silver threaded through his brown hair. "See that there?"

His minion's shoulders rounded, and a grimace flashed over his features. "Yeah, dammit. Sorry, Evan."

Evan straightened. "It happens. Just don't let it happen again."

"Got it," the younger man muttered.

Evan came out from behind the desk, his gaze aimed my way as I drew closer. The normally rock-steady electro mage looked more ragged than normal. Behind his glasses, his eyes were bloodshot, his ordinarily messy hair stood on end, and he sported an unusual well-beyond-five-o'clock shadow along his jaw.

I met him off to the side of the desk. "Dude, you look like crap."

"Feel it too." He waved me to the door that led to the back portion of the office, where the Guild's chaotic day-to-day operations were housed. "Spent the last forty-eight hours tracing down a runaway heir with delusions of anarchy."

Sounded like a typical bored, entitled Family teen. When someone had more magic than sense and felt untouchable, they tended to make spectacularly poor decisions. Even worse, when their family was keen to avoid public embarrassment, their mistakes were quickly swept away with the help of various tools, like the Arcane Guild. "How much damage did they do?"

He grimaced. "Enough that the Director punted the job to me as a priority."

"Lucky you." I grabbed the handle and endured the itchy wave of the magical scan as the ward did its security sweep. When the lock released, I pulled open the door.

Behind me, Evan continued his bitching as we wove our way through the workstations dotting the open space. "If you say so. You know, sometimes I wish these kids would pick a different way to get their parents' attention other than making my life hell."

I lifted a hand at some familiar faces. "Not sure they're specifically targeting you, Evan."

When he grunted in response, I shook my head and shifted my attention to the large whiteboard that dominated the back wall near a set of double doors. Next to my name, the mark of green for Señor Nutter's case now had a blue partner, indicating a potential job.

"Hey." Evan pulled up short, bringing me to a stop. "What are you doing here anyway? I thought we had a game night scheduled."

"Yeah, well, Lena got called out and won't be back until late." I leaned a hip against an empty desk. "She tried reaching you, but…"

He patted at his pockets, likely looking for his phone, and came up empty. He muttered an oath and ran a hand through his hair. "Yeah, I was dealing with Kel."

"The mini-you out front?"

"Yep, he skipped a search parameter." Thankfully, Evan didn't devolve into geek speak. He dropped into the empty seat and studied me. "She sound okay?" He strove for casual but missed by a mile.

"Stressed, irritated, pretty par for the course." I tilted my head. "What's up?"

He leaned back, a frown forming as he crossed his arms and stretched out his legs. "That's what I'm trying to figure out. Something's been bothering her the last few days. I wanted to make sure if she's not talking to me, she's at least talking to you."

As sweet as that was, it took us onto tricky ground. Evan was a friend, a good one, but Lena's friendship was older and longer, so I tiptoed carefully. "We've both been busy, haven't had much time to do anything more than wave."

"Hmm." The sound didn't say much, and the lines in his forehead deepened.

"Wine and dine her, then make her talk to you." I wasn't exactly the best person to offer relationship advice, but I knew Lena. She would keep things bottled up until they boiled over in the mistaken impression she was Superwoman and could handle it all on her own.

His brows rose as his gaze met mine, and a purely male smirk broke through. "Already got tickets for tomorrow for Platform 29."

"Nice." I was impressed. Platform 29 was a world-class cocktail bar in a restored Pullman car that wound through surrounding mountains outside of Phoenix while you enjoyed your drinks. It was also right up Lena's alley. "She'll love that."

"I hope so," he said. "So, you and Zev doing something tonight?"

I shook my head. "He's stuck in Vegas with Emilio."

Someone called my name, and I craned my neck to see one of the Guild's best investigators striding through the double doors at the back that led to the gym—a necessary amenity when ensuring your staff remained tight on both physical and magical self-defense techniques.

"Hey, Nat."

"Hey, Rory. You run out of contracts?" she teased.

"Nope, in fact looks like I caught another one." I jerked my head toward the whiteboard. "But first, I have to pay my debt to Adele."

That earned a chuckle from the formidable Hunter as she stopped next to us. "Wise move." She nudged Evan's foot. "Long day?"

"Aren't they all?" he drawled.

"Truth," she agreed. "Well, I finally have a free night, so I'm going to go enjoy it while I can."

"Netflix and chill?" I guessed. Rumor had it, her last

couple of contracts had been rough, lethally rough, and like most contractors, she spent her downtime just taking a breath.

She grinned and started walking backward. "Netflix and chill." With that, she turned and headed for the door.

"Enjoy," I called out as she walked away, then I turned back to Evan. "You should probably text Lena and then make the most of your solo evening to get rid of the luggage set under your eyes. You want to be pretty for tomorrow night's date," I teased.

He managed a credible derisive snort and pushed up from the chair. "I'm always pretty." He rolled his shoulders. "I might spice up my night by making sure my bunch of idiots don't end up dying while sitting around a campfire."

I knew better, but I did it anyway. "Say again?"

"My D&D group has a campaign tonight. Was going to ditch for our game night, but with those plans now out…" He shrugged. "They need me since last time, our bard was so caught up in teaching the sorcerer a song that he totally missed the bandits' flaming arrows that almost burned the forest down. Don't get me started about their fuck-up with the half-orc with OCD."

Right, shouldn't have asked. "Okay then, good luck with that." I straightened and motioned behind me vaguely. "I'm just going to go slave over some paperwork, check out the new job. You know, mundane things like that."

"Yeah, I like my plans better," Evan said.

Truthfully, so did I.

We said our good-byes and went our separate ways.

The activity on the floor had quieted down to near library-silent levels as the clock ticked past five and closed in on six. My pile of dead trees had dwindled, and my blurry eyes were grateful that the end was nigh. I signed for the umpteenth time and started on my second pass to make sure I hadn't missed anything because not only did I really like getting paid, I also did not want to tick off Adele. I heard my name and looked up.

Speak of the devil herself!

The Director's assistant was coming my way, and my pulse picked up speed. It was an involuntary reaction developed after years of braving the dedicated dragon housed in the cool professionalism of the efficient forty-something-year-old who guarded the hallowed entrance to the Director's domain. Whether Guild employee or independent contractor, Adele's patience did not extend to those who, as she said, "Waste my time by not managing theirs."

"Hey, Adele," I said casually.

She stopped in front of where I was working and offered a harried "I'm glad you're still here."

I blinked, not quite prepared for that comment. "Um, okay," I answered cautiously as I pushed back from the workstation. I was not used to seeing her so flustered. *Perhaps it's a phenomenon that only occurs after business hours.* "What's up?"

"Have you checked the board?"

I nodded. "See there's a job available. Haven't had a chance to review it yet."

"I just received a call, and they've switched it to an emergency courier request."

Ah, I recognize that tone. It was the one that said, "I'm not desperate," even though she was. "Let me guess—they need it tonight."

She nodded.

"Well, I'm available and interested." I stacked my paperwork into a neat pile and stood up. "But first, this is for you. The last of the Anwar paperwork." I handed over the mix of reports and invoices.

She took it, and I hid my grin as her shoulders went from rigid to a visible slump. "Thank you. I'll get this processed first thing tomorrow."

"Now, fill me in on the job details." I came around the workstation.

She started back to her desk. "Your notary certification is still up to date, isn't it?"

"It is."

"Lovely," she murmured. "The pickup address is the Red Maple Collection office in Dueñas Park, and the delivery address is in Sedona." She kept talking as she went to her computer and pulled up the information. "It appears the package is a gift that requires a notarized signature from the recipient."

Sounded fairly standard.

"Red Maple is offering a thousand-dollar bonus if the notarized receipt is returned to their offices by midnight." She straightened, and the printer kicked into life.

Two hours to Sedona, no more than a half hour to hand off the secondary package and get the required signature— maybe an hour, if the signer wasn't where they were expected to be—and two hours back. That was cutting it closer than I liked, but it was definitely doable. "I can do that."

As she waited for the contract to print, she said, "Wonderful. Thank you, Rory. I'm so glad you were here." She turned back to her keyboard, and behind her purple tortoiseshell frames, her eyes scanned the screen. "The package is listed as confidential, Level 3 security risk, which means you'll net the standard after-hours rate, plus thirty percent." The printer went quiet, and with the ease of practice, she quickly pulled out the pages I needed before handing them over.

A Level 3 security risk meant whatever magic the package

carried was stable, so long as it was handled with care. That didn't bother me, but the contents being listed as confidential did make me pause. "Should I be worried?"

Adele pressed her lips together and considered my question. Finally, she shook her head. "Cautious, not worried. Red Maple has a sterling reputation among collectors."

"Like art collectors?"

Her lips curved upward. "Art, antiques, and rare magical collectables. Based off previous contracts, they tend to be overly cautious on rating their packages."

Better safe than sorry. "Understood." I scanned the information provided.

Proving her depth of knowledge of those who work with the Guild, Adele said, "The delivery address is most likely residential, but I'll be happy to pull it up and double-check."

I shook my head. "Appreciate it, but I've got it."

Her earlier worry disappeared as she regained her typical brusque persona. "Right then, would you prefer a class-two vehicle?"

I frowned, thinking it through. Only so much would fit in the trunk of a Mustang. "Did they share package dimensions?"

She shook her head. "No, but my impression is the package would fit in a normal courier bag, so size shouldn't be a problem."

Good to know. For a courier run, I would normally turn down the offer of a vehicle with a magical containment box, mainly because it meant the Guild would increase their cut of the job and I would have to slog through a crap ton of insurance papers, but did I really want to risk transporting an unknown package that may or may not go boom in my precious Mustang? Thanks to my innate ability as a Prism, I would survive any magical attack. My baby might not be as lucky. That tipped the scales. "Actually, yes."

Adele nodded and turned back to her computer. "I'll send the request to Carl."

Carl was the head mechanic in charge of the Guild's fleet of vehicles. "Thanks." I folded the papers in half. "I'll head up now."

She looked up from her computer. "Be safe, Rory, and don't forget to get both sets of signatures on the invoice." The last carried an underlying hint of a threat.

"Got it." I flashed her a smile. "Have a good night."

"You as well."

New plans for the evening in place, I headed up to the garage to see what toys Carl had available.

THREE

WITH NOVEMBER well and truly underway, the stunning pinks and purples of sunset had disappeared about twenty minutes ago. The automatic overhead lights were on the job, spilling their glow over the parking lot. I guided the Genesis coupe into a spot facing the five-story building that housed Dueñas Park. I shut off the engine and stared through the windshield, fighting back a sense of déjà vu.

Just over a year ago, I had been in the same position, only then, I'd sat in my Mustang as I prepared to take on an unauthorized side job as a Guild employee. Despite some unexpected twists and turns, I had to say it was one of my better decisions because it had led me here. Still, I couldn't shake that trickle of unease. I considered bringing my Walther CCP with me, but I decided against it and left my gun secured in the custom holster tucked between the driver's seat and the center console.

I pushed open the driver's door, and the melodious chime of the open-door warning filled the quiet. I had asked the overly protective mechanic for something understated with power. I got the Genesis coupe, and its trunk, which doubled as a secured containment thanks to some creative aftermarket warding. The car would easily fit in with the rentals that flocked to Sedona or disappear among the career-minded rides of downtown Phoenix.

Although it had been out of production for a few years, Carl's love and care had kept it in pristine shape. Powered by a V-6 and three hundred forty-eight horses, the rear-wheel-drive cutie wasn't a showstopper, but she could definitely seduce someone into trouble.

I clicked the key fob then brushed my fingers over the security ward embedded in the frame. Considering there was a weapon in the car, it was better to be safe than sorry. Warding magic brushed against my Prism magic with a familiar tinge that nipped my fingers. The sting there and gone in a heartbeat. I cut through the landscaped patch of green dividing the lot and the sidewalk then jogged across the crosswalk to the stone steps that led to the glass entry for Dueñas Park.

Like most reflective surfaces, these were heavily tinted in an effort to hold off the near-nuclear rays of the summer sun, but tonight, they were slates of shadow reflecting my image. I reached for the metal handle wrapped in a door mitt, wondering if it would be locked like last time. Instead of the soft buzz of the lock being released, it opened easily, releasing a flood of light and the kind of after-hours silence that filled a normally busy space.

I walked through a tiled lobby decorated with muted colors, silk plants, and the same plush furniture I remembered from before. In an eerie echo of my previous trip, I headed toward the manned security desk situated to the right of the elevators. Thankfully, the person behind it wasn't the same as before. This time, instead of a he, there was a she.

"Good evening," she greeted with a polite tone, her expression suitably stern. "Can I help you?"

"Yes," I answered as I moved up to the desk. "My name is

Rory Costas. I'm with the Arcane Guild. I'm here to pick up a package from Red Maple Collections."

Her attention dropped to the computer terminal below the counter, and a few clicks later, she said, "You'll want to take Elevator Two to the fourth floor. Red Maple is the first office to your left."

"Thank you."

"I'll let them know you're on your way up."

"I appreciate it." I turned and followed her directions.

Once I was on the fourth floor, it was clear I was expected because a young man stood holding open the door to what I assumed was Red Maple's office. He spoke the minute I came into view. "We appreciate the Guild's quick response."

I waited until I stood in front of him to respond. "Of course, Mister..." I trailed off in a silent prompt.

"Simon," he filled in then stumbled over his words as he moved aside and waved me into an office done with dark wainscoting and wood tones. "I mean, my first name is Simon. Simon Moore."

"Rory," I offered in an attempt to ease his nerves. "Nice to meet you, Simon." I shifted out of his way as he headed to the reception desk. "I understand we are on a tight timetable tonight that requires a return of the notarized receipt?"

He rummaged behind the desk then set a piece of paper and a pen on the counter. "Um, yes, that's correct. Normally, we aren't so rushed, but this particular transaction, well..." He trailed off, a bit of color seeping under his cheeks as he stepped around me. "Our client is quite excited about its arrival, which is why we're offering the bonus."

That reaction made me think this young man was fairly new to his position. Well, that and the fact he was the one stuck waiting around after business hours for me.

"Well, the Guild is always happy to be of service." I picked up the pen and used a finger to pull the paper closer. A quick scan revealed it was a standard notice of transfer, including a statement about verifying the contents. I scrawled my name on the appropriate lines. "I'll do my best to meet your deadline." I pushed the paper back toward him. "Is the recipient aware the package is on its way?"

Simon nodded as he tucked away the transfer notice. "He is." He held out the file. "The notarized receipt."

I took it and scanned the contents to make sure everything was there.

Simon said, "I'll just go back and grab the package."

I nodded, closed the file, and watched him disappear down the hall. He was back within a couple of minutes, carrying a box that was roughly the size of a book, which made me think the containment ward might have been overkill.

"Here you go." He handed it over.

I took the box and noted it wasn't physically heavy. When there was no shift in weight, I decided it must be well padded. Magically… well, that was a different story. As soon as the box hit my palm, my Prism snapped into place, creating a barrier between my skin and the irritating scratch of magic. The contents were definitely magical in nature, but even my Prism decided it was more nuisance than actual threat. Adele had been spot-on when she said Red Maple tended to overestimate their security concerns. "Is it just this?"

Simon frowned. "Yes. The box is warded and can only be open by the authorized recipient, Mr. Maximiliano Vasquez. He'll be expecting you."

"Understood." Considering they dealt in priceless artifacts, the additional security measures weren't a surprise. "Any other precautions I need to be aware of?"

"Other than a reminder that the contents are breakable, so please be careful when handling it, no." His gaze lingered on the box for a moment before returning to mine. "I was hoping you wouldn't mind texting me your ETA before you head back as I'd rather not wait at the office the entire time." He rubbed his neck and offered a self-effacing half smile. "I mean, if you're planning on coming back tonight."

"That's my goal." I set the box gently on the desk and pulled out my phone. "If you give me your number, I'll shoot you a heads-up when I'm on my way in."

"Thanks." He rattled off his digits, and with them safely stored, I wished him a good-night and headed out to hit the road for Sedona.

•••••••••••••••••••••••••••

The GPS guided me along the Red Rock Byway, a two-lane stretch of asphalt that veered off the interstate and led into what the locals considered a village but tourists called Sedona. The drive up had been uneventful, and the package sat securely stored in one of the specialized compartments that doubled as a glovebox. Whatever magic the object had been leaking earlier was contained, at least from what I could tell from occasional check-ins with the Genesis.

It may have sounded strange to treat a car like a living entity, but because I was a Transporter, that was exactly what vehicles were to me, or at least to my magic. Most vehicles hit my consciousness like individual personalities. My baby was a tricked-out classic, all flirty attitude and edgy performance that equated to a sexy punk-rock speed demon. This coupe was all subtle handling with surprising depth that brought to mind a silver-screen queen who still made the boys drool. While I was behind the wheel, my connection to the car hummed in the back of my mind, and since it was staying quiet, the package seemed to be behaving. I settled in to enjoy the drive.

Since I had time to kill, I used my phone and its alter ego, which I'd named Alfie, to do a bit of a dive on Mr. Maximiliano Vasquez. As I'd learned in the past, it was best to know the customers. It hadn't been as necessary when I worked solely for the Guild because I trusted them to do their due diligence. However, once I became my own boss, only one person would cover my ass—me.

With a quick search of the internet, Alfie shared in a lovely male brogue that Mr. Vasquez was only about eight years older than me and was the heir apparent to a minor Arcane Family tucked under the more-influential Velasquez Family. I risked a glance down at his picture. Dark hair was swept back from a high forehead, the waves ruthlessly tamed but rebelliously curling behind his ears. His hazel eyes were bright with charm, and a dark, neat beard surrounded his full lips. Yep, Maximiliano Vasquez was the epitome of a successful businessman.

As for his ties to the Velasquez Family, that piqued my interest since I'd had the dubious privilege of meeting the head of the Family, Christina Velasquez. She was one of two women who sat on the Arcane Council, and she was a power to be reckoned with, not just because of the seat she held. I'd seen her in action, and I was not keen on an encore performance.

On the first pass, nothing about Max gave me pause. According to what was out there, he was well-liked, highly respected, and a generally all-around good guy. He worked with the family investment company and had his fingers in quite an array of businesses. There were no ugly scandals or rumors out there, at least not that I could find in a standard search. He sat on the board of a couple worthwhile charities, and rumors abounded that an engagement might be on the horizon between Max and his long-term girlfriend.

The sliver of tension in the back of my mind loosened, and I realized that on some level, I had been worried about the urgency surrounding this job. I poked and prodded until I unearthed the lingering trepidation that remained after my recent deep dive into the shark-infested waters filled with powerhouses in the Arcane world.

More than just my job status had shifted in the last few months. My accepted worldview had been blown apart then reformed into a patchwork of its previous self, complete with paranoid, conspiracy-laced scars that had me braced for treacherous machinations lurking around every corner.

I reminded myself that the world did not revolve around me, and I needed to get a grip, because it appeared that this job was exactly what it seemed to be—a simple expedited courier run.

The night sky was dotted with stars. As I came around the last bend, the narrow canyon walls parted, and the road widened into a divided two-lane ribbon. The good news was at this time of night, traffic wasn't bumper-to-bumper, but it was fairly steady.

I slowed and curved through the first roundabout as the GPS pointed me past the hotels and clusters of adobe buildings that catered to the gullible and curious. I kept my speed down, not just because Sedona liked their roundabouts or because of the steady trickle of traffic, but because unlike Phoenix, who adored their amber-colored streetlights, Sedona, as a Dark Sky city, didn't use streetlights. And desert nights were dark enough that the shadows could easily play tricks with a driver's vision.

The last thing I wanted, or needed, was an accident.

When I initially pulled up the address, it had appeared to be a private residence, and so far, that logic was holding. The road snaked into Oak Creek Canyon, leaving the art galleries and restaurants of uptown Sedona in my rearview.

The GPS continued to lead me along a winding road that slipped between red rock walls. Every now and then, the shadows would lighten enough to reveal faint outlines of the desert foothills. Eventually, Alfie directed me onto a private road. My headlights drifted over the opened wrought-iron gate and barely pierced the darkness veiling the space behind it.

I pulled through then rounded one last curve. When asphalt gave way to pavers under the Genesis's tires, I let out a low whistle of surprise. An impressive drive fronted the dramatically lit, sprawling Tuscan-inspired villa set against Sedona's infamous red-rock hills. It was stunning, and it knew it.

Based upon the top-tier collection of automobiles parked in the drive, there was one serious house party going on. I tried my best not to drool as I catalogued the recognizable names, including a couple of rare unicorns like a Bentley Bentayga and a Maybach. I hadn't expected Max to be hobnobbing at this level and questioned my decision to go understated with the Genesis.

Too late to change rides now.

I found an open space on the far side near another set of gates that appeared to guard an open-air courtyard. I popped the glovebox, grabbed the package, then picked up the file before getting out of the car. The minute my foot touched the pavers, magic raced over me, and my power met it head-on, like an invisible armor, an innate reaction that made me a tool to be coveted by the Arcane Families.

As history had proven, the powerful magical elite would go to unbelievable lengths to get what they wanted, regardless of the consequences. Since I happened to vehemently disagree with their perception, I tended not to advertise my ability. Funnily enough, this appeared to be a sentiment shared by generations of Prisms before me, and not just because Prisms had been all but wiped out when the Arcane Families used them as personal shields against magical attacks during the world wars.

Although that didn't help things. Neither did the fact that, either due to a desperate need to protect themselves or the selfishness of the Families in power at the time, historical records of Prisms were all but erased, leaving those like me to grow up convinced the only magic I had was the near-symbiotic bond I shared with vehicles.

All that changed when I discovered that the strange quirk that defended me from most direct magical assaults and ensured I wouldn't drop dead could also turn the same attack back on its users with lethal results. Then there was the revelation that I wasn't an orphan at all. Nope, in fact, I was the great-niece of Sabella Rossi-Giordano, the matriarch of one of the oldest and most powerful Arcane Families. She also happened to be one of my biggest contracts, but that was an entirely different story.

I crossed the drive as whatever magic surrounded the villa bit at my shield with an annoying itch, indicating a warding of some kind. With practiced ease, I ignored it and headed for the stone arch that guarded the front entry. The hairs on the back of my neck rose as I felt someone—or multiple someones—watching me. Not a surprise. A place like this wouldn't be unguarded.

As unobtrusively as possible, I checked for electronic or human security—and found both. Tucked under the eaves, little black security cameras were watching and recording. I took the two wide steps, but before I hit the top, a man slipped out of the shadows and stood in front of the wide, heavy wooden door.

"Good evening." His greeting was polite, but not exactly welcoming. He was undoubtedly security. Not just because he had the build and expression of a brick wall, but the irritating buzz of power ratcheted up a notch, indicating I might be facing a combat-level mage.

"Evening." I heeded the unspoken warning and stopped. "I'm with the Arcane Guild to deliver a package from Red Maple Collections to Mr. Maximiliano Vasquez. I believe he's expecting me."

"Credentials."

I shifted the package and file folder to one arm, retrieved my ID, and handed it over.

"Thank you." He did his due diligence before handing it back. "If you would please wait inside at the bar, we'll notify Mr. Vasquez of your arrival."

Bar? I put away my wallet then resecured the package and folder. "Of course."

He opened the door and motioned me through.

I stepped inside and quickly discovered this was no simple dinner party.

FOUR

HIDDEN inside the thick villa walls was a full-on nightclub masquerading as a mansion. The open interior was clearly designed for indulgent entertainment. An echo of a rhythmic beat pulsed through the tiled floor and pounded under the soles of my shoes. Somewhere, a DJ was set up, either tucked in a basement below or set up out on the patio that lay beyond the opening off the back of the house. Considering the glitter, glitz, and noise level, it might have been more than one DJ.

Sheesh.

Here, on what was clearly the main floor, furniture was sparse, leaving plenty of space for people draped in shimmering fabrics and tailored lines to drift among the crowd with casual friendliness under sparkling chandeliers. Flecks of light bounced off cut crystal stemware and various pieces of high-end jewelry like small fireflies. Balloons and streamers decorated the high ceiling, and a banner stretched across the room's far end proclaimed, "Congratulations Max & Devon."

Guess the rumors about Max's single status were no

longer rumors because I'd clearly crashed an engagement party.

"Ma'am," the bouncer-slash-guard said at my back as his arm motioned over to the right. "If you would?"

I followed his command and moved to the elegant bar set up along the right side of the room. He watched me as I took a spot near the end closest to the door and farthest from the woman deftly pouring drinks into cut-crystal glasses. Satisfied I wasn't going to wander off into the crowd, he turned away, pressing his hand against his ear, most likely notifying whoever was on the other end where he'd parked me.

Despite my tailored black slacks and short-sleeved, draped V-neck emerald-green silk blouse, I felt decidedly underdressed as I eyed the crowd. I recognized a few faces from various media outlets that covered the antics of the high-ranking Arcane families, but for the most part, the partygoers were simply a well-heeled crowd. Some sat in plush chairs nestled along the opposite side, and others spilled out into the night through the open doors at the far end. The air was full of music, murmured conversations, and laughter.

"A drink?" The melodious voice slid under the low din of noise.

I turned to find the bartender, her gaze aimed at me, pouring amber-colored alcohol into squat tumblers with seeming inattention. I met the deep-indigo lenses of her wire-frame glasses and shook my head. "Thanks, but no. I shouldn't be here long." I hoped. I tucked the file folder under one arm and kept a tight hold of the package. No sense in tempting good ol' Murphy. It would suck to lose my delivery to some sticky-fingered guest feet from its final destination.

"No rush. Stay as long as you like." She finished her pour and nudged the tumblers toward the young server who was clearly picking up an order. As he hustled off with the drinks, the bartender took another order, her hands moving behind the bar like a concert pianist.

The next few minutes ticked by, and I got a few curious looks that had me subtly wiping at my face. The third time I did it, the bartender closed in and leaned over. "There's nothing on your face, Ms. Costas."

I dropped my hand, my spine shot straight, and I narrowed my gaze on the fine-boned features of a woman I'd never met before. "I'm sorry?"

She flashed me an enigmatic smile. "You do realize you're building quite the reputation with this crowd."

I blinked at the unusual response. "I am?"

"You are," she confirmed as she half turned to prepare another set of drinks.

As disconcerting as it was to hear from a complete stranger, it didn't stop my ego from puffing a bit. I muttered under my breath, "Guess that's a good thing."

The bartender turned back to me, and this time, I was able to see the name on her discreet tag. Cass. Her hands paused midmotion, and with an unsettling seriousness, she said, "Not always, Ms. Costas."

Shocked she'd actually heard that, I opened my mouth, only to be stopped short when I heard my name. I turned and came face-to-face with Maximiliano "Max" Vasquez.

"Ms. Costas, I hope your trip was uneventful." He held out his hand.

Shifting the package, I took it, and still a little off balance, I managed a polite "It was, thank you."

He squeezed my hand then let it go. "Good to hear." His gaze dropped to what I held. "Good," he repeated to himself. Then his eyes came back to mine, and this time, a hint of excitement warmed his face. "If you wouldn't mind following me, we'll head up and get this taken care of."

"Of course," I murmured.

Behind me, Cass said in a low voice, "Smooth roads, Ms. Costas."

I looked back at her. She gave me another one of those inscrutable smiles and went back to work. I turned away and followed Max across the floor and up the curving staircase to the second floor.

As we made our way farther into the house, the noise below faded. Max stopped at a set of double doors and rapped his knuckles in a quick two-beat warning before opening it. A whiff of hot buttered corn laced with a hint of smoky spice escaped, as did a wave of laughter and conversation that seeped into the hall.

He held open the door for me. "After you."

Inclining my head, I went through into a large room, stopped just inside, and shifted off to the side. At the back of the room, a hostess served an older couple at a wet bar. Next to it, on the end, two thirtysomething professionals were helping themselves to a snack at an old-fashioned popcorn stand. The two pub-style tables with matching barstools that sat off to the right in front of a mesmerizing water feature were also filled. To the left, more bodies lounged on an L-shaped, low-slung couch that faced a massive TV with various electronic systems tucked neatly below.

My entrance barely made a ripple, likely because most of the attention was centered on the poker table that dominated the entertainment space. A mixed group of two men and three women sat at the table. Their hands were filled with cards, and a pile of poker chips was clustered in the center. A blonde in a sheath somewhere between bone and white slapped a string of cards on the felt and crowed triumphantly, "A straight flush, Kent, so pay up." She exchanged high fives with the other two females—one older, one younger, both dark haired.

From my earlier search on Vasquez, I matched the

carefully made-up face of the blonde to Max's girlfriend, Devon Olson. *Correction, fiancée.*

"Dammit, Devon." A dark-haired man with silver at his temples and suntanned skin tossed down his cards. "I'm done." He roughly shoved more chips into the pot, picked up a nearby glass, and shot the contents.

"It's just a game, man." This came from the other male at the table, a dirty blond this time, with an edge to his voice and what appeared to be a permanent sneer. He set his cards aside and sat back in his chair. "I'm sure you'll get a chance to win it all back next round."

"Like I said, Perry," the dark-haired Kent shot back, "I'm out."

"Don't be such a sore loser, Kent," admonished the older, dark-haired woman. "And Perry, stop making it worse."

Max came in behind me and headed toward the game, leaving me to follow. Devon, who was now raking in her winnings, looked up, paused, and grinned. "I won, babe."

"I had no doubt you would, Dev," Max said.

She stopped collecting her winnings and straightened, her attention shifting to me and the package I held. Excitement lit her face. "Is that it?"

"It is."

His pronouncement galvanized the room. The card game was swept away, and the table was cleared as chairs were neatly stacked off to the side, leaving a clear space around the table. It didn't stay clear for long. Guests began to gather round, and I stayed out of the way as Max walked over to Devon.

The milling guests hid the newly engaged couple from my view, and conversations tumbled over themselves. I caught a few phrases here and there, though, and if I hadn't been there in a professional capacity, they would have had me raising my eyebrows. I heard words like *hidden gold* and *lost treasure,* and one word I itched to look up—*pythagographs.* A few minutes passed in bustled activity, and a couple curious glances were thrown my way. I held my spot and ignored them, doing my best to become part of the décor. I managed a quick head count, and what initially felt like a crowd was actually closer to a dozen people.

Once everyone picked a spot where they could see the action, Max ushered me forward. "Ms. Costas, if you wouldn't mind putting it on the table?"

Faces turned to me, and a few whispers drifted around, but bodies parted, giving me a straight shot to the table. I took it, and when I got to Max's side, I noted there were four black-and-white five-by-seven photos laid out in a line.

Strange.

I set the package on the table, pulled the invoice out of the folder, and laid it next to the box.

Max picked up the invoice and scanned it. It didn't take long. He looked at me. "I'm assuming you'll be acting as a notary?"

"Once you confirm the box and its contents, yes."

Max dipped his chin in acknowledgement then turned to Devon. "Can you grab me a pen, babe? I think there's a couple in one of the drawers over by the TV."

Before Devon could do as he asked, Perry was digging in his pockets. "Hang on, I should have… right here." He pulled a pen out of his pocket and offered it to Max.

"Thanks." Max took it and bent over to sign.

I laid a hand over the invoice before he could mark it. "Mr. Vasquez, Red Maple asked that you verify the contents first."

Max paused, pen in hand, and blinked. A long moment passed, or at least it seemed long to me, but then he muttered, "Of course. Apologies, Ms. Costas."

"Rory is fine," I corrected quietly.

He set down the pen and carefully pulled the box closer. Standing as close as I was, I felt the moment he touched it. Not because the box began to emit a soft-amber glow, but because his touch activated the ward, and the magic pulsed against my Prism.

Devon's attention, like everyone else's, was on the package, but she sucked in an audible breath and clutched Max's arm. The ward shifted from a muted amber to a burning orange as the magic verified Max's identity. A second then two passed before it blinked out.

Max let out a slow exhale, continuing to handle the package with care. He began to undo the tape holding the box together. Tension swam through the room, as if something unique was about to be revealed. The reaction left me curious as to what was in the package.

"If this works, Max…" Kent murmured, his gaze focused on the box.

"Yeah," Max said, without looking away from the package. He pulled off the top and set it aside. The bottom half was filled with protective foam that surrounded a pair of wire-frame glasses.

Excited whispers erupted from those gathered around as Max pulled the glasses free of the foam. When he held them up, light from the fixture above glinted off the lenses. The glass was pitted with age, and the wire frame was a bit misshapen on one side. Clearly, they were old and well used.

"I was expecting something more…" Devon trailed off.

"Impressive?" The younger, dark-haired woman from the card game filled in with a quick grin.

Devon nodded.

Max pulled the earpieces out and held the glasses out in front of him as he peered through the lenses. "It's not how they look, but what they show you, that's impressive." He frowned then lowered them. "But there's a good chance the story behind them is just that—a story."

"You won't know for sure until you put them on," Perry said.

"And I have to once again warn you against doing that,"

Kent cut in. "Messing around with haunted items is the bedrock of any good horror flick."

A nervous twitter of laughter ringed the table, but Max, clearly undaunted, put on the glasses. "They aren't haunted, Kent. They're supposed to allow the user to see the actual map." He adjusted the glasses until they sat level on the bridge of his nose. Then he reached for the photos, picked them up one by one, and studied them closely.

I had no idea what he was looking at. The photos appeared to be random street shots from either the late 1800s or early 1900s, but I didn't know enough to be sure. Based on the topography in the background, it was somewhere in the Southwest, but just where in the Southwest remained a mystery to me. The road was hard-packed dirt, there were saddled horses tied to a wooden railing outside what looked like a general store, and women in long petticoats walked beside men in dark pants and suit coats.

Everyone waited with bated breath as Max picked up each photo, studied it, then set it down. He was on the last one when Perry's impatience finally snapped. "Well?"

Max lifted his head, and his mouth stretched into a wide smile. "They're definitely the real thing."

"Yeah?" Perry's sneer disappeared, replaced by a shocked excitement. "Seriously?"

"Seriously." Max lifted the photo he held. "Here, check it out."

Perry took the photo, and Kent leaned in over his shoulder.

Max started to remove the glasses, only to wince and give a slight hiss as one of the temple arms left a red scratch along his cheek. "Damn," he muttered, pulling the glasses away, then handed them to Perry. "Careful, those arms are a bit rough."

Devon turned Max's face her way and gently brushed the

small scratch. "You'll be fine," she reassured him then brushed a quick kiss over his owie before letting him go.

Perry got the glasses on and studied the picture. "Hot damn." He set the picture aside and picked up the next one. He studied the photos then looked at Max. A wide grin stretched over his face. "Looks like we're going treasure hunting!"

Cheers filled the room.

FIVE

AFTER PERRY'S rather dramatic statement, the party ratcheted up to the next level. Luckily for me, I didn't have to stick around. Since Red Maple required verification that the package was undamaged, Max had me examine the glasses. The still-red scratch on Max's face served as a reminder to handle the frames carefully, but the rough metal of one of the arms still managed to leave its mark on my finger. I set the old glasses back in their box, then Max and I signed the invoice. I notarized it and, delivery complete, took my leave.

My return trip downstairs was unaccompanied, and based on the increased noise level that met me as I walked down the steps, the party was in full swing. I pulled out my phone, checked the time, and was happy to see I was on schedule for the bonus from Red Maple. I hit the floor and wove through the crush of bodies that seemed to have multiplied while I was upstairs.

At the front entryway, I waited for the quartet coming in to move out of the way then slipped outside. I'd never been a fan of crowds, especially when the crowd included unknown magic users. I let out a relieved breath as I escaped the combined pressure of noise and power. After raising a hand to the doorman as he glanced up from checking in even more guests, I kept walking to the car. Headlights danced over me as another car came up, and I turned my head away to avoid being blinded. I hit the Genesis's key fob and heard the alarm system beep as I rounded the bumper. I reached for the door, still blinking annoying spots from my vision, then I caught movement from the corner of my eye. The base of my neck tingled in warning, and I turned to see who was lurking in the dark.

Nothing was there, just night shadows. I froze, one hand on the car, the other fisted at my side as I stared hard, trying to pinpoint what had set off my warning system. Behind me, a burst of laughter followed by a car door slamming broke the weird tension as new arrivals headed toward the villa. After another look around, I pulled open the door and got behind the wheel. I snapped my seatbelt into place, and my knuckles brushed over the gun still tucked away.

I could hear Zev's voice in my head now. *"Doesn't do you a damn bit of good locked in the car."*

"Yeah, yeah, yeah," I muttered, feeling a bit silly now that I was in the car. Still, I started the engine and did another scan, both visually and magically.

Nothing.

I shook my head, backed out carefully, and started down the long, curving drive. I considered stopping somewhere for coffee before I hit the freeway, but it was late, and time was tight. I didn't want to risk losing the bonus, so I settled in and headed back into the valley.

I used music instead of caffeine to keep me alert and decided to test the coupe's paces. I wound my way down the curves of the interstate and wove smoothly in and out of the late-night traffic. The Genesis and I were having a great time by the time we made New River, a small community about thirty-five miles outside of Phoenix. I had slowed back to posted speeds, not keen on dealing with a ticket and the mess it entailed, when the wheel jerked in my hands and the TPMS warning light flashed on the dash.

"What the hell?" I frowned, taking my foot off the pedal. The wheel vibrated, and I guided the car toward the exit just ahead. The car was equipped with run flats, so short of a complete blowout, which would have done a hell of a lot more than jerk the wheel, I had time to pull off somewhere I preferred. At the top of the ramp, I made a left toward the dark, empty shopping strip. I pulled into a parking space under one of the lot's few working lights and shut down the engine.

This time, I didn't leave the gun in the car. Middle of the night, flat tire, dark parking lot… Yeah, I'd watched enough crime TV to know that was a recipe for disaster. I got out, gun held down at my side, and aimed my phone's flashlight app at the ground. Faint sounds from the freeway whispered in the air, but tension crept up my spine and tightened my shoulders. I couldn't shake the feeling of being watched, which was ridiculous, but it didn't stop me from doing a slow circle.

Nothing.

I tried to shake off the uncomfortable feeling as I checked the driver's-side tires. Both the front and back were good. Adjusting my grip on my phone and gun, I rounded the trunk and looked down. The back passenger tire sat about three inches from the ground. "Well, shit."

I crouched, setting the gun on the ground in front of my toes. With the light of my phone shining on my hand, I ran my fingers over the tire. Metal brushed my skin, and I swore again. I'd picked up either a nail or a screw. Considering the near-constant construction the roads here endured, I wasn't surprised. Overhead, the light flickered and dimmed, and I shot it a disgusted look, hoping it wouldn't go out. It didn't, but it kept up its intermittent dance of illumination.

As if it wasn't creepy enough out here.

I braced one hand against the rear panel, angled my phone's light with the other, and leaned in until I could see under the wheel well. Shadows danced over the tire and glinted off something over on the tire's far edge. The angle was crap, but at least I could see whatever I picked up was nearly level with the rubber.

Dammit.

I pulled back, turned my phone's light toward the ground, and blinked away the lingering spots as my eyes readjusted. The run flats were good at low speeds for about a hundred miles because Carl didn't cheap out when it came to the Guild's vehicles. I ran my fingers along the tire's rim and found the slightly raised rune etched into the decorative chrome. A flex of will ignited the rune's magic, ensuring I wouldn't be running on those rims as I limped my way back into Phoenix. The tradeoff—I would be battling some serious magical exhaustion.

I picked up my gun and started to straighten, only to stop when something moved out in the darkness on my left. My phone clattered to the ground as I brought my gun up and stayed low, putting the trunk between me and whoever was out there.

A chill whispered over my skin, and my pulse thundered in my ears as I searched the dark parking lot, straining to see any minute differences in the shadows. Time seemed to stretch, marked only by my harsh breathing as I tried to spot the threat.

Rory.

My name and the accompanying icy touch to my shoulder had me spinning so fast that my back slammed into the car with bruising force. Panic held me in a tight grip for what felt like forever but couldn't have been more than a few seconds as I searched the darkness, but nothing was there. A blast of a passing semi's air horn from the highway snapped me out of my paralyzed state.

"Get your shit together, Rory." I kept my gun up, finger off the trigger as I crouched to pick up my phone, my eyes trained on the night. Once I had it, I wasted no time getting back inside the car. With the doors locked, I took a second to breathe away the adrenaline. When I was steady, I refocused, checked the time, factored in a reduced speed, and the route to Red Maple as it was closer than the Guild. My tight timetable had narrowed to seriously close, but there were a couple of shortcuts I might be able to pull off.

Wanting this run over, I tightened my magical reins on the Genesis, put the car into gear, and got the hell out of there.

By the time I pulled into Dueñas Park, my muscles were trembling, and a line of cold sweat ran down my spine as if I had spent the last forty minutes deadlifting weights with my pinkie. And not all of that could be attributed to overextending my magic. No matter how much I chastised myself for jumping at shadows, I couldn't completely shake off the unease that had trailed me back into town.

Fortunately, to make the deadline, I had to shift my attention to driving. My abilities were instinctive, and using them didn't typically drain me dry, but using them to combat the flat tire after already putting in a full day drained my magical tank to near empty, leaving me wiped, mentally, magically, and emotionally. Thankfully, I made it with five minutes to spare.

I grabbed the file with the invoice, got out, and hot-footed as best I could to the office building. I had sent Simon an ETA when I was about twenty minutes out, so hopefully, he was here and waiting. When I hit the top of the stone steps, the glass door ahead of me opened, and Simon stood in the doorway.

"I'm impressed." The light from the lobby behind him left his face shadowed.

I stopped in front of him, pulled the notarized delivery invoice out of the file, and handed it to him. "I did promise I'd make your deadline."

He took the piece of paper and scanned it. "That, you did." He looked up, a strange intensity sharpening his gaze. "Any issues with the delivery?"

I blinked at the unexpected question. *Did I miss something somewhere?*

Other than a flat tire and my weird moment of paranoia, the job had been fairly typical. He didn't need to know about either of those, so I shook my head. "Not that I'm aware of."

"Good, good."

Deciding to bring our transaction to an end so I could get the Genesis back to Carl and fall into bed, I thumbed the screen of my phone and opened the Guild's app. I turned my phone around until it was facing him. "To close out the invoice, I just need your signature that you're satisfied with the delivery and have received the notarized delivery receipt."

"Of course," he murmured, using his finger as a stylus.

I gave him the standard spiel: "The Guild would like to extend their appreciation of your business and hope you'll consider us for future needs."

When I was done, he offered his hand. "I'll authorize the bonus tonight so it will be in the Guild's account in the morning."

I shook his hand. "I'll let them know." I stepped back, offering a polite smile. "Have a good evening, Simon."

"You as well," he returned.

Business concluded, I turned and headed back to the car, leaving behind another satisfied Guild customer. If my name came up next time Red Maple needed a last-minute run, all the better. The urge to glance around chased me all the way back to the car, but I refused to cave, reminding myself that I was just tired and it had been a long day.

Once behind the wheel, I babied the coupe all the way back to the Guild's garage. I sent up a prayer to whoever was listening that Carl didn't have the night shift, but when I pulled in, I found no one upstairs was taking my request.

I was already talking when I opened my door and got out, holding my hands up in a placating gesture. "She picked up a nail on the freeway."

Carl's normally dour face darkened as he frowned. "Why didn't you call us to get a tow?"

I dropped my hands to my hips and arched a brow. "There's a rune for that, you know? They're called run flats."

"For emergency purposes only," he shot back.

It was the end of a long day, so it took a beat for me to quash my urge to snap back. Instead, with forced patience, I said, "Exactly, and the client's deadline made it an emergency."

Since the Guild generally held the client sacrosanct, that was the one argument he couldn't dispute. Instead, he shook his head in disgust and began circling the coupe. Cadaverously thin, the Guild's head mechanic and guardian of all things mechanical walked around the coupe, doing a visual inspection. When he got to the damaged wheel, he crouched down until I could barely see the top of his head over the trunk. His hand stroked over the rear panel as if he were petting the car.

"We'll get you all fixed up, sweetheart." His raspy croon accompanied another dirty look directed my way as he straightened.

I didn't bother defending myself, because he wasn't inclined to listen. His babies were precious, and anything that happened to them was the fault of the drivers they served. "I kept my speed down and took her on smooth roads." Okay, so I couldn't quite squash the need to defend myself. "It was maybe thirty miles."

More like forty, but who's counting?

His stink eye didn't fade, but he didn't give me any more grief as we got the Genesis checked in and I signed away my potential firstborn to attest that I hadn't maliciously hurt his girl. When he was finally satisfied, I beat feet, crawled into my precious, and escaped home, where I promptly stripped and fell face-first into bed.

SIX

THE SIREN'S call of cinnamon and caramel dragged me out of a restless sleep and into bleary-eyed wakefulness. A check of my clock on my nightstand showed it was almost seven o'clock. I buried my face in my pillow and groaned as the aroma of coffee continued to taunt me. Thanks to a nonstop reel of half-remembered nightmares, five hours of fitful sleep was not enough to leave me bright-eyed and bushy-tailed. Unfortunately, my boss was a real bitch, so calling in sick wasn't an option.

I rolled out of my bed, shuffled to the en suite bathroom, and did what was necessary to at least recognize my name. I left my room and made the very short trip to the condo's main living space, which was split between the open kitchen and living room.

"Morning, sunshine." My chirpy red-headed roommate stood at the stove with a spatula in hand.

I thought she grinned, but couldn't swear it, intent on getting to the dark liquid dripping into a pot. I skirted around her in my zombie-like shuffle, lifted a hand in acknowledgement, and muttered, "Coffee."

Lena waited until I had poured a cup and taken my first sip before she asked, "Late night?"

I grimaced. "Slept like crap." I took another fortifying sip, and the fog began to drift away. I rounded the island and took a seat on one of the barstools. "I didn't wake you when I got home, did I?"

She shook her head as she scrambled the mix of vegetables and eggs in the pan with a spatula. "I think you came in when I was in the shower." She set the spatula aside, dumped her egg scramble into a bowl, and put the skillet on the back burner. She collected her bowl and mug from the counter then hauled both over to the island so she could stand opposite of me while she ate. She paused with a forkful of egg halfway to her mouth. "When I got out, the alarm was set. Went out to see if you were up, but you were facedown in bed." She took her bite, chewed, then swallowed. "Thought you were going to chill last night. Did Zev get back early?"

It was my turn to do a head shake. "He got stuck overnight in Vegas with Emilio's thing." I took another fortifying sip then cradled my coffee mug. "I ended up doing a last-minute delivery run for the Guild."

"Anything interesting?"

I shrugged. "You know Max Vasquez?"

Lena frowned, took another bite, and chewed. Her gold-flecked green eyes narrowed as she ran the name through her memory banks. When she swallowed, she refocused on me. "Sounds familiar."

I set my elbow on the counter and rested my head in my hand. "He's the heir apparent to the Vasquez Family, and last night, he got engaged."

"To?"

"A Devon something or other." I couldn't remember her last name or if my search had even provided it. "Blond, classy, and apparently good at poker as she cleared a table last night."

Lena arched a brow, set down her fork, and picked up her mug. "Really?"

I nodded.

"Huh." She took a sip before asking, "So they held their engagement party at a casino? That's… unique."

My lips quirked at her attempt to be nice. "Actually, it wasn't a casino, but this tricked-out villa up in Oak Creek. Gorgeous place, but then again, up there, hard for it not to be." Since the caffeine was doing its job and I was starting feel more awake and aware, I sat back in my chair. "They had a couple of sweet rides parked out front, a bar set up on the main floor, and a DJ in the back."

Lena paused in the midst of taking another sip to say, "Only you would notice the rides."

I picked up my cup and grinned. "Best part of my night." Peering over the rim of my mug, I added, "Well, that and the thousand-dollar bonus I picked up."

"Score." She lifted a hand, and we exchanged high fives. When we were done, she went back to her breakfast. "For that kind of bonus, what did he do? Wait until the last minute to order her ring?"

I made an amused snort. "Actually, the delivery was for him, not her."

Lena blinked. "Wow, whatever it was must have been something."

It was on the tip of my tongue to share the package was an old pair of glasses, but while the contract didn't explicitly state confidentiality, years of erring on the side of caution kept me quiet. Instead, I decided to ease her unspoken curiosity while answering a question of mine at the same time. Two birds, one stone kind of thing. "Do you know what a 'pythagograph' is?"

Lena's semi-slouch disappeared as her attention sharpened. "A what?"

Worried I'd mispronounced it, I repeated a little slower, "A 'pythagograph.'"

"That's what I thought you said," she muttered as she took her bowl to the sink and rinsed it out. When she was done and drying her hands, she asked, "Where did you hear that?"

"Last night at the party."

"You know I want to ask for details, but I know the drill, so I won't." She carefully tucked the hand towel back on the handle of the dishwasher.

I voiced the unspoken, "But?"

"But"—she met my gaze—"you remember that case Evan worked about a month back? The one that was driving him nuts until he figured out someone buried electronic information in a picture?"

"You mean the WestMagi Union deal where the loan manager hid a bunch of off-shore account numbers in his computer's screensaver?" I drew one of my legs up, propped my heel on the seat of the barstool, and used the counter's edge to keep it in place. "Didn't Evan call him a brilliant idiot?"

She moved back to her original spot and leaned in, resting her weight on her folded arms. "Yeah, mainly because the guy was devious enough to use digital images to hide his trail, but stupid enough to do it on his work computer."

"You and I both know it doesn't take a PhD to be a criminal."

"True that," she said. "But to answer your question, pythagography is a close magical equivalent of image steganography, but instead of manipulating code to hide information in an image, you use magic to imbed a target-specific spell into an object and then mask it with an illusion."

Guess I picked the right person for an explanation, because Lena was a highly skilled Guild Key who specialized in spellwork, specifically curse breaking. "That sounds like a lot like a curse."

"Close," she said. "It's a unique blend of casting and illusion magic."

"So a pythagograph is a spelled image hiding some kind of information from someone?" I thought of the black-and-white photos laid out on the table at the villa. "Like in a photograph?"

She nodded. "That would be one of the easiest ways to set it up, yes, but the way I've seen it used and the stories I've heard about other cases is that another object needs to be used in conjunction with the image to reveal the true picture or information."

I frowned. "Kind of like a magical lock set where the object is the key and the image is the lock?"

She made a hum of agreement. "Do you remember that job I did for that museum in California a few years back?"

"The one with the weird art installment?"

"Yeah, that one. A series of paintings and objets d'art from one of the local families was left to the museum, and as part of the endowment, the paintings were required to be displayed in their own windowless gallery hall. Additionally, the family's trust required that two ornate chandeliers included in the endowment be hung in the gallery with the paintings. Further instructions stated that for a 'full experience,'"—she used her fingers like quotes—"visitors should spend time with the paintings illuminated only by the chandeliers."

"That's sounds a little over-the-top."

"It was," she agreed. "But the museum, used to dealing with eccentric requests, decided to test this art installation before subjecting their patrons to it. Safety protocols required a Key be in attendance during their initial viewing phase, so they call me in and set up a room with the paintings and chandeliers. It was me, the museum director, and some extended family member overseeing the installation. The paintings were done in oil and were beautiful landscapes. There were six of them."

She raised a finger as she counted each down. "There was a stormy seascape, a field of wildflowers, a quiet pond, a sunlit glade, a dark and wild forest, and a lonely mountainside. Despite their age, the colors were vibrant, and the artist was talented enough, it was almost like being there." She stopped talking, and her gaze turned distant, as if she were back in that room. Something disquieting drifted across her expression. "It wasn't until they flicked off the normal lights and left only the chandelier ones on that it all changed." She fell quiet, her gaze going somewhere unpleasant.

"Lena," I called gently then waited until she blinked and focused on me. "You okay?"

"Yeah." She gave a small shudder and seem to finally come all the way back. "Yeah, I'm good." She pushed up from the counter until she was standing straight. "Under the light of the chandeliers the paintings, hung as a set, became a larger scene of a figure who was navigating a maze. At the center, something dark waited, and at the far end, something bright waited."

That didn't sound so bad, but I could tell from her tone there was more to it than a simple change of imagery. "Was that all?"

She shook her head slowly. "There was a compulsion embedded in the artwork. It was subtle, and I almost missed it. If it hadn't been for the director's assistant coming in and flicking on the light, I think the three of us would still be standing there, trying to figure out how to get through the maze."

I couldn't remember how long she'd been out of town during that assignment. "How long did it take you to unravel the spell?"

"Three very long days."

I let out a low whistle. Lena was one of the top Keys in Arizona, so for a job to last that long equaled a seriously complicated casting.

"Yeah." She nodded. "I had to work in sprints because it was subtle as hell and hard to detect when it started to suck you under."

Totally into her story, I couldn't help but ask, "Why on earth would anyone want to leave something like that to a museum?"

Lena shrugged. "Why do people do any of the inane things they do?"

"Good question." I grabbed my cup, took another sip, then rested the mug on my knee. The heat seeped through the ceramic and the thin material of my sleep pants. "Did the museum keep the installment up?"

"They did, but only after the museum director confronted the trustee and told them to expect a bill for my work. They swore they had no idea about any of it, that they were simply following the last wishes of their client, who happened to be the last of his family."

"Did the director buy that?" Maybe I was tad cynical, but it was difficult to believe the trustee hadn't known, or at least suspected, something was up with a strangely specific request like that.

Lena grimaced. "I don't know, but he didn't strike me as a fool."

"They kept the installment," I pointed out.

"There is that," she agreed. "However, the museum made it clear that while they would display the paintings, they would be returning the chandeliers to the trustee."

"Guess that's one way to ensure your patrons don't lose themselves in the artwork."

She gave me a look. "Really?"

"What?" I asked, all innocence, even as I smothered my grin.

She simply shook her head. She started to say something, only to stop when her phone buzzed on the counter behind her. She turned, grabbed it, and checked the screen. "Great." She turned back around and told me, "Got to go. My nine o'clock just got moved up to eight."

I stayed seated and enjoyed my coffee as she rushed to gather her keys, sunglasses, and a lightweight sweater jacket. "Hey, any idea for when to reschedule game night?"

She pulled her hair out from under the collar of her jacket. "Maybe tomorrow?"

"That works."

She opened the front door. "I'll let Evan know. Can you check with Mari and have Zev touch base with Locke?"

"Yep."

"Cool, then I'm out." She flicked me a wave.

"Be safe."

"You too," she called back before the door closed behind her.

SEVEN

ABOUT AN HOUR AFTER LENA LEFT, I headed out to the first of my scheduled jobs. For a Friday, there was nothing too exciting on the docket, but it was enough to keep me busy. Unfortunately, my to-do list necessitated a return trip to the Guild garage to pick up one of their delivery vans. As an independent contractor, my transportation options were limited, much like my bank balance, so when my Mustang didn't cut it or I wasn't willing to put her at risk, I had an agreement with the Guild that allowed use of their standard-class vehicles for a cut of my fee. Of course, unlike when I actually worked for the Guild, this did not guarantee me my pick of options. Instead, my pool was limited to whatever was available.

Luckily, a recently acquired acquaintance-turned-friend who happened to also be a cutthroat lawyer had been nearby when I was reviewing the initial agreement with the Guild. Unable to sit by without inserting her opinion, she'd insisted I add an amendment to the agreement for jobs requiring a higher caliber of security and performance at a rate of five percent of the assignment's cost. Mindful of creating a solid bottom line, I'd hemmed and hawed until she rightly pointed out that since the Arcane Council was one of my contracted clients, high-risk assignments were inevitable. Since I couldn't argue, I amended the agreement and gritted my teeth as I included a five percent cut of my fee. The Guild pushed back for ten, and we eventually met at seven. Such a scenario had yet to occur, but I didn't doubt that clock would run out when I least expected it.

When being my own boss had been nothing but a pipe dream, I hadn't realized the plethora of parts that went into creating my own business. Yeah, it was great not having to punch someone else's clock, but since everything started and ended with me, my downtime was nearly nonexistent—especially during those first few weeks after hanging up my shingle. Even though I'd scored both Sabella and the Council as clients, there was a long road ahead of me before I left my mark on the Arcane world. Some days were harder than others, but with each new job and client, my determination to rise to the top deepened.

I spent my drive to the Guild mentally running through my upcoming jobs and their requirements, playing out a variety of what-if scenarios. I used the technique to keep my anxiety in check. Years of being a Guild Transporter had taught me that no matter how straightforward or easy a job appeared, the possibility of things going sideways was very real. Now that my assignments rested solely on my shoulders, with no Guild buffer, that truth haunted me. If I screwed up, my reputation would be damaged along with the job, and a sterling reputation was key to my end goal.

I guided my baby into the Guild's multilevel parking structure and tucked her into a parking spot guarded by Guild-monitored security cameras. I sent Evan a request to keep an eye on her and got his thumbs-up emoji back as I walked to the garage's office. Thankfully, one of Carl's minions was manning the office. He was checking out a level-four sedan to a man I recognized as one of the Guild's

Sentinels. Wearing a dark suit, he was built like a linebacker and kept his dark hair cut military short. Sean was a combat mage and one of the go-to names for personal security.

"Hey, Sean."

He glanced up from signing his name in triplicate and gave me a friendly "Hey, Rory, how's it going?"

"Staying busy. You?"

"Same." He swiped one more signature then handed the papers over to the minion, who then handed over a key fob. Sean muttered his thanks, turned, and walked by me with a "Later."

As he headed out, I called, "Stay safe."

He lifted a hand in acknowledgement and shot back over his shoulder, "You too."

Fifteen minutes and half a forest of initials and signatures later, I took the private elevator tucked behind the office to the garage's top floor, where the Guild stored all their vehicles. The doors slid shut, and I keyed in the access code as the Guild's protective wards activated. Years of practice made it easy to dismiss the annoying rasp of magic that guarded access from all but Guild-authorized personnel. When the doors slid apart, I stepped onto a floor that was miles away from the stained concrete of the lower parking levels. A wall of thick bullet- and magic-resistant glass stretched before me, and behind it lay a gearhead's utopia. The massive space was divided between what was affectionately called the showroom, which took up the first half, and the garage, which dominated the back half.

I stopped in front of the security glass and waited for the computerized voice to ask for my authorization code. "Mike, alpha, Charlie, hotel, one, zero."

It took a few seconds for the code and voice print to process, then the electronic voice directed, "Proceed."

The heavy glass doors slid open with a whoosh of air, bringing with it the scent of wax and oil as I crossed the multi-layered security ward that made the fine hairs along my arms stand on end. I adored the showroom. It was hard not to with the stellar collection of gleaming works of automotive art designed to hobnob with the elite while delivering protection, power, and performance.

I wove my way between some of my favorites, offering a slight brush of my hand as I strode past to the back half, where the Guild's workhorses sat. It was a ragtag collection of vehicles meant to blend into their surroundings, drawing nary a second look. Well, not until the driver got behind the wheel. It was what lay under the hood and was worked into the frame that set these unassuming vehicles apart from the norm. The Guild was not one to skimp on power or protection for their clients.

There were a couple of empty spots here and there, but Ike, the mechanic on duty, had offered me a choice of two late-model SUVs—a Honda CRV and a Nissan Murano. Sweet lines and smooth handling were my preference, so the Nissan won. I found it next to a minivan complete with a stick family on the side window and a Charger with a patchwork primer paint job.

Five minutes later, I was headed to my first stop, an address in Glendale. Unlike the heart-pounding thrill ride portrayed on the big screen, the job of a Transporter was basically a glorified delivery driver. Granted, the last year hadn't been quite that ho-hum, not after agreeing to a questionable delivery that had led to meeting Zev then eventually getting tangled up in a deeply twisted game of corporate revenge between three big-name Arcane Families. Not to mention that when all was said and done, one of the knots left unraveled was most likely tied to a shadow group of power-hungry, monied mages and scientists known as the Cabal. I tried very hard to ignore that last part since it was well above my pay grade and I wasn't looking to advance my career to that level. At least, not yet, but with both Sabella and the Council as clients, the ticking of that particular clock was getting louder.

For now, my focus was guaranteeing secured deliveries in a timely manner. That was why I spent the morning hauling twenty-five magically enhanced kitty litter boxes to a pet hotelier on the east side. The owner of the litter boxes was an older, rounded gent with a halo of pewter gray that left the top of his head bald. His worry about his patented odor spell falling into the wrong hands struck me as borderline paranoid, but my opinion of his mental state was beside the point, especially once he paid my fee. That job ate up the majority of my morning, thanks to the typical traffic snarls and headaches that plagued the overloaded and underfunded freeways of the Valley of the Sun.

After delivering the litter boxes safely to the exasperated pet hotelier, I hit a drive-through for more caffeine then aimed my wheels toward the next job, a package pickup from Tempe. Its final drop-off was over on the west side, which meant a return trip through construction and traffic. The thing about living in a metropolitan center like Phoenix was no matter how good a driver was at planning out the routes, efficiency was nearly unobtainable. Roughly a hundred fifty miles joined the SUV's odometer by the time I dropped a locked file box off at an industrial park. I was walking back to the SUV when my phone buzzed with a familiar ringtone. I couldn't stop my grin as I thumbed the screen and picked it up. "Hey, you! Are you back in town?"

Zev's chuckle filled my ear, leaving behind warm fuzzies. "Yeah, got in about an hour ago."

Only when the lingering knot in my stomach eased did it hit me that I had been low-key worried about Zev since his call the day before. "How was the dinner?"

"Uneventful, thankfully," he said. "Hey, I wanted to know if you're up for dinner tonight."

"For you, always." I got to the SUV, opened the door, and

got behind the wheel. I shut myself inside, shifted my phone to the other side, and held it in place with my shoulder as I started the car. "My place?"

"Love you, like Lena, but it's been a long couple of days. How about mine?" he countered gently.

"Just so you know, Evan's taking Lena out tonight, but I'm good with your place." I untucked the phone. "Hang on a second. I'm going to put you on speaker." I quickly synced the phone to the car. "You still there?"

"Yep." His deep voice rang through the speakers.

"Good." I swiped my phone to the maps app and pulled up my next job. "What are you thinking?"

"How do you feel about a night in and delivery?"

My imagination shifted gears. *Sounds damn good to me.* "Make it a sleepover, and you've got yourself a deal."

"Done."

I grinned to myself as I split my attention between backing out and my conversation. "What time is Emilio cutting you loose?"

"We've got a couple of things to tie up, but I should be home around four. What's your day looking like?"

"I've got one more run, then I should be free." I glanced at the time and did some mental calculations as I pulled through the parking lot and back onto the road. "I'll swing by my place, grab some stuff, and then head over."

"Sounds good. Shoot me a text when you're on your way."

"Can do." I hesitated a moment then added in a rush, "Love you, Zev. Glad you're home."

"Me too, babe." He sounded like it. His voice was sweet when he added, "I'll see you tonight, love. Stay safe out there."

Mushy emotions heated my face, and I managed to get in an "I will," before we both disconnected.

As I drove to my next pickup, it struck me just how much

my life had changed. I'd gone from being an orphan with a very small circle of friends and living in a crappy one-bedroom apartment while working with the Guild to pay off my training loans to discovering I was family to the matriarch of one of the most powerful Arcane Families, dating the lethal Arbiter for another scarily powerful Family, starting my own business that included the Arcane Council, and living in a sweet two-bedroom modern condo with my best friend.

Yeah, life had been a hell of a trip recently. Especially when I considered the not-so-shiny parts of that journey. Like the lingering guilt of my role in the death of a good man caught up in a monstrous plot, or the worry that a ticking time bomb was hidden somewhere inside me where no one— not even me—could see it after I'd been dosed by a madwoman and her even-crazier scientist boyfriend. And that wasn't even touching on the unknown threats that hovered around my DNA. There were reasons I'd been raised by the state instead of my great-aunt Sabella after the death of my mother, reasons why I hadn't even known of our familial connection until recently.

A sudden flash of red taillights in front of me had me easing off the gas before I finished processing the danger. I did a quick mirror check and glided over to the next lane to avoid adding my hood to the bumper of the sedan ahead of me.

Right, get your head straight, Rory.

I tucked my neurosis and concerns back into their corner where I had successfully kept them for the last few months with a promise of dealing with it later. If I stayed busy, that later would take a while to arrive. I flicked on the radio, determined to chase away my dark thoughts, and deliberately focused on the job ahead.

EIGHT

FIFTEEN MINUTES LATER, I turned into a large parking lot outside one of the many casinos owned by the First Nations. This one, Black Water, was one of the newer ones. Construction dumpsters still sat on the outside edges of the lot. It took a couple of minutes, but I finally scored a spot near the casino's entrance. I double-checked the contact's name for the job then got out of the SUV. I beeped the locks and ran my fingertips over the engraved sigil at the top of the driver's door. Magic sparked as the Guild's wards activated.

It took a few more minutes to find a path through the main floor cluttered with pale-faced, red-eyed customers enthralled by the annoying clash of flashing lights, electronic chimes, and blaring announcements of wins. Thankfully, there was no smoky haze to exacerbate the din. I followed the discreetly mounted signs to the casino's offices. I pulled open the door, stepped inside, and went up to the receptionist, a young man dressed in a dark suit coat, white shirt, and dark tie. The door behind me clicked shut, and the noise from the floor dropped several decibels, proof of good soundproofing.

"Good afternoon," the young man said. "Can I help you?"

"Yes, my name is Rory Costas." I unlocked my phone,

thumbed the screen until my ID pulled up, flipped it around, and set it down for him to see. "I'm here to pick up a package from Rebecca Tsosie."

He picked up the phone, studied it then me, and handed it back. "If you'll give me just a moment, I'll go back and let her know you're here."

"Thank you." I reclaimed my phone and put in my pocket. Then I waited.

A couple minutes later, the young man returned with a dark-haired woman at his side. Something about her seemed familiar, but I couldn't place it. She was older than me, and the air of unapologetic maturity had me thinking she might be in her late thirties, possibly early forties.

She caught sight of me and offered a polite smile as she moved around the edge of the counter to meet me. She didn't offer her hand, but her greeting was warm. "Ms. Costas, lovely to meet you."

"Ms. Tsosie," I returned, taking no offense at the lack of a handshake as such caution wasn't unusual when dealing with those outside the Arcane community. Both Traditionalists, those who possessed little to no magic, and First Nation members were understandably leery about outsiders.

"If you'll follow me?" She waved me ahead of her out of the office.

I stepped out of the quiet office and into the din of the main floor. Neither of us talked, mainly because we would have to yell to be heard. She led me around the main floor to the back side of the casino and through a set of doors marked Employees Only that spilled into a wide service hall.

I didn't bother with polite chitchat. Since I considered it annoying, I wasn't inclined to inflict the irritation on others. However, I couldn't help but notice the small sidelong glances she kept giving me.

Finally, when we hit the double doors at the end of the service hall, she stopped. "You don't remember me, do you?"

I paused and studied her for a moment. A little taller and less curvy than me, she was attractive, with her dark hair, dark eyes, and striking features. Again, there was that sense of familiarity, but I couldn't quite place her. "I'm sorry, I don't." I didn't want to offend her, but I really couldn't figure out where we'd met.

She smiled. "Last night—"

Her wry grin made it finally click into place—the younger dark-haired woman in Sedona. "At the poker game," I finished. "You were at the table with Devon and the others."

She gave a small laugh and pressed open one of the doors. "I was," she confirmed as she waved me through the opening.

I waited until she followed me in. "That was a beautiful venue for their engagement party."

She stayed at my side as she continued our journey through what appeared to be where the casino accepted deliveries. It was a large space with huge rolling metal doors opened along the back, some blocked by large trailers filled with various boxes. Workers milled around, loading and unloading, their work interspersed with the occasional shout.

"Dev and Max are nothing if not dedicated to being memorable." There was nothing mean in her voice, just a gentle note of teasing. "Here we are." She stopped near a narrow window and an electronic keypad. She pulled out a keycard, swiped, then pulled open the door.

I moved inside to a neatly arranged storage room and stood off to the side as she entered. It was cooler than the main warehouse behind us. A long, tall table stretched through the center space, matched with equally tall chair-like stools. Bits and pieces of packing materials were scattered across the surface.

"Well, that villa is definitely memorable," I offered.

Rebecca laughed as she stepped inside, and the door closed behind her. She headed toward the metal shelves on the back wall, lined with boxes. "It belongs to his firm, and since they like Max and Dev tends to get what she wants, they were happy to offer it up."

I'm sure Max's connection to the Council didn't hurt either. Instead of sharing my rather cynical comment, I kept quiet.

She ran a finger along the cardboard faces until she found the one she wanted. She pulled it down, brought it over to a relatively clear space on the table, and set it down. "Let me grab the documentation."

"However it came about, the party seemed to be a success."

She headed toward the far-back corner, where a cluttered desk held a computer and a battered filing cabinet stood guard. She yanked opened one of the metal drawers, and it screeched in protest. She spoke as she searched the files. "That, it was, but it's not the only thing people are talking about now." She found the papers she wanted, pulled them out, and brought them over to the table.

"Oh?" Maybe it wasn't wise to indulge my curiosity, but Rachel seemed willing to chat. I moved closer to the table, watching as she sorted the pages into recognizable piles that revealed what was in the box on the table—the provenance report, supporting literature, then the condition and appraisal reports—which all equaled artwork, specifically museum-grade artwork. Lena's story whispered through my head, but I shook it off. This was not some weird, cursed set of paintings. Something like that would never fit in such a small box. Still, I pulled my Prism a little closer, just in case.

Rebecca set aside a single sheet of paper. "Everyone's speculating on whether or not that map really leads to anything." She searched through the packing debris, found a pen, and signed the paper. Then she slid it toward me and offered the pen. "If you wouldn't mind?"

"Not at all." I took the pen, read through what appeared to be a fairly straightforward package acceptance. There was one additional line with a condition. I looked up. "This requires I verify the object. Are you willing to open the package for me?"

"Not a problem." She found a pair of scissors and carefully cut through the packing tape. Then she dug through the box, spilling Styrofoam popcorn over the edges, and pulled out a heavily wrapped object. She gingerly unwrapped it to expose a stunning pair of kachina dolls. She set the pair on the table.

Power whispered along my Prism, but that was all it did. There was a depth to that touch, a depth that spoke to age. "Those are gorgeous."

With their bright colors, soft feathers, dyed leather, and wood, nothing about the dolls was mass produced. The two pieces of artwork were clearly hand-crafted masterpieces and worlds apart from the ones found around town.

"Aren't they, though?" There was a quiet pride in her voice. "They belong to one of our oldest families, and they are lending them to the university for an exhibit that opens in a couple of months."

I had no doubt the university was beside itself with glee over this, but I was here to do a job. "Do you have the photos? I can use those for a visual verification."

She went straight to the second pile and separated the photos. "Here you go."

"Thanks." After confirming these were, in fact, the two dolls I was to deliver, I signed below her signature then handed back the package acceptance form.

Rebecca set it aside and rewrapped the dolls. Then she stacked the documentation into a neat pile, slipped it into a manila envelope, sealed it, and touched an embossed rune on the flap. The bright spark of a privacy ward flared. She handed it over with a half-apologetic smile. "The university requested authentication, so be sure they sign for both the dolls and the report, please."

"Of course." I took the envelope and ignored the magic prickling along my fingers as she re-packed the dolls. Since she'd started it and I was curious, I went back to our original conversation. "Do you think Max's map will lead to anything?"

"Honestly? I don't know." She swept up the escaping popcorn pieces and dumped them into the box. "For his sake, I hope it does." Before I poked at that comment, she asked, "Do you know the story behind the map?"

"No."

She picked up a tape gun and shot me a look. "Do you want to know?"

Actually, yes. I tried for casual. "Sure."

The tape rasped as she sealed up the box. She set down the tape gun, nudged the box closer to me, and settled in against the table. "How strong is your grasp of Arizona history?"

Truthfully, it was probably better than most since I'd spent a few years searching through lesser-known historical texts when I was looking for information about being a Prism. I learned quickly that recorded history was colored by the one telling it, but I didn't think this was the time or place to delve into the darker accounts of Arizona's volatile beginnings. I'd run across quite a few seriously heartbreaking and horrifying survivor accounts of that time, but that was not why I was here, so I gave her the school-approved version. "Sometime in the late 1800s, a group of Families allied with the First Nations, and the two managed to keep the US government from wiping out the First Nations people and stealing their land. It wasn't until, I think, fifty, sixty years later that the First Nations negotiated an agreement with the government on land usage. A few years after that, Arizona ended up being one of the states covered in the First Nations Agreement of 1925."

Rebecca, lips pressed thin, folded her arms. "So you know the G-rated version."

Hearing the weary bitterness in her voice, I added quietly, "I know it was never that simple. I've read the other accounts."

She studied me for a long moment and dipped her chin. "Thank you." She unfolded her arms, braced her palms on the table, and went back to the story of the treasure map. "The map's story belongs to the Velasquez Family."

"As in the Council's Christina Velasquez?"

Rebecca nodded. "You know her family is one of the originals, right?"

It was my turn to nod.

"Right. The most popular story goes, after the Redondo Uprising, deserters from the US militia set down roots with the local communities. Many of these 'deserters'"—she used her fingers to make quotes—"were Traditionalists."

"That must have been awkward." Traditionalist were those with little to no magic, thanks to diluted bloodlines. They believed that magically strong portions of society were too arrogant and entitled. While I personally thought there were more than a few grains of truth to that thought, I wasn't in a rush to jump on the "magic is evil" bandwagon. Considering how few of them identified as Traditionalist, neither were most of the Arcane society.

Rebecca's lips curved with a hint of amusement. "Probably, but for this story, one of those Traditionalist deserters was named William Rutherford, and he ended up married to a woman with ties to the Velasquez Family, Maria Velez. She was a second or third cousin, I think."

"That must have made for an interesting marriage."

A short burst of humor escaped Rebecca at my dry comment. "I'm sure it was, but however they managed to get along, it worked for them, because the story claims they loved each other madly. Their respective families, on the other hand, not so much."

I grimaced. "Yeah, I'm betting family dinners were a nightmare."

"In more ways than one," Rebecca agreed. "In fact, William's older brother, Edward, really detested his younger brother for going AWOL. So much so, he hunted William down and dragged him back to be tried by a military tribunal, who found him guilty then sentenced him to hang. When Maria heard the news, she was devastated. Even more so when Edward managed to take anything William had of worth away from Maria by claiming that their marriage was invalid because William was a deserter. He left Maria with basically nothing."

Knowing how stories like these went, I added, "I foresee some serious revenge brewing."

"Oh yeah," Rebecca said. "Maria's ties to the Family might have been slight, but in the end, she proved she could be just as vindictive as any of them. She discovered that the real reason Edward turned William in was because Edward wanted the gold William had stolen during the Civil War. Gold that William hid when he settled down with Maria."

"And the map Max was talking about leads to that gold?"

Rebecca shrugged. "Supposedly, but it's not just the map that Max will need to find it. You see, Maria may not have flaunted her magic, but she had no issue nailing good ol' Edward with everything she had, and what she had was a doozy. Although her main power lay in necromancy, she had a secondary ability of illusion, specifically that of a Nightmare."

I let out a low whistle as a shiver crept down my spine. A mage who could manipulate the dead and magnify deep-seated fears until they became reality was not someone you wanted to cross, no matter how minor their power. "That's a hell of a combination."

She made a sound of agreement. "And motivated by grief and anger, she poured all that emotion into creating a curse that would last for generations. Maria, who knew about William's gold, decided that if Edward wanted it so bad, he could have it, but she didn't make it easy. Instead, she created a map masked in illusion. The only way to see the real map was to view it through a pair of William's eyeglasses. Then she began the whispers of the map's existence, enough to lure Edward into looking for it."

I had to give Maria props; she was devious as shit. "Let me guess. She cursed the glasses."

"Mm-hmm, she did." There was a hint of delighted glitter in Rebecca's dark eyes, as if she too wanted to high-five Maria. "According to legend, anyone with a selfish heart who wears those glasses will be haunted by those they wronged, until they pay in full the debt they incurred."

I raised my brows. "I'm assuming that debt ended with someone not breathing." That was how stories like this typically played out.

"So it seems," Rebecca replied. "Edward was dead within a year of his brother, and the map and the glasses disappeared soon after. There are stories throughout the following years of others chasing after the gold and then ending up dead under mysterious circumstances, but until last night, the glasses, like the map, remained lost to history."

"But if those are the right glasses, now it's Max's turn." I thought about the excitement that had filled the room the night before and the vivacious blonde who'd held on to Max. "Why on earth would he risk it?"

Rebecca sighed then said, her voice laced with frustrated acceptance, "Because he's a wannabe treasure hunter determined to leave his mark."

I wasn't sure that kind of glory was enough to risk a generations-old curse, but then again, what did I know? "Perhaps he plans on donating the treasure to charity, maybe get his name on a foundation or something," I said. When Rebecca gave me a puzzled frown, I elaborated. "To sidestep the whole 'selfish heart' part of the curse."

She choked back a giggle. "I'll have to share that solution with Devon. She'll totally push him to do that."

"Well, I wish her, and Max, the best of luck with the treasure hunt." If any part of the story Rebecca had just shared was true, they would need it. Maybe I should give Lena a heads-up that a call from Max's family might hit the Guild boards sometime soon. Rebecca came around the table as I grabbed the box then settled the weight of it under my arm. "As for me, I'll stick to more-mundane ways of making my mark in history. Like getting this package safely into the hands of the university."

Rebecca grinned. "Well, the university *and* I appreciate your dedication, Ms. Costas." She walked with me back to the door. "Although your reputation is starting to precede you, you know."

I shot her a glance. "Hopefully in a good way."

She made another one of those noncommittal hums. "We wouldn't have called if that wasn't the case." Her fingers flew over the keypad on the wall. The electronic lock clicked open, and she pushed the door wide, gesturing me through. "But I'll admit that curiosity also played a part. Everyone's trying to determine what it is that caught the Council's eye."

"Besides the obvious family connection?" The cynical question escaped before I could censor, but the unspoken hint of judgement rankled me.

Rebecca's eyes flew to mine, carrying a trace of surprise, as if she wasn't used to being called out on her behavior, and maybe she wasn't. She quickly reclaimed her composure. This time, something a little more wary lingered in her gaze. "Besides that, yes."

My annoyance took a step back at her admission. I stepped through the doorway then waited as she closed the door and reset the lock. "I would never presume to understand the Council's logic, Ms. Tsosie. What I do know is I'm good at what I do, and I hope that will be the reason my name is recognized, not because I'm the current object of curiosity."

This time, her laugh was soft. "I'm sure you are, Ms. Costas," she murmured as she led me back through the warehouse, "but may I offer you a bit of advice?" She waited for my nod. "Use that curiosity wisely, because things have a way of changing when the Families take an interest in your business."

NINE

I WAS INITIALING the return forms under the eagle eye of Ike, who had replaced Carl's earlier minion, when the Guild's custom ringtone interrupted. A quick rearrangement of items allowed me to answer my phone and sign off on the last page at the same time.

"This is Costas."

"Rory." Adele's voice filled my ear. "Do you expect to be at the office today?"

There was an unusual formality to her tone that made my spine stiffen as I gave Ike the forms and turned away. As far as I knew, there were no Guild jobs waiting for me. "I'm actually at the garage right now. Do you need me to come in?"

"Yes, that would be good," she said, that careful tone still in effect.

"Adele, is everything okay?"

"No need to rush. I just need your signature on the Anwar invoice."

Anwar invoice? The one I handed over yesterday? I frowned and said slowly, "Okay. I'll be there in five."

"Thank you." With that, she hung up.

I lowered my phone and continued to frown at the screen. "You're welcome," I muttered as I tried to figure out what the hell was going on. I shook my head and put my phone in my pocket. I lifted a hand as I pushed through the door. "Later, Ike." Without waiting for his response, I hot-footed it to the main lobby.

I sent Zev a quick text, letting him know I might be late, as I rushed up the stairs to the second floor. I came out of the stairwell and took a second to steady my breathing and nerves, then I calmly walked toward the Guild's offices. I had my hand on the handle of the glass door when I realized it was good that I had taken that second, because what would normally be a deserted lobby at nearly four o'clock on a Friday now held a stern-faced Adele facing down a man and woman while a wide-eyed Kel observed from the front desk.

I walked in, and the two strangers turned toward me. Recognition hit and explained Adele's earlier tone. I pasted on a polite smile and braced. "Detectives Hall and Rendón, isn't it?"

"Hello, Ms. Costas," Hall, the older male, said, while Rendón, his partner, simply dipped her head in an unspoken greeting.

I joined the trio in front of the reception desk. "Hello again."

I ignored the muttered "That was quick," that came from Detective Rendón. Clearly, time hadn't dulled whatever issue she had with me.

Since it wouldn't do me any good to call her out, I played deaf and turned to Adele. "You needed a signature?"

"I did, yes." She offered me the electronic tablet she held. "If you could just initial here"—she pointed about halfway down the screen—"and here." She indicated another section just below that. "And then sign at the bottom. We should be good."

"Of course." I took the tablet and quickly scanned the

indicated sections of what was clearly not an invoice. I was, in fact, signing an addendum between the Guild and myself for legal representation.

Legal representation?

The waiting detectives and Adele's demeanor came together in a rush of nerves. I didn't hesitate to initial each section, confirming I accepted the Guild's legal representation, access to any additional resources as needed, and the warning regarding client confidentiality.

Something big was up, and since I didn't have time to reach out to my legal counsel, Adele was stepping in. The Guild didn't mess around when it came to covering its ass, and as a contractor, I would now benefit from that coverage. I scrawled my final signature on the bottom of the page then handed it back to Adele. "Thank you for following up. I'm not sure how I missed that."

"Easy enough to do." Adele's smile didn't touch her somber eyes. "By the way, the detectives here have some questions for you."

Acting surprised wasn't difficult. "For me?" I turned to the watching duo. "About?"

"You delivered a package last night?" Detective Rendón asked bluntly. "To a Maximiliano Vasquez?"

I looked to Adele, who inclined her head, silently giving me permission to answer. "I did, yes."

The detective looked between Adele and me, clearly not missing the silent exchange. I waited for her to comment. Instead, she continued with her questions. "And that package was?"

"I'm sorry, Detective, but you know I can't answer that."

"Can't or won't?"

"Both." I refused to let her rile me. She had been just as snippy in our first meeting when I was laid up in a hospital bed. "First, I was under Guild contract for that delivery, which means I'm subject to their confidentiality clauses. Second, as a Transport—"

The lobby door behind me opened on a whoosh of air, and a voice ordered, "Don't say another word."

I turned to see a man bearing down on us. He was average height, a little round around the waist, but impeccably dressed in a tie, collared shirt, and pressed pants. The overhead lights glinted off his polished shoes. I snapped my mouth closed and mentally searched for a name to go with the face.

Before I could find a match, he was at Adele's side and addressing the detectives. "Carson Harrington, Guild counsel." He held out his hand to the two grim-faced detectives.

With no other choice, they shook his hand and exchanged names.

When they were done, Carson continued in a pleasant, noncombative tone. "While we're happy to answer your questions, I'll remind you that Ms. Costas was acting on behalf of the Guild during the delivery in question, and in accordance with her contract, any official inquiries necessitate counsel presence."

Detective Hall cleared his throat, which didn't mask Rendón's dismissive snort. "We appreciate your cooperation," Hall said. "However, we aren't here to interrogate Ms. Costas. We're simply interested in retracing Mr. Vasquez's movements last night."

"Then the question regarding the contents of the package is moot, isn't it?" Carson's smile didn't waver as he politely reinforced his point. "Ms. Costas confirmed she delivered the package. Unless that package was damaged in some way, I'm not sure what other information she can offer you."

I wasn't either, but I didn't dare interrupt. The relationship between the Guild and local law enforcement was touchy at best, and navigating it was like walking through a minefield while blindfolded. I left it to those better qualified than me to make that journey.

Hall stepped lightly. "We're not here to impugn on the Guild's reputation"—he looked at me and added—"or Ms. Costas." He turned back to Carson. "We're simply touching base with all those who interacted with Mr. Vasquez last night. Ms. Costas's name has come up during these interviews, so we are here to follow up."

Interviews? As in plural?

Even though I'd done nothing wrong, my nerves shifted to anxiety at the direction their questions were taking and what it implied.

"Perhaps," Adele interrupted smoothly, "we should continue this conversation in the conference room?"

Hall smiled, deepening the sun-worn lines around his too-grim eyes. "Of course."

Adele took the lead, and when Carson motioned for me to follow her, I did. Adele waited for me to move into the back office space. I barely registered the uncomfortable itch of the protective ward as I crossed the threshold. I stepped out of the way of the others and looked to Adele. "Room two?"

"That should work," she confirmed.

I led the way to one of the smaller conference rooms. The door was unlocked. The blinds were drawn, leaving the room dark, so I flipped on the lights. A dark oval table surrounded by eight high-back chairs sat in the space. I picked a seat on the far side and waved the detectives to the seats across from me. Carson claimed the seat to my left, and Adele, after closing the door, came over and took the seat to my right.

Once we were settled, Carson took charge, his amicable expression firmly in place, his hands folded in front of him on the table. "Now, we're happy to assist so long as your questions do not violate our client's privacy. However, I'm curious as to why you are here."

Hall and Rendón exchanged a look, then Hall answered,

"Earlier this afternoon, Mr. Vasquez was involved in an accident."

Carson's eyes narrowed. "What kind of accident?"

"We're not at liberty to share those details," Hall said. "I can tell you that he's currently in the ICU at Desert Memorial."

My mind whirled with images of a laughing Devon and an excited Max. "Oh my god," I murmured. "Poor Devon."

Rendón's attention shot to me as Hall started typing something on his phone, notes probably. "You know Ms. Olson?"

I felt a hand brush my thigh—Adele's version of a warning. I ignored it and shook my head. "I met her, briefly, last night at their engagement party."

Hall didn't look up from his screen as Rendón took over the interrogation portion. "Guests indicated that you arrived around nine thirty."

I shook my head. "Closer to nine, actually."

"And what time did you leave?"

"Around nine forty or so."

She raised her eyebrows. "Do you have any way to verify those times?"

Carson answered before I could. "If records are required, you'll need to submit a warrant, Detective."

Rendón's lips tightened. "You're certain of the times?"

"Because of the urgency attached to the delivery, yes, I am."

Her brown eyes sharpened as she focused on one word. "Urgency?"

"Mr. Moore contacted our office after hours and asked to upgrade the delivery status to immediate," Adele clarified. "He also indicated there was an additional bonus if the notarized receipt was returned to Red Maple's offices by midnight."

"And you're sure it was Mr. Moore you spoke to?" Hall asked.

Adele cocked her head. "He identified himself as Mr. Simon Moore, an agent with Red Maple Collections. I verified that the number he was calling from belonged to Red Maple, and his name was included on our contract with the same."

"It's my understanding that the Guild employs its own Transporters, correct?" Rendón cut in.

"That's correct," Adele answered. "However, based on the limited notice, none of our in-house Transporters were available. The offer was presented to Ms. Costas, as she has provided excellent service on Guild jobs in the past."

I didn't get much of a chance to bask in Adele's compliment before both detectives turned their attention back to me.

Hall took the lead. "Ms. Costas, did anything unusual occur during your delivery?"

It was clear they were looking for something specific, but other than getting a flat, nothing stood out for me. I wasn't pretty sure they didn't give a damn about my tire. "No. I picked up the package, took it to Sedona, handed it over to Mr. Vasquez, and got back to Red Maple just before midnight."

"You mentioned you met Ms. Olson briefly at the party." Hall waited for my nod. "Did you meet anyone else?"

"There was the doorman, another security personnel, the bartender, and those in the room with Mr. Vasquez and Ms. Olson."

"Do you have names?"

I looked to Carson, who nodded, so I took a deep breath. "For security and the doorman, no. The bartender's name tag said Cass. I spoke to her for a few minutes while I waited for security to inform Mr. Vasquez I was there. Obviously, Max Vasquez, Devon Olson, but there were two men who were playing poker with Devon. I think their names were Perry and Kent. There were two women at the table as well. One was Rebecca Tsosie, and the other was an older lady, but I didn't catch her name."

"Rebecca Tsosie?" Hall arrowed in on the name. "How do you know her?"

"I don't, other than I did a recent delivery for Black Water Casino, and she was my point of contact."

Hall made a note on his phone while Rendón continued to study me in that particular way cops had that made a person feel like they were minutes away from being handcuffed. "While you were at the party, did anyone appear to be upset with Mr. Vasquez?"

"No," I said.

A flash of frustration was there and gone, then she and Hall circled around the same questions a few more times. Each time they overstepped, Carson politely reprimanded them, until finally they gave up. I stood with Carson as Adele led the detectives out, both of us quiet until their voices disappeared.

Carson held out a business card. "If they reach out again, Ms. Costas, refer them to me."

A little dazed by the whole situation, I took it. "I will, thank you."

He studied me for a moment then offered a friendly smile. "Ms. Costas."

"Rory, please." My response was automatic.

"Rory," he corrected. "There's no reason to let them worry you."

My gaze jumped to his.

"Their questions were fairly standard, considering, so I'm sure you have nothing to worry about." He patted my arm awkwardly then wished me a good evening.

I returned the same and slowly followed him out of the room. Unfortunately, his reassurance did nothing to ease the knots in my gut.

TEN

I STRODE into the garage where my Mustang was parked, distracted by the interview with the two detectives. Worry and a slow burn of resentment created tight bands of tension across my neck and shoulders. I tried to reassure myself that Hall and Rendón were simply doing their job, but it wasn't working.

I'd never been the trusting type, and my relationship with authority figures was rocky. I had cultivated a few helpful connections with the local law enforcement throughout my years with the Guild. However, when Zev and I were attacked in a different garage by a team of mercenary mages months ago, those relationships had fallen short, hence my initial meeting with Hall and Rendón where it was made crystal clear she didn't like me. As for Hall, he played things close to his vest, so I had no clue how he viewed me.

Truthfully, Rendón's dislike had more to do with who I chose to hang around with, specifically the Arcane Families. It hadn't taken me long to recognize the chip she carried when it came to the elite and powerful because a similar one weighed heavily on my shoulders for years before practicality had whittled it down to cynical size. In the Arcane world, the

Families held all the cards. They had the money, the magic, and the power, both personal and professional, to get the results they wanted. It made things difficult when an individual was caught between serving the public and answering to their politically motivated boss.

Knowing this, I tried not to take offense at Rendón's attitude, but I wasn't stupid enough to ignore the potential trouble it could create. I made a mental note to put in a call to my personal lawyer, Maribel Ortiz, to ensure my legal assets were covered should the detectives decide to make a return visit. Not that I didn't trust Carson's advice, but, well, he was answerable to the Guild, and Mari had to answer to Sabella, and my great-aunt was much scarier than the Guild.

Evening shadows and the electric hum of the overhead lights filled the interior of the parking structure. I was cutting through the now-empty spaces on a direct approach to my baby when a flicker of movement off to my side caught my attention. It was just enough to bring me to an abrupt halt. My Prism snapped into place.

Magic hummed in my veins as I peered into the heavier shadows along the unlit edges of the garage. Standing in the middle of the space left my back exposed, so I began to inch toward one of the thick concrete pillars. It wasn't much, but it was something. A scramble of claws rasped over concrete, and the flicker of movement came again, this time from my right.

I gave up stealth and sprinted for the dubious protection of the pillar. Something flew at me, and I raised my arms to protect my head and hunched my shoulders, bracing for impact. Instead, an ice-cold wind streaked across me, so cold it hurt, leaving a stinging brand across my cheek. A high-pitched shriek ripped through the quiet as a trail of tiny fireflies of silver-and-white sparks flashed in front of me, leaving me blinking away distracting afterimages of a monstrous visage that was terrifyingly familiar.

Terror wrapped around my throat like a talon, choking my startled scream short, and held me in place. That face—bloodied, crazed, and filled with malicious intent—belonged to the possessed man I'd killed to protect Zev. The same one that haunted my recent nightmares.

He's dead. He's dead. He's dead.

The panic-stricken mantra didn't do jack, and it took my brain a second to re-engage. When it did, I locked my magic in place and slammed my back against the pillar. My heart raced as I frantically searched the garage for whoever was behind the attack. I tried to calm my harsh breaths so I could hear, but fear made that difficult. I lifted a shaky hand and brushed my fingertips along the still-burning mark on my cheek. Something warm met my touch, and when I pulled my hand back and looked down, my fingers were stained with blood. I curled my hand into a fist to hide the disturbing proof that it wasn't just a figment of my terrified imagination.

Bryan is dead.

The reminder didn't help. If anything, it made the whole situation worse, because whatever had flown at me was real enough and carried enough threat to not only activate my innate defensive power, but also cause physical harm. Shaking, I waited for the next strike, praying it would give me some idea of how to fight back.

But seconds ticked by, and nothing happened. I let even more pass before I cautiously moved away from the dubious protection of the pillar. My hand shook as I dug my phone out of my pocket. I started toward my car and was halfway through a text to Evan when I remembered he wasn't in the office. I gripped my phone and sprinted the remaining distance to my Mustang.

I brushed my empty hand across the hood as I rounded the 'Stang, recalibrating my warding from sentry to active mode. I just needed to get behind the wheel, then I was out of there. My hand was on the door handle when a small, distressed squeak sounded from behind the trunk. My magic had hit something near my car.

"Don't do it, Rory." Despite my muttered warning, I let go of the door, wishing I hadn't left my gun behind this morning. *Might be time to rethink my stance about concealed carry.*

Taking a deep breath, I crouched and crept along the Mustang, keeping it between me and whatever was behind it. I eased my hold on my magic and let it spill out around me. The move had become instinctual after hours of endless practice at Zev's insistence. As my power flowed over my car and across the pavement, a small round object rolled under the trunk and past the rear tire. As I stared at the glowing object, another unknown magic licked at the leading edge of mine as it crept stealthily toward my baby.

Oh, I don't think so.

I bit my lower lip and carefully lowered my hand. I used one finger to draw an attack ward in the thin layer of dust and dirt covering the concrete floor. As soon as the last line of the ward was completed, my magic snapped closed, capturing the invisible whatever behind my trunk.

The squeaking came again, this time more agitated and accompanied by a rattling sound. Power spilled from whatever I caught, slamming into the unforgiving wall of mine. The impact triggered a flash of power that strobed the garage. A glowing walnut stopped inches from my back tire. Whatever I'd caught wanted out, which was too damn bad. I tightened my magical hold in warning. "Don't do that again."

That earned me another squeak. I studied the glowing object lying on the concrete. *Who in the world would use a nut to...* Realization struck. "Are you kidding me?" I got to my feet and rounded the trunk.

Dark, beady eyes met mine, and a furry snout lined in brown and white was wrinkled in a snarl. A very pissed-off chipmunk was caught in my ward. Its brown-and-white fur stood on end as it emitted a sharp series of squeaks, trills, and hisses.

I stood there, hands on my hips, and shook my head. "Seriously?"

I considered my next steps, but I didn't get far before more of those high-pitched noises emerged from the surrounding shadows. I shifted my position until my trunk was at my back and my captive was held between me and the three new chipmunks that skittered forward. With a flex of magical muscle, I widened my Prism, holding the three advancing critters at bay.

They furry rodents hit the barrier, and magic erupted like static over their fur, sending the one on the left back about a foot. The other two held their ground and fell ominously silent. The one trapped between us scrambled around until he could see both me and his rescue squad.

I folded my arms over my chest and directed my question to the bigger one in middle. "What's going on?"

He rose onto his back legs, his fur still on end, and his forehands twitched nervously. His mouth opened, and all that came out was a series of click, trills, and squeaks.

I held up my hand, palm out. "I don't speak chipmunk."

It was hard to tell with the stripes in his fur, but I thought he frowned at me. Or maybe he had a prime resting bitch face. He looked to the one I had trapped, and another series of undecipherable noises emerged. My captive shook his head. More growls, squeaks, and trills followed.

Finally, my prisoner turned to me, and in a tinny voice, he carefully enunciated, "Other is where?"

Other who? I took a guess. "You mean Mr. Nutter?"

He managed a jerky nod.

"I turned him over."

My captive leaned to the side as if searching for something, and I realized I needed to be a bit more direct in my answers.

"He's not here."

Those beady little eyes stayed steady as he processed my answer. Finally, he turned back to his friends and shared. After another back-and-forth, he turned to me. "Where?"

Explaining contracts and client confidentiality to a chipmunk was beyond me, so I kept it simple. "His boss has him."

Another round of chipmunk speak ensued. This time, the one on the left stood on its hind legs, chest puffed out. Arms held out and down, it strutted back and forth for a few seconds. The middle one shook its head, and the one stuck in my ward made a sharp disgruntled noise. The strutter stopped and said something that made the middle one and the trapped one exchange a long, considering look.

Finally, my captive turned back to me. "Boss is where?"

I sighed and dropped to a crouch, getting eye level with all four of them. I had no idea how I managed to get into these situations, but I swore next time I went after something like Mr. Nutter, I would up my fee. I studied each of them a moment, thinking. Giving them Beto's office address wasn't breaching confidentiality, not when they had followed me there yesterday. Plus, considering they could track me to the Guild, it might take them a few days, but eventually, they would return to the scene of the crime, or worse, make their way to Beto's office. But what gave me pause was what would happen if they confronted the financier, so I couldn't help but offer a warning. "It's not good to go after the boss."

Undaunted, the captive chipmunk stared back. "Boss is where?"

Right, okay, so if they want to go after Mr. Nutter, it's their funeral. I sighed and pulled out my phone. I pulled up the address to Beto's office and switched the maps setting to satellite, figuring it was the easiest way to get them recognizable visuals. I added the construction site address then zoomed in until the path between the two was clearly marked. I had no idea if these chipmunks could follow a map, but short of taking them to Beto's offices myself, this was all I was comfortable giving them.

I set my phone on the ground so they could see the screen and pointed to the construction site. "This is yours." I traced the path to Beto's office. "This is the boss." I removed my finger and rested my arms on my knees.

The chipmunks inched closer. The middle one reached out for my phone, and I did the same, stopping him from moving it. "Uh-huh."

He hissed at me but motioned the other two closer until all three stood staring down at my phone. They chittered back and forth for a few more moments before backing away. Deciding they were done, I reclaimed my phone and turned to the one still caught in my magic. "You got your information. We're done."

His narrow nose wrinkled, flashing a glimpse of sharp teeth. "We done."

Business concluded, I straightened, and without turning my back, I walked to the ward. I didn't look away from my furry watchers as I scuffed the markings with my foot and released the captive chipmunk. He scurried to his friends and stopped. They all gave me identical glares then disappeared into the shadows.

ELEVEN

I FINALLY MADE IT HOME, and when I pulled into the condo's garage, I saw a familiar black-matte Harley parked in my visitor's space. *Guess Zev got tired of waiting.* Thankfully, my ride up to the eighth floor was uneventful, and when I walked into my condo, the scent of seasoned ground beef woke my stomach, which protested its lack of food with a loud rumble.

I cleared the entryway and hit the open kitchen, where I tossed my keys and phone on the island counter. I headed toward the tall, dark-haired man standing in front of my stove. "Something smells good." I wrapped my arms around his lean waist and pressed my cheek to his spine, inhaling his familiar sandalwood scent. "Hi."

Zev angled his body so he could wrap his free arm around my waist and bring me into his side as he pressed a kiss to the top of my head while he continued to stir the meat in the pan. His teeth flashed in his closely cropped beard that matched the equally dark hair that brushed his broad shoulders. "Hi yourself."

I leaned into him, one hand on his flat stomach, my other

arm curled around his waist, happy to have him there. "I thought we were having a sleepover at your place?"

His lips quirked. "Figured your kitchen was better stocked and, since you were working late, decided to move our date to your place. You did say Lena was out tonight."

"Yeah, Evan got tickets to Platform 29, so I don't know if she'll even make it home."

"Isn't that the train bar place?"

"Mmhmm." My answer was distracted as I rested my head against his chest and stared, mesmerized, as he stirred the browning meat. "You're making tacos."

"I am." Barefoot and dressed in well-worn jeans and a faded T-shirt, he was a delightful addition to my kitchen.

I finally shook off my daze, looked around, and noticed the uncut tomatoes, avocado, and lettuce sitting on the counter. "I'll start the veggies."

"Works for me."

I got to work dicing, slicing, and shredding. "Sorry about running late."

"Everything okay?"

I shrugged as I continued to dice the tomatoes. "I don't know. When I got back to the Guild today, Detectives Hall and Rendón were there."

The spatula paused as he looked back over his shoulder and frowned. "Aren't they the ones who worked our assault case?"

I nodded.

He grunted and tapped the spoon he was using against the pan. "And they were there for you?" He set the spoon on the counter and turned down the heat. Drawers opened and closed as he pulled out potholders. He picked up the pan and brought it over to the double sink in the island.

"Yeah."

He spooned out the oil. "Why? Our case has been shut tight for months."

"They weren't there about that." I finished the tomato and grabbed the lettuce. "It had to do with a job."

He stopped and looked up. "Which job?" He gave a sharp shake of his head. "Sorry, is this a job you can share?"

"Yeah." His question was legit, since both of us handled things with a high level of confidentiality. "Last night when you got stuck in Vegas, Adele asked me to take a last-minute Guild run to Sedona, a commission plus bonus." I shot him a tiny grin. "Since you weren't here to distract me…"

He snorted.

I went back to sous chef duties. "Actually, their questions weren't about the job exactly, more like the person I handed the delivery to since he got in an accident sometime this afternoon and is in the hospital."

"Is he okay?" He went back to draining the meat.

I shrugged. "I'm thinking no, since Hall shared he was in ICU at Desert Memorial."

"That doesn't sound good," Zev said, "but what does that have to do with you?"

"Normally, nothing." I looked up from my cutting board and met his heavily lashed deep-brown eyes. "But the detectives made it clear that they're questioning everyone who interacted with him."

He finished at the sink and took the pan back to the stove. "Okay, so why do you sound worried?"

I shredded the lettuce into a neat pile next to my tomatoes as I struggled to put my emotions into words—not an easy thing to do since it wasn't natural for me, especially as I'd spent years keeping things to myself. That was a habit I was trying my best to break because Zev and I were working hard to make this relationship thing work. Thanks to our histories and jobs, neither of us had a good track record, but we'd agreed to give it our all this time around. "Two reasons. First, they came to me because some of the others at the party mentioned me. Second, I can't shake the feeling that I missed something last night."

He ripped open the taco spice mix, dumped it into the pan, and added water. "I get the first half of that."

I grabbed the avocado. "You do?"

He nodded, the muscles in his arms flexing under his T-shirt as he kept cooking. "You have a love-hate relationship with unwanted attention."

Heat flooded my face as I carefully sliced the avocado. "I'll admit I'm a little freaked that complete strangers seem to know my name." I snuck a glance at him from under my lashes.

He turned around, spoon held aloft, and caught my eyes. "You do realize that is exactly what you want when building your reputation?"

I sighed. "There's a difference between publicity and notoriety."

"Really?" His sarcasm was hard to miss.

I stopped my culinary activities and met his gaze. "Yes, really."

He cocked his head, and a puzzled frown marred his forehead. "You're serious."

"Of course I am." I set down my knife and flattened both hands against the counter. "I don't mind my name bandied about if it's about my job performance, but when I walked into that room last night, that wasn't what the whispers were about." Because I was watching him, I didn't miss the flash of compassion before it disappeared.

His voice was gentle but firm. "I did warn you, babe."

I grimaced. He had, multiple times, reiterating what I was getting myself into when I got involved with the Families. "I know, and logically, I get it." Because when shit went down with the Arcane Council, which involved powerful names, whether I was in the middle or on the edges wouldn't matter.

It all became fodder for gossip. "I just didn't realize how much it would get under my skin."

He studied me for a long moment. "It's not going to get any better."

"I know." I picked up my knife and finished slicing the avocado. "It's just annoying." I knew I was just bitching to bitch because with him, it was safe to do so. He was the one person who wouldn't use my insecurities against me. When he didn't say anything else, I looked up to find him still watching me, a hint of worry in his gaze. "Honestly, Zev, I'll get used to it." I didn't have much of a choice, not if I wanted to succeed professionally. "Between the cops and the damn chipmunk mafia, I'm just having a bad day."

He blinked. "Chipmunk mafia?"

"Long story."

"Sounds like it." He turned back to the stove and stirred the simmering meat. "You want to share and maybe talk through what's bothering you about last night?" A deliberate casualness to his tone caught my attention. "It might help."

I looked up, and his back was to me, his shoulders stiff as if he were bracing for a rejection I had no intention of delivering. Our relationship was still in the early stages, and both of us struggled with the whole open communication thing since neither one of us was the most trusting. Sometimes that ingrained restraint played havoc with what we shared, but we were determined to make it through together. "Yeah, actually, I'd love that."

The tight set of his shoulders relaxed, and he turned his head to look back at me. "Then let's get our food and settle in."

Unable to resist, I set down my knife, closed the short distance between us, and cupped his jaw in my hands. The soft rasp of his beard tickled my palms as I rose to my toes and pressed a kiss against his lips. "I missed you, Zev."

Without letting go of the pan or spoon, he leaned in and brushed his nose against mine. "Missed you too, Rory."

Butterflies erupted, and I held him for a moment longer before finally letting him go. "Right. How many do you want?"

We spent the next ten minutes prepping our tacos then set the kitchen to rights. We took our plates to the sofa in the living room and settled in. Zev had his legs propped up on the coffee table, his plate balanced against his stomach. My plate rested on the arm of the sofa as I angled into the corner and tucked my toes under his thigh.

For a few minutes, the only sounds were the crunch of taco shells as we ate. I was polishing off the first of my two tacos when he spoke. "So, what's first? Chipmunks or Sedona?"

After deciding to start at the beginning, I ran through the whole Mr. Nutter situation, keeping specifics like names out of it. My retelling earned a chuckle or two that quickly turned to an irritated frown. Then it was on to the party in Sedona. That explanation was a bit more challenging thanks to my unease, plus it required Zev's insight. He had an advantage I didn't—not only was he the Cordova Family's Arbiter, but he'd grown up in the world of the Arcane Families. Up until recently, my involvement with them had been limited to Transporter jobs.

What little I knew of the power players in the local Family scene wasn't nearly enough to understand the undercurrents surrounding Max, hence my need for Zev's perspective. "So once Perry confirmed the glasses worked, everyone got all jazzed about doing a treasure hunt."

"Not a surprise," Zev said. "If they're the real deal, then Max finally has a chance at finding an actual treasure."

I figured the chances of that were about the same as winning the lottery. "Does Max do this a lot?"

"You mean the treasure-hunter thing?" Zev took another bite of his taco and chewed.

I nodded.

He swallowed and nodded. "Yep. He gets ahold of some passed-down story or supposed treasure map that will lead him to a fortune, then convinces his friends to pitch in financially. If his family hadn't put their foot down, he'd be knee-deep in dust and cobwebs and broke." He took another bite.

I picked at the vegetables on my plate, popped a piece of tomato into my mouth, chewed, and swallowed. "I'm guessing it costs a pretty penny for these hunts of his?"

"Lots of pretty pennies, actually. It's why he ropes his friends into it. My guess, Kent and Perry, and most likely others in that room, had all invested in whatever search he's got going."

Must be nice to have that much cash just lying around. "What happens if it doesn't pay off?"

Zev shrugged. "My guess? They write it off, like any other investment."

"That happen a lot?"

He gave me a look. "What do you think?"

"It happens a lot." It amazed me how blasé people could be with their finances. "Seems a waste."

"Everyone has their vices, babe. Max's is chasing the pot of gold at the end of the proverbial rainbow."

Remembering my conversation with Rebecca about the legitimacy of the map, I asked, "How does he make sure he's not getting scammed? I mean, yeah, the glasses worked, but who's to say the map is real? Forgeries happen all the time." There were tons of grifters out there, and it seemed to me this would be the perfect in to fleece someone of serious cash.

Zev shrugged. "Don't know, but from what I heard, Max isn't totally stupid. He does his research."

I made a soft hum, neither agreeing nor disagreeing with his assessment. "Do you know a Rebecca Tsosie?"

He set his now-empty plate aside. "The name seems familiar, but no, I don't think I do."

"She's a friend of Max's fiancée, Devon, and happens to work at Black Water Casino. I ran into her on an unrelated job yesterday, and we got to talking about the story behind the glasses. Then she made a comment that makes me think it wasn't just his friends that Max hit up for his financing."

"How so?" He wrapped his fingers around my ankle and gave it a tug.

I let him pull my foot into his lap. "I asked if she thought Max's map actually led to something, and she said she hoped for his sake it did."

His fingers went to work on my arch. "Did you share that with the detectives?"

I bit back my moan and shook my head. "I kind of forgot about it until just now."

"You may want to call Mari and fill her in on all of this," Zev suggested. "Just in case."

"Had it on my to-do list." I dumped my empty plate next to his then leaned back, rubbing my hands over my face.

"Tired?" His fingers dug deep into my arches, easing the dull ache of the day.

"Didn't sleep well last night," I admitted.

"Bad dreams?"

His question was casual, but I couldn't help but tense up. "Something like that."

His fingers stilled, and he gave my foot a nudge. When I raised my gaze to his, he said, "Spill."

I nibbled my lower lip and tried to verbalize my churning thoughts. "Honestly, I don't remember much of them, just that they were disturbing." I rubbed a spot in the middle of my forehead and closed my eyes. "Maybe it was just leftover stress from the flat."

"What flat?"

Right, I didn't share that part.

"The Guild Genesis I used for the delivery run picked up a nail or something just outside Phoenix." I opened my eyes to find him watching me. "The Guild uses run flats and a protective rune, so I made it back by the deadline, but it made for a nerve-wracking drive." I grimaced. "It didn't help that when I pulled over to check it out, I got spooked."

The fingers on my foot tightened then relaxed. "What happened?"

"That's the thing. Nothing." I readjusted a pillow under my arm. "It was a shopping center parking lot with crappy lighting." I managed an awkward shrug, even as the memory of my whispered name sent chills racing along my arm. "I think the whole situation just got to me." I looked away as I admitted in a low voice, "It felt like someone was watching me, and I thought I heard someone call my name. Thing is, there was nothing and no one around."

Unlike this afternoon. I brushed my fingers over the thin cut on my cheek.

Zev didn't miss the move. His gaze sharpened, but he nudged my legs down then pulled me against him. Only when his arms wrapped me tightly did I realize I was shivering. Thankfully, he didn't try to placate me with empty reassurances and just gave me space to talk.

So I did. Muscles tightening, I admitted, "And today, after the whole interview thing, I was heading back to my car, and I... saw something."

TWELVE

CLUED in by my tone and stiffness, Zev's hold tightened reassuringly. "What?"

My voice was low, and I didn't move from where I lay against him. "Bryan."

His arms around me flexed, and I felt his chin brush the top of my head. "Babe…"

I turned just enough to press my forehead into his chest. "I know, Zev."

He didn't say anything for long minutes, and neither did I. I turned so my ear rested against his chest, and the steady beat of his heart provided a comforting anchor as I tried to untangle my worry that my paranoia would be too much for him.

Bryan Croft had been the Clarke Family Arbiter and had worked with us on uncovering the madmen—and women— behind an experimental serum that acted like steroids on a mage's inherent magic. Bryan, a laid-back charmer, had been unknowingly dosed with the serum, and the results had been monstrously lethal. In the end, it was a combination of Zev's skill and sheer, desperate luck on my part that had managed to stop him.

Finally, Zev broke the silence with one word. "Guilt."

The rumble of his voice echoed under my ear, and I tilted my head to look up at him. "What?"

His dark eyes searched mine. "You're carrying around guilt for his death."

There was no use denying it, because he was right. For the most part.

But Zev wasn't done. "He'd hate that for you."

I wasn't so sure.

Whatever Zev saw on my face had him adding, "Bryan knew the risks, just like I do. Being an Arbiter…" He shook his head then fell quiet. It was obvious he was picking his words with care when he continued. "When you're the last line of defense for a family, it's a given that any time you step in front of a threat, you may not walk away."

I fought the urge to cover his mouth with my hand to make him stop talking. For the most part, I did a good job ignoring the inherent risks of his position as the Cordova Arbiter, but having him state it so bluntly was like tempting fate.

Zev clearly had no problem flipping fate the finger. "When you accept the position, you accept all that it entails. Right or wrong, you do what's needed to protect those under your charge."

I swallowed hard. "But what if—"

"Don't," Zev warned before I could finish. "Don't go there. It's a waste of time and emotions to play that game. You did what was necessary to keep everyone safe." He held my gaze with his. "And that's something an Arbiter understands and respects."

I wasn't sure I believed him. The conviction in his voice was unmistakable, though, easing the sharpest points of my guilt, but not all of it. That, I knew, would take time. "Okay, but guilt doesn't explain the feeling of being watched."

His eyebrows rose. "The chipmunk mafia?"

I shook my head, trying to figure out how to put my nebulous concerns into words. "I don't think so. It felt more… ominous, almost like I was being… hunted." Even to me, it sounded borderline paranoid, but that threat, both in the parking lot and in the garage, had felt all too real.

"Okay, if not the furry brotherhood, then who else could be targeting you?"

I gave his question serious consideration, but every name I could think of was either dead or locked up, so I was drawing a blank. "I don't know."

He studied me for a moment. "Piss off anyone in a race lately?"

I snorted. "Nope, I haven't been to a night race since…" I counted back. "Since you and I went back in late summer."

A flicker of disbelief washed over his face. "Seriously?"

I pushed up so I was sitting upright in his lap. His hands dropped to my hips as I faced him.

"What's that?" I circled a finger around his face.

His lips quirked. "What's what?"

My temper sparked. "That… that… look. Like you think I'm lying."

He chuckled. "I don't think you're lying, babe. It's just hard to believe you've gone that long without getting your fix."

I folded my arms over my chest and glared at him. "Well, I've been a bit busy between, you know, my job, you…"

My grumpy response garnered another chuckle, this one accompanied by his hand curling behind my neck and dragging me down so he could kiss me. It was hard to stay mad as he took his time raising my blood pressure and body temperature. By the time he let me up for air, I had lost track of what we were arguing about.

He had me flat on my back, one leg hitched over his hip, and his solid warmth trapping me against all that was him and the sofa. His hair fell forward like a silky, dark curtain.

Unable to resist, I tangled my fingers in the warm strands. He leaned in and blazed a trail along my neck with his lips.

I tried to reciprocate, but my attempt ended on a breathless moan as his wicked mouth and clever hands got busy. It wasn't long before my shirt and his were gone. A muted clatter broke through my sensuous haze, and I realized our activities had knocked my empty plate to the carpet.

Zev lifted his head, his face flushed and eyes filled with desire. He pushed up. From my close-up position under him, watching that move stole my breath and raised the heat burning through my veins.

He stood next to the couch and leaned over me. His voice was a dark rumble as he caught my wrist and gently pulled me to my feet. "Bedroom."

"Bedroom." My agreement came out on a breathy giggle as we started the sleepover portion of our night.

The cold woke me first. Icy teeth gnawed at my bones and crept through me like a slow-moving glacier. Awareness bled into nerve-rattling dread, and I tried to pry open my eyes but couldn't. Panic sawed through my chest, and my heart raced so hard, it actually hurt.

A sibilant whisper filled my ears, drowning out all other sounds. At first, it was just indecipherable noise, then it morphed into recognizable words.

"You killed me!"

Darkness held me trapped as the unnerving voice grew louder with each repetition, and the weight of accusation threatened to crush me into nothing. Desperate to escape, I opened my mouth, and a soundless scream bounced off the inside of my skull.

Something moved in the inky blackness, prowling closer on a wave of breath-stealing foreboding. My heart raced as I tried to move but couldn't. The voice warped, changed into a haunting familiarity, then rose into a deafening roar.

"Kill you!"

Flickers of movement at the edge of my vision had me spinning in panicked circles, but all I caught were flashes of Bryan as he'd been when twisted by the demonic magic creeping closer, the feral madness focused on me.

Trapped in an unmoving body, I struggled to tear my mind free of the entangling cobweb of fear.

Wake up, wake up. Wake! Up!

My brain kicked into gear with a painful lurch, as if up-shifting from first straight to fourth, and my body jerked as my eyes snapped open. Unseen menace stalked out of my head and into the night-drenched shadows. Fear held me in a paralyzing grip as my breaths escaped my dry throat in sharp pants.

He's dead. Not real. He's not real.

Despite the logical reassurance, I couldn't force myself to move. My eyes darted around, and the solid darkness slowly morphed into various shades of black and gray. The familiar lines of my bedroom came together and stepped the panicked fear back. Not much, but enough that the world reformed around me—the cushion of my mattress under me, the brush of the blanket tangled in my legs and around my waist, and the chill air against my exposed skin.

I held my breath, pulse pounding in my ears as I dared to stretch one arm toward my nightstand, where I kept my Glock. My fingers brushed the solid edge of the drawer. Sharp needles of ice speared my wrist then bit down, and an invisible grip yanked me out of the bed.

I hit the carpet with a short screech that ended in a pained grunt. I wrenched my wrist, trying to free it from the frigid hold, but it wouldn't loosen. I kicked out in a desperate attempt to get them away from me. Pain, bright and sharp, engulfed my toes and arrowed up my leg as whatever held me tightened its hold until I couldn't feel my fingers.

Undeterred, I struggled against whatever held me, twisting, turning, and striking out with my other hand and my feet. Still, it didn't budge. Clawing at my wrist, I finally realized there was no hand or physical object to fight against —just that invisible cuff of icy knives that was now pinning the arm against the floor. Since my other hand remained free, I balled it into a fist and swung out. This time, it hit, and the impact reverberated up my arm and into my shoulder, sending shooting pains through both.

Thoughts connected like lightning strikes in the panicked haze. This was a dual attack—physical and magical. My Prism could hold the worst of the magic at bay for a bit, so I focused on the physical. I got a hand and foot under me, then something heavy landed on me, and I grunted under its weight. The rough fiber of the carpet abraded tender skin, and only then did I realize I was buck ass naked. A very real fear piled on top of the existing maelstrom, then fury edged it out, creating an opening for actual thoughts.

Where the hell is Zev?

I twisted my hips, trying to throw whoever had me off and get to my knees. When that didn't work, I slammed my head back, hoping to smash it into their face. The back of my skull hit something hard enough to rattle me and elicit a bitten-off curse. Emboldened by the tiny success, I twisted and bucked like a madwoman, trying to get them off my back. I even curled the fingers of my free hand into claws, and despite my shitty position, I raked them down whatever I could reach.

"Godsdammit, Rory! Wake the fuck up!"

I froze at Zev's familiar rough growl. My harsh breathing filled my ears as I lay trapped facedown on the floor. "Zev?"

"Right fucking here." This time, his voice was right next to my ear, and the weight at my back pressed in. "Are you awake?"

"Ye… Yeah."

Little by little, reality intruded. His body, also naked, trapped me against the carpet, squashing my boobs painfully flat. A hand was in my hair, holding my head in place. Another had locked around my wrist.

I made a tiny movement. "You're heavy."

He shifted his weight, easing back, and the hand against my head disappeared. The one on my wrist did not. It was the same wrist caught in the icy cuff, except… except the ice was gone, replaced by his unrelenting hold. I sucked in a sharp breath and jerked.

His grip tightened. "Easy."

A pained *eep* escaped. "Dammit, let go, Zev. It hurts."

He did as I asked, then his weight shifted off me. I sucked in air and started to roll over, only to make another undignified squeak when he wrapped his arms around me and dragged me into his lap. One of his arms was a steel band around my back. His hand curled at my hip, but he used his other hand to brush my sweat-matted hair out of my face. "I need light so I can see you."

That was my only warning before a pulse of power brushed against me and a small ball of illumination sparked into life, throwing shadows over Zev's face as he nudged my chin upward.

Shivers wracked my body, and I gripped his wrist, my nails denting his skin, my eyes darting around my room. Whoever had attacked me had to still be here, hiding somewhere. I wrapped my Prism around Zev, determine that what lurked in the shadows wouldn't get a second chance at either of us. "Where is he?"

"Who?"

"Bryan."

"He's dead, Rory." His voice carried that careful note of someone trying to talk a jumper off a ledge.

Irritation sparked. "No shit, Sherlock, but he left something behind." I held up my aching wrist, the illumination showing the red blotches that were deepening into a bruise. "And whatever it was dragged me out of bed."

"You were having a nightmare." He caught my wrist and pulled it closer, examining it. He frowned and brushed his thumb over the marks. "I tried to wake you, and you jerked back and fell out of bed."

Clammy sweat left my skin sticky and chilled. "Nightmare, my ass." I tried to pull free of his grip. My rising temper, his body heat, or both, eased the shudders wracking my body until only a random tremble remained. "Someone… Something yanked me out of bed."

He kept ahold of my arm, lifted his gaze, scanned the room, and came back to me. "The room's empty, Rory." He frowned as his thumb continued to feather over the marks on my wrist. "It was just a nightmare." The certainty of his statement did not match his tone of doubt.

I shook my head and carefully tugged free of his hold until I could lace my fingers with his. Logic shouldered its way through the lingering traces of panic. Yeah, Bryan was dead, but whatever I'd just fought with had carried enough of a presence to leave its mark. "It was more than that."

I burrowed into him and tried to make some sort of sense out the last few minutes. It wasn't easy, but one thing was true—it had started when I was asleep. "Can someone attack you through dreams? Like magically?"

The muscles in his chest rippled as he shrugged. "It can be done, sure, but you're the one who told me Lena has this place warded up the wazoo." His arms tightened around me. "If you're up for it, we can see if anything's broken through."

Maybe he was trying to humor me, maybe not. Either way,

I was taking him up on his offer, but… "Give me a minute." I wasn't sure my legs would hold me.

We sat there for more than that as I pulled myself together. My pulse dropped out of stroke range and leveled off while the tremors from earlier finally disappeared.

"Can you tell me what happened?"

I tilted my head back so I could see his face. Not wanting to rock the emotional boat that had just calmed, I kept it short. "Overwhelming fear, panic, like I was being hunted. Bryan's voice. Flickers of him chasing me."

His dark eyes drifted over my face, concern clear in their depths. "You get nightmares like this often?"

I shook my head. "Had a few after Bryan and the thing with Imogen, but for the most part, no."

His eyebrows lifted. "No Imogen, just Bryan?"

I read between his unspoken lines. "Imogen attacked first. Bryan…" I looked away and shifted uncomfortably. "It wasn't his fault."

His hand drifted along my spine in comforting strokes. "Maybe talking about things tonight stirred things up."

Adamant denial burst to life, but instead of spitting it out, I shrugged, not willing to argue until we checked the condo's wards. I dropped my head against his chest, and a startled snort escaped when I realized we were sitting on the carpet next to my bed, naked. I shifted in his lap and leaned over him, intending to liberate the hanging sheet next to us. It put certain soft bits of mine in his face.

His petting stopped as he took advantage and nuzzled me. The rasp of his cropped beard sent a totally different type of tingle through me.

I dropped my hand to the back of his head and gave his hair a tiny tug. "Behave." Then I let him go and dragged the sheet free.

His head thumped back against the bed, but his arms stayed around me. "I'd rather not."

His tease pushed away the last lingering tendrils of fear and dread. Grateful, I pressed a quick, chaste kiss against his lips and pulled back. "Up, my horny one. I want to check the wards."

"Killjoy," he muttered, but let me go.

I used his shoulder for balance as I got to my feet and wrapped the sheet around me. Then I held out my hand to help him up. As he pushed to his feet, I couldn't help but take advantage and cop a feel of my own. "Don't worry. I'll make it up to you."

THIRTEEN

I EXCHANGED the sheet for Zev's discarded T-shirt while he pulled on a pair of sleep pants, then we made our way into the living room. It was just after four in the morning, and I really didn't want to have call Lena and have her cut short her time with Evan and come home. I hit the switch for the string of fairy lights decorating the media wall. Small stars ignited, and their illumination was enough to chase away the deeper shadows. As Zev headed toward the door where the security rune and keypad were, I asked, "Do you know what we're looking for?"

"I'm sure we'll figure it out when we see it."

Glad one of us believes that. I walked over to the short entryway, where he stood punching in the code for the electronic alarm. "Doesn't that need to be on too?"

There was an electronic beep as he shook his head. "Nope." He brushed his fingers on a blank spot just above the pad. The customized rune that Lena had created for Zev ignited in a blue shimmer then deepened as it snapped to life. "If Lena set this up like most security wards, it should act like a magical backup to your system."

A pulse of power rushed over my skin, waking my Prism

and setting the hairs on my arm on end. With the ease of months of practice, I held the automatic magical reaction in check. Magic wasn't easily explainable and tended to be driven by will and instinct. When it came to intent, I could out-stubborn the best of them, but my Prism was all about instinct. If that instinct scented trouble, well then, it stepped right the hell up and shut shit down quick. This wasn't the time for my defenses to click in, but smothering all of my power was out of the equation. Tamping it down through sheer will? Yeah, that was doable.

Zev half turned and motioned me closer. "Your turn, babe."

I sighed, slipped into the opening he'd left, my back brushing his chest, and swept my fingers over my sigil. A flash of red winked awake and joined the swirls of blue. I turned and tipped my head back. "Now what?"

He cupped the back of my head, his fingers sinking into my hair, and his warm palm eased the strain on my neck. "You remember what we did when we broke Lena out of the Drainer's Circle?"

"We combined our magic to overload the caster's power." I frowned. "I'm not keen on blowing out Lena's wards."

He grinned. "We won't." He carefully drew his fingers down and out of my hair, letting me go. "I'm hoping that Lena followed typical warding structure when she set this up. If so, I should be able to walk you through a check by piggybacking on your signature."

"Mine?"

"Yep, yours." He nudged me around until I was facing the still-glowing runes. He pressed in, one hand cupping my hip, while he straightened his other arm and used his index finger to trace just above the sigils. "See how bright yours is compared to mine? How it appears to almost be carved into the wall a bit?"

I leaned in and peered closer. "Yeah." I pulled back. "I never noticed that before."

"Most generally don't. It's something that occurs with deeply anchored wards, and since you're one of the two homeowners—"

"Mine and Lena's wards will be the oldest."

He dropped his hand. "Exactly, and I'm betting she set it up so one or both of you can access the warding structure."

I was not keen on messing with the wards, mainly because I'd been procrastinating about taking the time to familiarize myself with the ins and outs. I knew it was necessary, but with Lena being readily available and my time being eaten up with getting my business feet under me, it had dropped on my priority list. *Guess I should've moved it up.* "When she first set it up, she spent like twenty minutes trying to explain it all to me, but, honestly, she went into so much detail, she lost me. Finally, we decided I just needed to be able to activate it and understand the various warnings. Changing it is all her."

The hand on my hip squeezed gently. "We aren't going to mess it up. We're just going to check it, like making sure everything is plugged in and working, okay?"

"All right." I gave my agreement a tad reluctantly. "Do we have to do a casting circle or something?"

"Nope, we don't need that much power to do this, but..." He tugged me back until he could wrap his arms around my hips, holding me against his front. "We do need to be touching." The last part was said near my ear in his low voice as his bare chest pressed against my spine, his heat seeping through the T-shirt.

Mmmm. My pulse picked up, and I couldn't stop the tiny shiver. "Focus, Zev." My admonishment came out on a husky reprimand.

"Oh, I'm focused," he muttered. He lifted his head, and his voice returned to normal. "Okay, since both of our magics are Mystic based, this should be fairly easy."

Famous last words. "Right."

His arms tightened then eased. "Okay, so keep your Prism in check and activate the ward."

Sucking in a deep breath, I reinforced my hold on my Prism and did my best to ignore the itch the vulnerability created. Then I touched the rune. A flare of magic ignited, sparking neurons and igniting the piece of me that recognized active magic.

The majority of the Arcane abilities landed in one of two camps, Mystic or Elemental, with a rare few in a third, Divine. As a Transporter who also happened to be a Prism, I was solidly in the psychic camp of Mystics. Between his combat skills and his innate connection to various animals, so was Zev, which made working our abilities in tandem easier.

Zev's right arm left me, and he lifted it until it hovered right above my outstretched arm. "Ready?"

For what? Instead of asking, I just nodded.

He gently laid his arm over mine, his long fingers curling around my wrist carefully. The minute he touched me, a surge of power zipped between us like a burst of static electricity.

Startled, I sucked in a sharp breath.

Zev stilled. "You okay?"

I took a couple of seconds on an internal check. Nothing hurt. I just felt...wired. "I'm good."

Taking me at my word, Zev guided me through stretching my magic along Lena's wards. By the time we finished, that wired feeling had dropped to normal levels. Handling the additional magic didn't hurt, but it was a strange feeling, like holding two electrified strands steady so they wouldn't touch and explode.

When we were done, blue-tinged red sigils were alight on every wall. "Wow." I blinked at the pretty illumination. "Is this what Lena sees all the time?"

"Probably," he said. "Let's get to work. If you hold this too long, you're going to be beyond drained."

He wasn't wrong. We spent the next half hour going through Lena's intricate warding runes that kept the riffraff out of our home. It was like steering an overpowered compact on a narrow road. I had no idea what we were looking for exactly, but working with Zev on a magical level created a unique sense of intimacy that went beyond the physical and into the mental. Not surprisingly, he took his time. With his experience, he was more likely to spot trouble outside the obviousness of a broken ward.

At a couple of spots, he stopped, fell quiet, then shook his head before moving on. The third time that happened, my curiosity won out. "What?"

His attention shifted to me even as we froze in place. "*What* what?"

"What's with the quiet thing?"

His lips quirked. "Lena left a few surprises in her structure. I just want to make sure we don't trip them."

Yeah, my roomie was sneaky that way. "Probably a good idea."

He chuckled, then we went back to it. We went through each room, but nothing seemed broken. When Zev finally had me stop, my eyes burned as if I'd spent too long staring at a computer screen, and the lack of sleep was dragging at me.

I dropped into one of the barstools and rubbed my aching eyes. "Dammit."

Zev stood behind me, his fingers digging into my shoulders as he tried to ease the tension that had gathered there. "I'm thinking the wards are fine, but you may want to have Lena check just to be sure."

I kept my eyes closed and my hands over my face. Zev's fingers found a sore spot, and a groan escaped. "I don't want to text her for another couple hours. It's still too early."

"Well, then your choices are going back to bed or staying up."

"I vote for staying up." No way in hell did I want to chance a repeat of my recent nightmare experience.

"Coffee and a movie?"

I sighed, propped my chin in my hand, and stared blearily into my kitchen. "Works for me."

After one last squeeze of my shoulder, he left me on my stool and headed toward where I kept my precious java beans. He opened the cupboard, pulled out a bag, and dumped the dark beans into the grinder. A few minutes later, the scent of a chocolate-caramel roast filled the air as my coffeemaker gurgled quietly.

Zev leaned a hip against the counter as we both silently waited for the pot to fill. When it was done, he poured two steaming cups then added a bit of sweet and cream to mine and nothing to his. He picked up both mugs and came around the counter. "Up, babe." He tilted his chin toward the living room. "Couch."

I slipped off my stool and stumbled over to the sofa, where I dropped into the cushions. He handed over the mugs, and I held them both as he settled in next to me, remote in hand. Once he was down, I handed over his, then mindful of my cup, I snuggled into him. We found a classic comedic tale of airline travel on one of the streaming services and settled in to pass the next hour and half with bad puns, witty double entendres, and slapstick humor that defied decades.

After the credits rolled, neither of us felt like moving. Instead, we stretched out on the sofa, dozing as the next movie scrolled past. When we finally roused, it was close to eight in the morning, which I decided was polite enough to send Lena a text. Then I asked Zev if he wanted breakfast. We were finishing up our pancakes when my phone rang, and Lena's number flashed over my screen.

I had a forkful of syrup-dipped pancakes in one hand, so I used my unoccupied one to thumb the screen. "Hey, Lena. Sorry to call so early."

"What's wrong?" Lena's voice, still husky with sleep, came over the speaker.

I winced. "Right now? Nothing, but I was hoping if you had time, you could swing home soon and check out something for me."

There was the sound of rustling, and her voice cleared. "Check out what?"

"The security wards." Zev joined the conversation, so I shoved my bite into my mouth and chewed.

"What happened to the wards?" Lena's voice sharpened.

"As far as we can tell, nothing," Zev said, "but if you can double-check, that would be appreciated."

"Rory, start talking," my roommate demanded.

I quickly swallowed and launched into an abbreviated version of my night. When I was done, Lena was quiet for a moment. Finally, she asked, "Rory, do you really think someone or something got through the wards?"

In the light of morning, I had my doubts, but they weren't enough for me to ignore the niggling worry. "I don't know, but I'd feel better if you could confirm I'm just being jumpy."

"You're not the jumpy type, so what aren't you sharing?"

I grimaced. "The police cornered me at the Guild. They had some questions about my run to Sedona."

"Why?"

Zev answered, "Max Vasquez is in the hospital in a coma."

There was a sharp inhale. "Holy shit, what happened?"

I wasn't keen about getting into it over the phone, but luckily, it seemed she wasn't either, because she quickly said, "Never mind. Zev, you sticking around for a bit?"

"Yep."

"Good." Jostling noises filled the line, then she said,

"Hang on." A low murmur of conversation replaced the noises, then she was back. "Give us a few. We should be there in about an hour."

I stared at my phone, feeling something in my chest loosen. "Thanks, Lena."

"You're welcome, but heads up, girl. Be ready to spill when I get home."

"Deal," I agreed. With that, we said our good-byes and hung up.

On the other side of the island, Zev braced one hand on the island as he studied me. "You doing okay?"

I managed a nod. "But I'll feel better once she double-checks things." I picked up my plate, got up, and headed for the sink. Reminded of Max's situation, I wondered aloud, "Do you think Max will be okay?"

"Without knowing what happened to him, I don't know." He watched me come closer. "You know, if he's at Desert Memorial, we might be able to check in with Devon and find out."

I got to the sink and rinsed our dishes. "I don't know. Wouldn't that be weird?"

"How so?" He drained his mug and set it in the sink.

"We don't really know him, and we're not family." I nudged Zev out of the way so I could drop the dishes in the dishwasher.

"True, but I'm sure the word is out by now. Friends and business acquaintances are probably in the know, so they'll drop in because it's expected." He grabbed a cloth and started wiping down the counters. "I've met him a few times when he did business with Emilio."

Following his logic wasn't difficult. Zev's cousin and boss was a big shot and pretty much did business with everyone in the Valley. "Maybe we can bring him flowers or something?"

"And ask a few questions." He joined me at the sink and rinsed the cleaning cloth.

"And maybe get a couple of answers." Plans made, we headed back to my room to get dressed before Evan and Lena showed up.

FOURTEEN

I SAT on the couch while an incandescent net of power washed over the walls. "Okay, this doesn't look like what Zev and I were able to pull up."

By the front entry, Lena traced another brilliant line with one polish-tipped finger. A complex pattern of runes lit up like tracers chasing her touch. "You think I'd let just anyone mess with my creation?"

Hey, now. "Since when did I rate as 'just anybody'?"

Without stopping what she was doing, she shot me a look. "About the same time as when you tripped the damn thing at two in the morning and woke up the dog pack down the hall."

I remembered that night. Kind of. I had stumbled home after a very long day and missed a sigil while disarming the alarm. The resulting electronic screech wasn't nearly as panic-inducing as the screaming wails that erupted from the disrupted magic. I managed to shut off the electronic alarm before the police were notified, but then the trio of furry mutts staying with our next-door neighbor, Angie, decided to join in, creating an impromptu gathering of irritated residents. Lena had stepped off the elevator about the same time as the mood detonated from irritated to dangerously grumpy. She'd deactivated the security ward and dragged me into our apartment just in the nick of time.

"Okay, that's fair," I muttered.

Her soft "mmm-hmm" said "told you so" louder than words. Her magic flexed, and the interlinked sigils came alive, shifting positions and rearranging from a jumble of lines and squiggles into a grid of arcane keys. It was fun to watch Lena work, like sitting in the center of a revolving light show, but the battering magic waves left me fighting the urge to scratch my skin off.

Lena brushed off her hands and turned to face us. "All right, time for a few tests."

More skin-ruffling power swept through the room. Zev and Evan remained sprawled in their seats, unaffected. Meanwhile, I clutched the decorative pillow tighter against my stomach so I wouldn't give in to the urge to scratch. Thankfully, my Prism had chilled out, probably because Lena's magic wasn't coming across as an attack. When the power finally leveled off, I breathed a sigh of relief.

"The good news," Lena said as she walked over to join me on the couch, "is that nothing's gotten through or attempted to get through the wards." She dropped next to me and propped her feet on the edge of the coffee table. In faded tailored jeans and a gorgeous bronze tunic, my auburn-haired bestie was disgustingly gorgeous.

"And the bad news?"

She gave me a long look. "If you really believe someone used your dreams to attack you, then I need to check you haven't been hexed."

I didn't think it was possible for my stomach to get any tighter, but boy howdy, it cramped right the hell up. "Would that even be possible? I mean, I'm a Prism. Isn't that, like, impossible?"

"Nothing's ever really impossible," Evan chimed in unhelpfully.

"While annoying, he's right," Lena said. "I could get into the whole science behind the spell crafting of hexes, but I'll do my best to keep it simple."

"Appreciate it." My knowledge of curse-based magic was pretty basic. The power to create one was convoluted, and the result could range from pesky to deadly, depending on the caster's intent. The curse, or hex itself, could be a one-shot deal or span generations. The wide variety and depth of skills needed to play in that arena meant Keys specialized. In Lena's case, she was all about high-value targets who tended to earn really nasty hexes.

"Curses are like macarons."

I gave her an incredulous look. "Like the cookie?"

She nodded. "They look easy, right? Pretty colors, top cookie, bottom cookie, creamy filling, voila! Easy peasy." She repositioned to face me, her back tucked into the corner of the couch and her leg propped on the cushion between us. "But actually baking those suckers?" She shook her head. "Hours later, after the sugar burns, the cream breaks. The cookies turn into flat crackers. You're in tears. The kitchen is a mess, and there's nothing left to do but drink."

Okay, someone needs to cut back on their Bake-Off shows.

Blithely, she continued her strange example. "At first glance, a curse can appear pretty straightforward, but once you dig into it, it's all about the caster's skill and their attention to detail. If you're dealing with a line cook, that's one thing, but if you're dealing with a Michelin-level chef, that's a whole other stitch."

"You're forgetting intention," Evan added.

"Right, the caster's intention plays a part as well," Lena agreed. "The more focused the intention, the more complex it becomes."

"I don't think I'm the focus of anyone's wrath lately." The

main names I came up with were no longer an issue. Then I thought of the furry ambush in the garage and grimaced. "Well, maybe the chipmunk mafia might want to make an example out of me."

Confusion scrunched up Lena's face. "Chipmunk mafia?"

I shook my head and waved a hand. "Long story for another time. Keep going with your pastries of persecution."

Zev's amused snort was drowned out by Evan's muttered "Nice one."

Lena's grin was quick, but she got back to her lecture. "Once a hex is crafted, the caster has a couple of options, depending on what they're trying to achieve. Generally speaking, most hexes are all about personal payback. You hurt me, so now I'll hurt you and yours, right?"

I nodded. "And the caster's will also determines how strong that curse is. Kind of like wards and how strong or weak they are, right?"

She nudged my hip with her foot. "Hey, you really were listening."

"I always listen." For the most part, I did, but yeah, there had been days she'd come home and needed to vent over a particularly frustrating job, and some of her comments had stuck. I knew the more stubborn a mage was, the more difficult it was to break their hexes.

"Once the hex is set, it comes down to attaching it to your target, and that, my friend, requires an in of some kind."

"Biological," Zev chimed in.

"Physical," Evan added.

"Psychological," Lena finished up. "The first two are the easiest and most common. Think blood, skin, an everyday object, something like that. The last, though—that requires intimate knowledge of your target. Their fears, their nightmares, their doubts, all of that creates emotional cracks that most mages instinctually keep hidden."

"A weak mind is a broken mind." I repeated a mantra the Guild had drummed into us during our initial training.

"Exactly. So if someone is attacking you through your dreams—"

"Or you've recently pissed off a combat-level Nightmare mage," Zev cut in.

"Or that," Lena said. "They'd have to really know you." She studied me, and her voice softened. "I love you to pieces, girl, but I know the number of people you let close can be counted on maybe two hands."

I fought the urge to squirm. It was more like one hand, but she had a point. "Okay, so we can cross off the dream route, unless one of you three or Sabella has a bone to pick with me." That got me a round of head shakes and scoffing snorts. "That means we're down to a physical or biological anchor."

Lena tilted her head. "Which is why I wanted to check you."

"I don't have a problem with you checking." It just made me nervous to be that... vulnerable, magically. "But I don't get how a curse would find an anchor on someone like me."

"Prisms aren't invulnerable, Rory." Zev leaned forward in his chair, his arms braced on his knees. "Your magic reacts to active power on an almost-instinctual level, but when it comes to passive magic..." His shoulders rose and fell. "Not so much."

"So it wouldn't be out of the realm of possibility that you got tagged with a hex that remains inert until something triggers it," Evan said, as he drummed his fingers on the chair's arm.

"Or you accidentally picked up residue from someone else's hex," Lena added. "You know, like a cold or something."

Everything they said made sense. Unfortunately, it didn't make me feel any better. "Fine, so there's a chance I've got someone's curse cooties or something then." I worried my lower lip, thinking things through. "If I've picked up some kind of magical germ, wouldn't I be able to tell?"

My question garnered a puzzled look from Zev and a frown from Lena, but it was Evan who answered. "Not necessarily. Sticking with the cold germ example, you generally don't realize you caught someone else's cold until you're blowing into a Kleenex and downing pain relievers, and by then, it could be days later."

Good point. "Fine." I looked to Lena. "Do your thing, and let's see if I'm infected."

She held out her hand, and when I stared at it for a long moment, she teased, "You won't feel a thing. Promise."

I shook off the strange flash of anxiety and put my hand in hers. A shiver of power washed over me, and my Prism shimmered to life. It was like pressing down on an accelerator on a muscle car, while simultaneously keeping the other foot on the brake. The two competing urges fought until I was able to wrestle the Prism under control.

"Ready?"

At Lena's quiet question, I lifted my gaze from our hands to her eyes. "Ready."

The gold flecks that floated in her green irises brightened. Her magic swept around me like an invisible wind.

My Prism bucked against my hold, wanting to charge forward and lock out the encroaching power. I held it back through sheer will and stubborn determination. I needed to know if I was compromised or just dealing with suppressed guilt.

I wasn't sure how long we sat there, staring at each other, while Lena did her thing. But when she finally pulled back, magically and physically, my every muscle quivered as if I'd just finished working out. As I shook out my hand, I asked, "Well?"

Wearing a small frown, she shook her head. "Nothing's there. You're clear."

"That should be good news, right?" When her frown didn't fade, I motioned to her face. "What's with the frown?"

She bit her lip and blew out a breath. "There's a bump or two, but nothing that indicates an active curse."

I wasn't sure I liked how careful she was in her phrasing. "I hear a but in there."

"So do I," Zev said.

Lena shared a look with Evan, who obviously read something in their exchange.

"Trust your gut, baby," he said.

"Why does she need to do that?" I glanced between the two of them then turned to Lena. "What is it?"

"I don't know." She pulled both legs up onto the couch until she was sitting cross-legged, a throw pillow tucked against her stomach. "There's nothing there right now, but you're not the type to jump at shadows, which makes me think I should probably call in another Key, one who specializes in latent hexes."

"Latent? Like lurks-in-the-dark, waiting-to-strike type latent?" My voice gained a slightly panicked pitch. I did not like the sound of that at all. Unable to sit still, I shoved off the couch and started to pace over by the sliding glass door that led to our balcony. "Do you really think that's necessary?"

Lena braced her arm on the back of the couch and propped her chin in her hand as she watched me. "I think I'm being overly cautious, but knowing you, I think it will keep you from obsessing if I bring someone in."

I wanted to argue with her, but she knew me too well. So long as I had even one iota of doubt, I wouldn't be able to stop worrying. Maybe I hadn't really dealt with everything that had happened. As a matter of fact, I tried my best not to acknowledge that I had been injected with a derivative of a magic-altering serum. Granted, nothing showed up in tests, and my magic hadn't disappeared or suddenly increased exponentially, but something had been in that syringe. That lingering worry haunted me. Maybe its impact wasn't as strong as being directly responsible for Bryan's death, but just those two concerns alone were enough to create some heavy-duty emotional trauma. Call it paranoia, worry, or obsession —whatever it was, I just wanted to make sure this thing chasing me was born from my own neurosis and guilt, not crafted from someone else's magic.

I stopped in front of the glass door and stared out blindly, not really seeing the buildings that made up downtown Phoenix. Instead, my mouth was filled with the metallic taste of fear, and I couldn't swallow it away.

"Call them." My voice was rough, so I cleared my throat and half turned back to the three watching me. I forced a grin, trying not to show how rattled I was inside, even as my hands rubbed up and down my arms. "Go ahead and call them. Better safe than sorry."

Concern darkened Lena's eyes, but thankfully, she didn't call me out. "I'll reach out. Once I hear back, we can clear this up once and for all."

"Sounds like a plan." I turned to Zev. "In the meantime, we should go see Max."

Zev pushed up from his chair, walked over, and pulled me close. "We'll swing by the gift shop and pick up flowers or a balloon or something."

I laid my head against his chest, and under my ear, his heart beat a reassuring cadence. "Works for me."

FIFTEEN

WE PULLED up to Desert Memorial on Zev's matte-black Harley. With Zev driving, I didn't mind riding because there were some enjoyable benefits to being his passenger. We locked our helmets to his bike and hit the gift shop on the first floor. Ten minutes later, we left with a ubiquitous Get Well Soon card and a sleek smoky-gray vase filled with bright carnations and brilliant sunflowers interspersed with pretty green-and-purple flowers that looked familiar. Zev offered to carry it, but a little uncomfortable about visiting someone who was essentially a stranger, I refused. The vase gave me the appearance of being a legit visitor, and not just Zev's plus one.

We rode the elevator up to the intensive care unit. The quiet ping of our arrival barely penetrated the heavy hush that filled the halls. A soft murmur of activity seeped from open doors and farther down the hall. Scrubs-covered figures slipped between rooms and medical carts, pausing now and then to share abbreviated conversations.

Zev led the way to the empty nurse's station. A young man dressed in scrubs decorated with—I had to double-check what I was seeing—laughing cucumbers, smiling tomatoes, and dancing heads of lettuce came around the corner. Zev managed to get his attention, and he met us at the desk. Although clearly exhausted, the nurse managed a welcoming smile and a gracious greeting. Zev quietly inquired for Max's room.

After a quick computer search, the young man walked us down the hall to our right. "Visitors are limited to two at a time, and I believe his parents are with him currently. You're welcome to wait with the others." He stopped near the end, where a waiting room was marked as private. "Here you go."

Zev and I murmured our thanks and stepped inside. The room wasn't crowded, but it was full. Our entrance didn't go unnoticed by the small gathering. Pale, grim faces and red-rimmed eyes turned our way. I searched the grief-stricken visages, recognizing a few from the engagement party, but there was one notable absence—Devon.

Before I could say anything to Zev, a man with dark hair that was silver at the temples broke away from a small group hovering protectively around an older man wearing a shell-shocked expression and headed our way. He waited until he was close to hold out his hand. "Zev, thank you for coming."

"Kent." Zev shook his hand. "Wish it was under better circumstances."

"Me too." His attention shifted to me and sharpened. "Ms. Costas, yes? You were at Max's engagement party."

Startled by his memory, especially considering the circumstances, I covered my reaction with a sympathetic smile. "I was, yes."

His gaze drifted from me to Zev, and he frowned, clearly forming questions, but he was too polite to ask. Instead, he glanced around then gently herded us away from the others and toward the seating area on the other side. "Shall we?"

We followed him toward the small sofa and a pair of

matching chairs. A sleeping teenager filled one, so Zev and I sat on the couch, our hips pressed close. Unable to relax, I perched on the edge of the cushion, my spine stiff as I held the vase tightly in my lap.

Kent sank into the chair, and his gaze fell on the bouquet. "Here, let me take that." He reached forward, claimed the vase, then set it on a nearby side table. When Kent turned back, he sank back into the chair. The urbane gambler was gone, washed away by stress and exhaustion that left the dark hair sticking up every which way while the healthy tan had drained to a sickly olive tone. He looked to Zev, who set the card next to the vase. "I don't mean to be rude, but I'm surprised to see you here. I wasn't aware the news had made the rounds already."

Zev matched Kent's low tone, ensuring their conversation didn't carry to the other side. "Honestly, I don't know if it has. Emilio and I were out of town and just got back yesterday." He threaded his fingers with mine and held my hand against his thigh. "When I called Rory to let her know I was back, she informed me the police were at the Guild to interview her."

I let his minor revision of history play out and stayed quiet.

Something worked behind Kent's eyes, and a dismissive snort escaped. He rubbed his palms over his face. "Sorry, I'm just..." He didn't finish but lowered his hands and rubbed them along his thighs before he slumped back in the chair. His gaze dropped to our joined hands, but it was as if he weren't really seeing them—or us, for that matter.

Zev leaned forward, his concern evident on his face and in his voice. "How long have you been here, man?"

Kent's lips curved, the intended smile closer to a grimace. "Since I got the call yesterday, so..." He checked his watch. "Twenty-two hours or so. Max is... and Devon... I can't..."

Once again, he trailed off, misery darkening his reddened eyes.

A sick feeling squirmed in my gut. I squeezed Zev's fingers, praying I was wrong. "How is Devon doing? Has she been in to see Max?"

"See Max?" Kent's forehead was furrowed, his tone confused. He must have connected the dots, because his frown cleared, but his voice was rough. "Devon was in the car with Max. She didn't make it."

"I won, babe." Devon's joyful face, filled with excitement and love as she shared her victory with Max, when we'd walked into the room rippled through my mind. Reconciling that memory with the current situation was heartbreaking.

Kent turned to look at where the others were still gathered. "The doctor came in just before you arrived and broke the news to her father."

The older man's ravaged, stunned expression now made horrible sense. I swallowed against the lump in my throat and managed a soft "I'm so sorry."

Zev echoed my condolences then added, "And Max?"

Kent turned back to us, the white lines bracketing his mouth deeper than they were a moment ago. He ran a hand through his hair. "Not good. Due to the swelling and bleeding on his brain, they put him in a medically induced coma."

Zev's grip on my hand tightened. "Do you know what happened?"

Kent's nod was jerky. "According to the cops, witnesses claim that Max swerved across the road when he was headed down from Sedona. No one saw what caused him to lose control, so the cops can't tell if it was deliberate or accidental, but however it happened, the car went over the side and rolled multiple times." His hands fisted.

That particular stretch of road was infamous for accidents. The steep downgrade proved to be too much temptation for many drivers, and the sharp curves could catch the mildest speed demons by surprise. Despite's Kent's disbelief, it wouldn't be a stretch to think that maybe Max hadn't been able to outrun the temptation to speed. "I'm sure the investigators will be able to get some answers for Devon and Max's family."

Kent's lips curled into a bitter sneer. "The police aren't interested in finding out what really happened. They just want to close it as fast as possible so their asses aren't in the crosshairs of the Arcane Council."

"That may be," Zev said, "but if Christina's influence means they prioritize the investigation—"

"That's just it," Kent cut him off with a banked fury. "I'm telling you, based on the questions they were asking here, they're going to push the story it was a deliberate move on Max's part, even though no one believes it. Even if Max's aunt throws her weight around, I'm not so sure they'll take this investigation seriously. They'd rather blame Max than find out what really happened."

"Max never struck me as the suicidal type," Zev said.

"Because he's not." Kent leaned in, his face set in hard lines, as an undeniable intensity vibrated in his voice. "I will never believe Max deliberately caused this. If he swerved, it was because he was trying to avoid something. I've been with him when he's made this trip before. Years ago, he almost got shoved off one of those curves by a passing semi. Since then, he's been paranoid about that stretch. There's no way in hell he was speeding, especially not with Devon in the car. He's not reckless, and he would never put her in harm's way. He adored her."

There was no doubt Kent believed everything he said. It was there in his fervent denials fueled by righteous anger. When I looked to Zev, it was clear Kent's faith in Max was creating slivers of doubt.

Sure enough, Zev asked, "Did the police mention if there were any skid marks?"

"They di—"

The door opened and a tall, Rubenesque woman swept in, her intimidating presence quieting the room. Dark eyes bright with an uncomfortable mix of fury and grief swept over the people gathered in the waiting room. They landed on Zev and me and sharpened. Christina Velasquez inclined her head in acknowledgement then turned to say something to the older couple who accompanied her.

Somewhere in their sixties, the couple had at least fifteen years on the councilwoman. The gray-haired man listened to whatever Christina said, then he nodded. Using the arm holding his petite partner close, he guided her over to the others as she wept silently into her fistful of Kleenex. His shoulders were hunched under the invisible weight of worry and grief, yet he still managed to convey a sense of regal dignity.

"Max's parents," Kent murmured.

Christina left Max's parents and headed our way. Kent, Zev, and I rose to our feet to meet her. She reached out to Kent first, who took her hands, pulled her close, and brushed her cheek with his lips before pulling back.

"Kent, thank you for being here." Christina's typically smooth voice held a hint of roughness. She turned to Zev and me. "Zev, Rory, I'm surprised to see you here."

"Christina," Zev greeted her, taking the hand she offered. "We came to see how Max was doing."

Then it was my turn to take the councilwoman's hand. "Ms. Velasquez," I murmured, "I'm so sorry about your nephew."

She frowned, clearly puzzled. "Did you know Max?"

I swallowed down the nerves that always rose when I dealt with members of the Arcane Council. Not only were their personalities off-putting, but the power leaking from their pores scraped against my magic, making me antsy. "Not personally, but I made a delivery to him at his engagement party in Sedona."

Something dangerous flitted through her dark eyes. Up close, they were raptor sharp and just as disconcerting. "Is that so?"

The silky hint of menace in her voice tripped every instinct I possessed, and my Prism snapped into place with a teeth-gritting quickness.

Before I could say more, Kent stepped in. "She made Max and Devon's night." He rubbed the back of his neck. "Well, more like the delivery was the cherry on top of their night. They were so excited about those glasses, it was all they could talk about. I had to coax Devon into a game of poker so she'd stop pacing and driving me nuts."

"Glasses?" Christina's attention shifted to Kent.

Kent sighed. "Part of Max's latest treasure hunt, the Kidder coin collection. One of three hexed objects that help reveal the true map to the coins. He spent months tracking them down and finally got Red Maple to acquire them."

She turned back to me. "I was under the impression Red Maple worked with the Guild."

"They do, but the delivery request came in after hours. No one else was available, so they offered me the contract." There was no reason not to share, since nothing about it violated my noncompete clause with the Council's contract.

"Small world," Christina murmured.

Too damn small if you ask me. Since she hadn't, I didn't offer my opinion.

A surprised burst of sound erupted from the other side of the room. We turned in time to see Max's father catch his wife before she fell to the floor, sobbing. He led her to a nearby chair. Devon's father, face marred by tears, watched with a detachment that came from one too many emotional hits. Clearly, the news about Devon's death had been shared.

Sympathy and sadness washed away the cold edges of Christina's face, leaving it strangely vulnerable. "Poor Andrew. First his wife, now his daughter."

"He's going to want answers," Kent said softly.

Her eyes closed for a moment as she regathered her composure. When her lashes lifted, her familiar icy mask was firmly in place. I didn't think her shoulders could straighten any more, but she proved me wrong. "He's not the only one."

Kent's jaw tightened as his attention stayed on the scene playing out across the room. "I'd like to have those answers when Max wakes."

"So would I," Christina added.

Kent turned and met her gaze. "Then might I suggest you have a discussion with the police chief to share your desire?"

The undisguised bite to his request did not escape the councilwoman. "Is there a problem I should be aware of?"

Kent turned to face her fully and crossed his arms over his chest. "The police are convinced Max deliberately swerved off the road."

"Is that so?" The chill in her question raised the hair on my arms.

Undaunted, Kent continued, "I think they've made up their minds and won't waste resources to look elsewhere."

Christina gained a predatory demeanor as she studied the infuriated man in front of her. "You think this accident wasn't an accident."

I wasn't sure if Kent's grief was making him an idiot or brave, but he didn't back down.

His jaw inched up, a clear sign he was digging in and digging in deep. "I think this whole thing stinks to high heaven. You're Council, which makes you the only one I can think of that can make sure the truth comes out."

Clearly unoffended by his outburst, Christina considered him for a long moment. "You make a valid point." Her attention shifted to Zev and me. "What good is power if you can't use it?"

Her rhetorical question made me brace. Next to me, Zev stilled. We both waited for the metaphorical ax to fall.

Christina's smile was far from reassuring as she invoked the power of her position. "Zev, Rory, I'd like to request your assistance. Find out who targeted my nephew and killed his fiancée."

SIXTEEN

CHRISTINA WASTED no time in pulling her strings. With one call, she not only got Zev and me access to the case, but also arranged an appointment with the lead investigator of Max's accident. She sent the name and number to Zev's phone. Surprisingly, it wasn't either of my two favorite detectives. Guess the lowly delivery person didn't rate the top-tier interrogation, which was fine by me.

"For someone keen on avoiding the Council's attention," Zev drawled, interrupting my musings, "you have an absurd knack for getting it, sweetheart."

"It's not my fault," I said as we walked down the hospital hall toward the elevators. "I didn't know she'd be here." Or that the councilwoman would neatly corner my ass and, by extension, Zev's. I might not have been able to refuse, thanks to my contract with the Council, but Zev… "Is this going to cause you issues with Emilio?"

That earned me an amused snort. "Doing Councilwoman Christina Velasquez a personal favor?" He gave me a sidelong glance as we stopped at the metal doors. "Not likely. A favor asked is a favor earned, remember?"

Right, I should've known. Zev's involvement meant the

councilwoman would owe the Cordova Family a favor, something much more valuable than money in their world.

The elevator arrived with a soft ding, and the doors slid open. A trim, attractive man in his mid- to late thirties, with short, professionally styled brown hair and a strong jawline covered in a neat beard, stepped out, dressed in what I considered the corporate uniform—pressed slacks, button-down, collared shirt and understated tie. Nothing too flashy, but tastefully put together in a way guaranteed to earn a second glance from most females. He was the epitome of the successful corporate businessman.

He pulled up short when he caught sight of us, his hazel eyes sweeping over me dismissively before narrowing in on Zev. He cleared his throat and said, "Zev."

"Jayson." Zev's return greeting carried a cool tone. "Are you here to see Max?"

"Ah, yes." Jayson fiddled with his tie with his free hand. His other held a card, which he waved in the direction of the halls behind us. "I just heard he was in an accident. I wanted to stop by and wish him well." There was an underlying hint of nervousness in his voice, as if he were intimidated by Zev and trying not to show it.

Zev's eyebrows rose. "I didn't realize you and Max were friends."

A surprised bark of sound escaped Jayson before he quickly cut it off. "Friends? I wouldn't go that far." Something slid across his face too quickly to catch, then he regathered his composure. There was a hint of arrogance in his voice when he went on. "Business associates mainly. We've been working on finalizing an agreement between our two companies for the last month or so." His gaze shifted to behind us before coming back. "We were supposed to sign the papers on Friday."

The elevator doors started to close, but Zev's hand shot out to hold them open. His lips curved into a smile, but it wasn't amused or polite. It was just cold. "Your father must be thrilled."

A flash of anger was there and gone as Jayson managed an equally insincere grin. "Dad stepped down about three months ago, which is why I'm here."

"Congratulations."

Jayson inclined his head. "Thank you. How's Emilio doing? I've heard things have been challenging lately."

"No more than normal," Zev said. "How is Valerie doing? Last I heard she was getting ready to launch her nonprofit venture. That must keep the two of you busy."

Jayson's face froze, and his body stiffened. "It would if we weren't separated."

Oh, ouch! I hid my wince at his frigid response.

Pity or sympathy, even I couldn't tell which, swept through Zev's face, and his voice eased a bit when he said, "I'm sorry to hear that."

"Yes, well, life likes to take unexpected turns." Jayson stepped around us carefully. "Please, don't let me keep you. I'm sure you have a lot on your plate." His brush-off was unmistakable.

Zev's smile sharpened. "As, I'm sure, do you."

For a long moment, the two men stared each other down. Finally, Zev motioned me to the elevator and said to Jayson, "It was nice to see you again." Zev followed me into the elevator and hit the button for the lobby.

"You as well." Jayson's attention stayed on us until the door cut him off.

As we rode down, I looked at Zev. "Who was that?"

He watched the numbers count down above the door. "I'll tell you outside."

Mmm, story time.

I waited until we were out of the antiseptic air of the hospital and standing at his bike before I demanded, "Okay, so share."

Zev unlocked our helmets and handed me one. "Jayson Guzman."

I took the helmet he offered and mentally ran through the list of local Arcane bigwigs, but I came up blank. "You say that like I should know him."

Zev shrugged. "Not unless you're fascinated by the valley's economic development plans. He's the middle child of Saul Guzman, CEO of Guzman and Sons Development. They're one of the leading commercial construction companies in Phoenix."

So that made him at least a mid-level mover and shaker. "So, if he's the middle child, why isn't his older brother taking over the company?"

Some of Zev's tension disappeared as he chuckled. "Don't let the name fool you." He settled his hip against the Harley's seat. "The 'sons' part came about in previous generations. I believe the senior Guzman had a brother who didn't want to continue the family legacy. Which left the burden to him, and Jayson is his only son."

"Only son?" I rested my helmet on the padded leather next to Zev's thigh. "Sounds like there's a daughter or two in there somewhere. What happened? Did they not want to run the company or something?"

"Just one," Zev said. "And it was more like she decided to marry a high-ranking German politician about a decade ago. She has no interest in running the family company since she's perfectly happy swimming in the political pools of Europe." He shared the last bit with a hint of a sneer.

I angled my head and studied his expression. There wasn't much to go on. "What's the deal between you two?"

Any trace of amusement disappeared, and his tone turned curt. "I don't like him, and the feeling is mutual."

Hmm. "Yeah, I got that. Want to share why?"

Zev folded his arms over his chest, and a muscle in his jaw

jumped. "The Guzmans are Traditionalists with some fucked-up ideas they don't mind sharing."

In my opinion, fucked-up ideas and Traditionalists tended to go hand in hand. Curiosity got the better of me. "Like?"

"Jayson's father is one of a handful of loud voices behind the movement for the Arcane Registry."

"Oh gross." That conversation crawled out every election cycle. In the Arcane world, magic equaled power, and those who held the most made up the Families. Those who held little to no magic in their bloodlines were known as Traditionalists, and by their nature, they were very anti-Family. It was the old tale of the haves versus the have-nots, where the have-nots would go to any length to level the playing field. "So they're fundamentalists?"

"More like unhinged bigots, but yeah."

I could agree with the bigot sentiment, but it made me wonder. "So why is he doing business with Max?"

"At a guess?" Derision was clear in Zev's voice. "Guzman and Sons ran out of options and most likely went to Watershed Investments for financial backing on a project."

"Which is the agreement Jayson mentioned."

"Probably."

That explained the sour-grapes attitude. Well, that and losing his wife. The guy was obviously hitting a streak of bad luck.

A nasty smile creased Zev's mouth. "Would've paid good money to sit in that meeting. Whatever their agreement was, I'm betting Max made sure it hurt."

It couldn't be that easy, could it? I shot Zev a look. "Jayson the type to strike back?"

Zev snorted. "Totally, but I can't see how he'd be involved. Jayson and his father have made it very clear that they're proud not to have any magic of their own. Besides, if he's desperate enough to go to Watershed for financing, the last thing he'll do is endanger getting that money. Power may not rule his family, but money? That's a different story."

Maybe Zev was right. Maybe he wasn't. But since we'd been tasked with finding out if Max's accident *was* an accident, I was keeping Jayson on my mental list of bad guys. At least for now. "Fine, but you know you don't need magic to cause an accident, right?"

"I do." Zev straightened and picked up his helmet. "But let's start with the easiest thing first."

I grabbed my helmet. "Which is?"

"Answering the question of skid marks or no skid marks."

Zev turned into the cracked-asphalt lot and brought his bike to a stop under one of the palo verde trees that offered a bit of shade. This time of the year, with the cooler temperatures, the fight for such protection wasn't as intense as it was in summer, but the drifting storm clouds hinted that rain was a possibility. Three one-story dusty white buildings surrounded the lot like a blocky U. Blue awnings jutted out here and there over heavily tinted windows. We headed to the center building, where a square patio roof kept the elements from the entry.

Zev pulled open the door, and the bell tied to the inside bar jangled. I started to cross the linoleum floor to where a paper ticket dispenser sat next to the plexiglass-protected stations lining the main space, but Zev caught my wrist. "Where are you going?"

I motioned to where the number seventy-six hovered in midair above the ticket dispenser. About half the seats were filled with bored faces, and each open window was occupied. "If we don't grab one now, we'll be here forever."

"Don't need it." He pulled out his phone and started texting.

As Zev sent off his message, I wasted half a second considering the hard plastic chair that reminded me of my elementary school days and decided it would be safer on my spine to stay right where I was, so I shifted to Zev's side. His shoulder brushed mine as he folded his arms, and together, we stood near the back wall by the door and waited.

We got a few curious looks from those who were waiting to be called to a window and a couple of the employees. Thankfully, it was only a few minutes before a heavy door off to the side opened. A woman strolled out, her gaze zeroing in on us. Her hair was in a neat, short cut but was doing that slow-fade-to-gray thing. On the lean side and a couple inches taller than me, she wore knife-creased black slacks and a short-sleeve muted-green shirt that complemented the air of authority wafting around her.

Zev and I straightened and started toward her.

She met us halfway. "Zev Aslanov and Rory Costas?" There was a cool politeness to her voice. Clearly, she wasn't keen about dancing to Christina's tune.

"Trooper Greene?" Zev asked.

"Sergeant," Greene corrected then motioned to the door she'd emerged from. "If you'll follow me, we can talk in my office." Without waiting, she spun on her heel and headed back.

I shared a look with Zev before we both trailed behind her.

The woman stopped and pressed her palm against a clear resin square set in the wall. A sigil ignited, and the sound of the lock releasing followed. She pulled open the door and waved us through. "We're heading toward the back to the third room on the right."

A cluster of cubicles filled the main space, along with the chaotic hum of voices, ringing phones, and electronic equipment. Unlike the almost-uncomfortable quiet of the lobby, the noise was a clear indication that this was where the bulk of the work got done. The back wall was lined with offices, some open and some closed.

I stayed a step behind Zev as he waited for Greene to take the lead. We wound our way back, drawing only a few glances, but the sergeant's presence legitimized ours, so the curiosity was brief. We followed Greene into her office.

She rounded the desk and dropped into a rolling chair behind it, leaving Zev and me the two seats in front. A credenza stood below the narrow window behind her. Files, books, an overflowing box, and a few other items filled the top. Various awards, certificates, and a couple of hand-shaking pictures hung above the two filing cabinets against the wall to my right.

Once we were all seated, Greene folded her hands over a couple of files on her desk, her gaze steady but unreadable. "It's my understanding that Councilwoman Velasquez requested we give you access to the accident report involving Mr. Maximiliano Vasquez and Ms. Devon Olson. While we're happy to assist the Councilwoman, especially during this difficult time, I would like to stress that this office holds the integrity of its investigators and their investigations in high regard."

Translation: I don't know what dirt the Arcane Council is looking for, but I won't let you screw my department over.

Zev offered her a polite smile and a consolatory "We assure you, Sergeant Greene, that Councilwoman Velasquez does not question the validity of your office or your investigators. We are here simply to confirm every possible angle has been reviewed. Max and Devon's family are struggling, and she felt an extra set of eyes would offer them much-needed comfort."

Her lips thinned. "Are either of you trained investigators?"

"I am," Zev said. "However, Ms. Costas is an automotive expert."

Greene's gaze landed on me, and I did my best not to squirm. Unpolished nails drummed against the files as she studied us both, clearly debating just how blunt she wanted to be. She finally came to a decision. "Look, I don't know what it is you're hoping to find, but unless there's something else going on that we're not aware of, this has all the hallmarks of an accident. If the councilwoman's concern is truly for the families, dragging this investigation out would do more harm than good."

"On that, we can agree," Zev said. "Which is why she asked us to review a copy of the accident report. Her intent is to indulge the family and their concerns by having us confirm your office's findings."

Color me impressed. Zev's polite dance was a thing of beauty.

A long, tense moment passed, then Greene finally blew out a long breath. "Fine." She took the top file and handed it over to Zev. "Typically, you have to wait six days for the report to be officially processed. The Colonel personally passed along Councilwoman Velasquez's request. I'm sure I don't have to remind you that this information is not to be made public."

Zev took the file. "You do not, and it will not." He pulled it back and, surprisingly, handed it to me. "However, please know how much we appreciate your cooperation."

I took the remarkably thin file and flipped it open, letting Zev handle the pleasantries. My initial scan of the accident report noted three witness statements were taken, and that the responding officer took detailed notes. The diagram on the second page showed the path of Max's vehicle as it traveled southbound in the right lane, swerved across both lanes, then veered off the road, which matched the story Kent shared. But I would need time to read through the rest of the report. "Where are the photos?"

My abrupt question cut off the conversation between Zev

and Greene. When I looked up, both were staring at me—Zev with a bemused look, the sergeant with a scowl.

Greene asked, "Pictures?"

"Of the scene." I closed the file and lifted it. "This is just the report. Could we get copies of the photos?"

Greene's shoulders stiffened. "We were asked to share the report. The photos are not part of the public record until the investigation is complete."

I tapped the file against my knee. "All right, then I assume you're holding Max's car, correct?"

Her scowl deepened, and her reluctance was clear. "We are."

Recognizing that she was stuck between a rock and a hard place, I channeled Zev's diplomatic approach and tried for a conciliatory tone. "If we could, we'd like to see it."

A muscle in her jaw jumped as she considered my request.

I felt for her—I really did—but she wasn't the only one who had to answer to someone who could make her life difficult.

Finally, she gave a sharp nod. She pulled her keyboard over and spent a couple of minutes clicking through screens. When she stopped, she looked at us. "The vehicle is being held in the property and evidence lot, just down the street. I'll let them know you're heading over."

"Thank you," Zev said as he stood.

I echoed him as I did the same then followed him to the door.

Greene rose behind her desk, and just before we could step across the threshold, she called out, "Mr. Aslanov, Ms. Costas."

We turned back.

"No pictures." The command was clear.

"No pictures," Zev confirmed.

Her gaze shifted to me.

"No pictures," I promised.

SEVENTEEN

SINCE THE PROPERTY and evidence lot was down the block and behind the main buildings, we left Zev's bike and walked the short distance. Deciding to multitask, I flipped through the report, trusting Zev not to lead me into a ditch or something.

"According to the witness statements, one minute Max was calmly passing a semi, and the next, he was picking up speed and weaving erratically between the two lanes, before shooting over the side. None of them report seeing anything lying on or darting across the road."

Zev touched my arm in warning. "It's surprising that he didn't hit someone."

I sidestepped a lifted piece of the concrete sidewalk. "He came close. According to one person, he almost clipped an SUV, but they managed to brake short, which almost caused the driver behind him to hit him."

Out on the street, a car drove by. I lifted my gaze and watched it slow to a stop at the sign at the end. "Not one of the witnesses remember seeing his brake lights."

"Any notes on how fast he was going?"

"One witness said he was at eighty-five when Max blew

past. Because of the downgrade, that stretch is marked at sixty-five."

Zev caught my wrist and brought me to a stop by the crosswalk. "The only ones who actually stick to the speed limits are the semis and the snowbirds."

He wasn't wrong. I used the file folder to shade my eyes from the sun's glare and looked up at him. "If Max 'blew past' a witness at eighty-five, it's safe to assume he had to be doing ninety plus."

He studied me. "Which adds weight to the initial report of the accident being deliberate."

"Maybe," I agreed. "Another explanation is that someone tampered with the car, maybe disabled the brakes or messed with the ECU." Either of those should show up once a mechanic or electro mage checked out a car. I dropped my attention back to the report and studied the initial notations on the accident diagram. "But I'm not seeing anything in here about skid marks or fluids on the road. Not that the lack of either of those signs are conclusive evidence of sabotage."

"ECU?" He put his hand against the base of my spine and gave me a nudge.

I closed the report as we stepped off the curb and crossed the street. "Engine control unit. It's the computer brains of most modern cars."

"Like a plane's black box."

"Yep." We hit the sidewalk on the other side, and I lost his touch as he moved to take the lead. "If I had known we were going to check out the car, I would've brought Evan along," I told his back.

Without looking back, he said, "I'm sure DPS has their own electro mages to run diagnostics."

I'm sure they did, but who knew how long it would be before they would share the results. Plus, Evan was in a league of his own. And he was sneaky. Sneaky would be good since we weren't allowed to access anything anyway. Still, it was a nice thought.

We followed alongside a tall wall topped with curved iron spikes and stopped at a locked security gate. I kept my voice low. "You do realize that just because I'm a Transporter doesn't mean I'm going to be able to take one look at the car and determine what happened, right?"

Zev shot me a look as he pressed a button on the pad above the gate's lock. "Maybe, maybe not, but you can see things I can't."

"Yes?" a disembodied voice crackled.

"Zev Aslanov and Rory Costas. We were sent over by Sergeant Greene."

After a long pause, she answered, "Please have your IDs ready. I'll have the yard manager meet you momentarily."

"Thank you." Zev pulled his wallet from his back pocket.

I wasn't a fan of purses, not when things tended to get lost in them. Instead, I kept a couple of cards and my ID with my phone. We both had IDs in hand when a short, burly bald man with a handlebar mustache appeared around the corner and headed our way.

He eyed us both as he punched in a code and yanked open the unlocked gate. He moved into the opening and barked, "IDs."

We handed them over.

He eyed them both then handed them back. "My name's Will. It's my understanding you're here on behalf of the driver's family to see the Vasquez vehicle." He handed me back my ID then Zev's.

Zev put his away. "That's correct."

"A few rules, then I'll take you back." Will nailed us both with a flinty gaze. "You are not allowed to take any images or recordings of any kind of the vehicle as it is still being processed. Nor can you take any personal items from the vehicles. Those will be returned to the family once it has fully been processed. Do you understand?"

Zev's expression remained unchanged. "Yes."

Will's attention shifted to me.

"Yes," I said.

"Good." The older man stepped back, giving us permission to walk through. "You've got fifteen minutes."

We followed him toward the huge garage dominating the yard. Inside, there were racks of parts and tools neatly lined on metal shelves along one wall. The opposite wall held various labeled bins and more equipment. The familiar scents of oil, grease, and dust filled the space, but an additional brush of magic jangled over my nerves, rousing the power that lived in me. I rubbed at the itch as the Prism slid into place like a bird settling its feathers.

Will stopped us just inside the structure. "You need to glove up first."

He dug gloves and protective booties out of their boxes and handed them to us. I set the file on the rolling cart that served as a computer station and slipped the paper booties on first. A soft, cool breeze blew through the opening on the far end that looked out on a collection of cars in various conditions, but it was the crumpled hunk of metal hovering a few feet above the ground in the center that held my attention.

"Holy shit," I muttered under my breath, wondering how in the hell Max and Devon had managed to get out of that alive.

Next to me, Zev asked, "Is that it?"

"Yep." Will's answer was brisk.

I tugged the gloves on and walked forward.

"Ma'am," Will called, stopping me.

I looked back. "Yes?"

"Watch your step." He indicated the floor near the wreckage.

It was only then that I noticed the markings on the ground below the twisted metal. "Got it."

I paced a slow circle around what was left of what had once been a sedan. The front and back ends were nothing but mangled metal and plastic. The front tires were folded back under the engine block, and the main cage of the driver and passenger seats, front and back, were the only thing that held any sort of shape. Curtains of white from the deployed airbags dropped from the inside roof, and a thin film of dust decorated the battered dash. A mass of cracks snaked through the safety glass, looking as if something simple like a breeze would shatter the precarious windshield into a million pieces.

The passenger door was caved in, and the black paint was scraped down to white in some places. I moved around to the driver's side, following the long gouges marring the metal. The door was gone, revealing the broken seats stained with a mix of brown and rust-colored spots. The steering column was jacked, and the wheel itself hung lopsided. I was betting that was due to whatever tools the responders had used to pry Max out.

I clasped my hands behind my back so I wouldn't touch anything and leaned in to get a closer look at the interior. A pair of familiar coffee cups lay on the floorboards next to what looked like a phone with one of those circle things people put on them to make it easier to hold, and there was a high-heel shoe over in the passenger side. In the back, the partition between the trunk and rear seats had burst open, spilling clothes and toiletries through the opening.

I straightened, stepped back, looked around, and spotted the door among the other pieces sitting off to the side. Some, I recognized, and some, I didn't. I turned back to the wreckage as Zev came over to stand with me. I leaned back so I could see Will as he stood watching us, his thick arms crossed over his chest.

"Any idea how many times it rolled?" I asked him.

Magic brushed along my senses, and the car's remains tilted slowly in the magical net suspending it, until the roof became visible. The ease of the movement indicated Will was either a metal mage or a mech mage. Considering his job, I was betting on the latter. Zev stepped back, giving me room to move in closer.

Will spoke as he came over to join us. "My preliminary findings indicate that it rolled at least twice." He stopped next to me and used his finger to trace above a gouge along the roofline. "Do you see this gash here?"

There were multiple scrapes and scratches, but I followed his path over the two longest carved along the frame just above the driver's side. One was deeper than the other. "Yeah."

"The first time it rolled, it landed on something hard enough to embed it into the metal. See how the bottom of this one is marked up?"

"Looks pitted."

"Not a surprise. The initial roll would pick up rocks and such, but the second roll would tear it loose, leaving behind ragged edges like this."

Not wanting to tumble into the casting circle or the twisted metal it held, I put a hand on Zev's arm for balance and leaned in closer. Sure enough, on one side of the deeper marks, the edges were bent out as if the metal had expelled something. "Wow, I never would've noticed that."

Will made a noise that sounded like a grunt.

I pulled back, let go of Zev, and asked, "Have you been able to find any signs of impact not consistent with the rollover?"

"I haven't gotten that far yet. I barely got it this morning, so we've a ways to go yet." Will's gaze shifted from me to Zev's silent presence then back to me, as he correctly put the pieces together. "Are you a mechanic?"

I shook my head. "Transporter."

"Guild?"

I nodded.

"Right then." He stepped back, apparently satisfied I knew my shit. "What do you know about Audis?"

I studied the mangled metal and flipped through the mental files I kept for my job. "Just the high points on speed, handling, and performance."

"And safety?"

"They tend to score higher than most."

"Yep," Will agreed, dropping his arms. He turned his attention back to the remains and waved a hand at it. "This particular model was rated one of IIHS's top safety picks for its year. Someone spent a pretty penny on this one here, because it was decked out in safety features. If it was offered, this had it."

That explained how Max and Devon had survived. "So it had an AEB?"

"An automatic braking system? Yeah, it did."

The grim note in Will's answer made me look at him. "Why does it sound like there's a but to that?"

"AEBs can be disabled."

Catching Zev's raised eyebrow, I elaborated. "Because people find the constant warnings annoying." I looked to Will. "Was this one disabled?"

He shook his head. "I can't answer that until all the evidence is processed."

We had more than driver error to worry about. Disabling the AEB or interfering with the ECU could be done remotely, without the driver's knowledge. Someone just had to be damn good at hacking the car's computer. "When everything is processed, will you be able to tell how and when any interference occurred?"

"Most likely." Will cocked his head, his eyes sharp. "You think someone hacked the car?"

"It's an option we have to consider," Zev said.

A flash of sympathy moved through Will's stoic mask. He turned away to study the wreck for a long moment. Finally, he said, "Right now, the only thing I can rule out is mechanical interference."

"So no cut brake lines?" I murmured.

Will nodded. "We still have to run both electrical and magical diagnostics."

It was Zev's turn to do the arm-crossing thing. He even added a glower. "How soon will that be done?"

"This time of the year, we're short-staffed. My best guess?" Will scratched his chin. "A week, two at most."

We didn't have a week or two. Zev and I shared a look, then I started my second walk around the car. Zev said that I might see something he would miss, but I wasn't sure what he… The mental light flicked on.

Oh, yeah, that might work.

I snuck a glance at Zev and Will. I might not have Evan's level of know-how, but I could do something that might give us a leg up. However, I couldn't do it with Will breathing down my neck. Distracting him would be up to Zev, but he would need a good reason. Zev caught my gaze, and I tilted my head in a silent nudge.

He turned to Will. "You mentioned personal items. Do you have a list I could share with the family?"

"Over on the computer. I'll pull it up for you." Will led Zev over to the cart with the laptop.

Utilizing the opportunity presented, I flexed my magical muscle that let me "see" magical signatures. It was uncomfortably draining to use, but if magic was involved, I might luck out and catch an echo of it. This particular trick was a quirk of being a Prism, one I'd discovered by accident. Now, after months of practice, I took the mental half-step to the side, and my perception shifted with me.

Silver and green burst to vibrant life. I blinked in an effort to regain my focus. When my vision cleared, the green settled into the casting circle on the garage's floor. Silver lines were anchored at various points of the car and ran up to the ceiling, where a smaller power circle was set in the roof.

Realizing silver and green would be tied to Will, I walked around the remains again. I let my magic unfurl and drift inside the car, searching for any other colors and taking mental notes to go over later. There was a flicker of pale orange with snaps of even paler blue near the center console. *Heating-cooling element?* Broken strands dripped from the glove box. *Probably a ward of some kind.*

I was on the passenger side when a silver flare spilled down the anchoring lines and the wreckage slowly shifted its tilted position back to its initial position. I stepped back until it settled in place. There were vibrant strands, some intact and some broken, threaded along the passenger's door and across the front dash and wrapped around the driver's seat. "Will, did emergency services have to use magical means to get Max and Devon out of this?"

There was a pause, then he answered, "Yes. Notes I have indicated a metal mage was on scene and had to move parts of the seats and dash out of the way."

That explained why that magic was so clear. I leaned in to look through the windowless back door. There was a grayish smudge of some kind on the seat behind the driver, but I couldn't make it out with all the clothes scattered on top.

I strolled around the rear and back up the driver's side, stopping once again at the driver's seat. I started reeling in my power, then something snagged it, like claws catching on a spiderweb. I froze, not daring to move lest I lose the fragile connection. I studied the interior carefully as I narrowed my focus to where the magical vibrations seemed to originate.

There, under the seat.

I slowly dropped to a crouch, trying to get on eye level. A weak yellow glow trickled from under the driver's seat. The echo was fading as I watched. The urge to reach out and grab whatever it was rode me hard, but somehow, I managed not to violate Will's circle. "Um, Will? I think I found something."

I heard feet coming closer, then Will was at my shoulder. "What?"

I pointed to the shadowy edge of something wedged under the seat and leaned back so he could see. "That."

He peered in, muttered something under his breath I couldn't catch. "I see it."

Taking him at his word, I straightened and backed away so he could do what he needed to. Since a headache was starting up, I reclaimed my magic, and the colorful tapestry winked out.

Will wasted no time in reaching in and working out the object. When he pulled back, he pivoted on his heel and, without rising from his crouch, held out his hand. "Got any idea what this is?"

Seeing a familiar box, I cleared my throat. "It's a pair of glasses."

Zev, who had followed Will over, shot me a questioning look, and I nodded.

"Glasses?" Will frowned as he straightened. "Like for driving?"

"No, those are antique." When he looked at me, I said, "I delivered those the night before the accident."

EIGHTEEN

"DO you think it's worth our time to talk to the witnesses?" I asked Zev before taking a bite of my dill pickle spear.

"Probably not." He had his back to the wall and one arm lying across the top of the booth's seat. He caught the eye of a passing waitstaff and lifted his glass, requesting a refill. "I don't think they can add much more than what's in that." He lifted his chin to indicate the file that sat off to the side of our table.

After leaving the evidence garage, we'd decided to plot out our next move while enjoying a late-lunch-slash-early-dinner. I dragged a French fry through the puddle of ranch on my plate. "Yeah, that's what I'm thinking."

"Walk me again through what you found," he said.

I blew out a breath and sat back, pulling my leg up and tucking my foot under my other thigh. "Okay, so there were the obvious signs from the emergency workers. There was a temperature ward in the console, most likely to regulate the drink holder."

Our server approached and set a new glass of soda in front of Zev, smiling pleasantly. "Here you go."

He gave her an absent thanks, and she bustled away.

I waited until she was out of earshot before continuing. "I think the glove box doubled as a lockbox."

"That's fairly standard, isn't it?"

"On high-end cars, definitely, but it's also an easy after-market addition." It wasn't that difficult. I'd done a few, with Lena's help, including the one in my Mustang. It was a great way to keep minor valuables safe. The Guild used the space to double as containment. Anyone with the money could do the same on a private vehicle. In Max's case, the magical echoes weren't enough to determine which role his had played. "I'm thinking that's where the glasses were until the crash, which broke the hinges."

"And somehow they got thrown over to the driver's side and wedged under the seat?" There was a skeptical note in Zev's voice.

"Actually, yeah." When he continued to study me with obvious disbelief, I shrugged. "It's not unheard of. You'd be amazed at where shit ends up when a car gets tossed around."

"I'll take your word for it." He drummed his fingers against the table. "You said there was something in the back?"

I nodded. "A gray smudge of some kind on the seat behind the driver, but it was hard to tell what exactly with the clothes and crap all over."

"Smudge?"

"Yeah, normally echoes are like strands—different colors, sizes, thicknesses, that kind of thing. Think of it like a rainbow spiderweb. But as magical signatures fade, those strands tend to lose their shape, almost as if they turn into smoke." The phenomenon was a recent discovery from work I'd done with Sabella and Lena. My aunt was a hard-ass who continually pushed me and my abilities. I hadn't appreciated it at the time, but in situations like this, it paid off to understand what the hell I was looking at.

"So it could be an old working of some kind?"

"Probably?" Since this was a new-to-me skill, I was still figuring out the particulars. "I can't be a hundred percent sure, but I'd assume so."

"Which means no obvious magic at work." He fisted his hand and knocked his knuckles against the table. "Which leaves us with nothing."

As much as I felt the dismay in his tone, I couldn't ignore the other possibilities. "Not nothing, Zev."

He looked at me.

"There's still the possibility of physical tampering."

"Which they won't share for weeks."

"So?" When he just sat there looking grim, I set my arms on the table and leaned in, keeping my voice low. "If we believe Kent and Christina—that Max was not at fault, and there's no sign of magical interference—then we're left with sabotage. Whether it's physical tampering or hacking the onboard computer systems, there's more than one way to screw with a car. We don't necessarily need to know how it was tampered with. We just need to figure out who's behind it." I held his gaze. "So maybe what we need to look at is who has it out for Max."

Zev's fingers stilled as he stared at me, but it was clear he was thinking things through and not really seeing me. He blinked, his attention coming back online. "Not just Max."

Not quite following, I asked, "What?"

He shifted in his seat and mimicked my pose. With his arms folded on the table, he leaned in. "Max wasn't the only one in the car."

I sat back and cocked my head. "Wait. You think Devon was the target?"

"I don't know what I think, but if we follow your logic, we have two potential targets."

He wasn't wrong. I frowned down at my plate, picked up a fry, and doodled in the ranch as my mind spun. Because of Max's relationship with Christina and the fact he was the one behind the wheel, I'd automatically focused on him. In my mind, when someone was tangled up with anyone on the Council, the avarice of others turned them into a target. Power, jealousy, greed, and all those ugly demons would come out to play in the worst possible way. Granted, that was my personal bias talking, but I didn't think I was too far off the mark. However, that kind of behavior wasn't just limited to the Council. Something I would do well to remember.

I set down the fry next to my half-finished hamburger and pushed my plate aside, no longer hungry. "So, who do we start with? Devon or Max?"

Zev nudged his plate to join mine, then he sat back, his foot bumping mine as he stretched out his legs. "Why not both?"

Our server collected our plates and set a faux-leather holder with our bill on the table. "Can I get you anything else?"

Zev took the bill before I could blink. While he dug out his wallet, I looked out at the half-full dining room then turned to the server. "You mind if we sit here for a little bit longer?"

She shook her head. "Not at all. Our dinner rush won't hit for another hour."

"We should be done by then," I assured her. "Could you bring us a pot of coffee?"

She accepted the bill from Zev and tucked it into her apron as she resettled the dishes. "Of course."

"Thank you."

She flashed another smile and bustled off.

"All right," I said to Zev as I pulled up the notepad on my phone. "Who do we start with?"

Zev quizzed me on who was at the engagement party, and based on my descriptions, he proposed names that matched. Outside of Kent, there was Rebecca Tsosie, the petulant blond named Perry, and the older woman at the poker table, who Zev thought might be Barbara Warren.

He did a web search and pulled up her photo to show me. "This her?"

When I nodded, we added her name to the list. I also put down the weirdly friendly bartender, Cass, with a question mark.

Zev's brow furrowed. "A bartender?"

I made a note to find out who'd catered the party so I could track Cass down. "Why not? You'd be surprised at what they hear. At events like that, bartenders and servers fade into the woodwork. The partygoers barely pay attention unless they're out of alcohol or food. All sorts of dramas play out in front of them."

Zev made a "huh" noise but didn't argue.

I looked over our very short list. "I think we should start with Rebecca."

"Why?"

"Because when I ran into her, I got the impression she was close to Devon and Max. She not only mentioned the villa belonged to Max's 'firm,' which I assume is his family's company, but she was familiar with the story behind Max's treasure hunt." And remembering her retelling of betrayal and revenge, the hair on my arms stood up. "No way."

Zev's gaze locked on to me. "What?"

"The glasses." When he continued to look at me without comprehension, I shared, hoping he would confirm my logic was just paranoia. My heart raced, but I kept my voice level. "Okay, so Rebecca told me the story behind Max's treasure map and the glasses. Long story short, the map is supposed to lead to a lost cache of Confederate gold buried somewhere in the desert. However, the map's true route is hidden by illusion, and you need the glasses to see it." I took a deep breath. "According to legend, the glasses are supposedly cursed by the widow of the man who took the gold. That widow was a Nightmare who also created the map."

Zev didn't take long to connect the dots. "The glasses you delivered to Max?"

My nod was slow. "Yep. Everyone was so excited when he put them on and stared at a bunch of old photos."

"Old photos?"

"Yeah, they called them pythagographs. I asked Lena about it, and she confirmed that pythagographs are a magical equivalent of hiding information in an image. My guess—they were a test to make sure the glasses were authentic."

"And were they?"

"According to Max, they were."

Zev's face darkened. "The Nightmare's curse—what was it?"

A clammy sweat broke out over my spine, and I tried to shove down my anxiety, but my voice shook a little when I answered. "According to Rebecca, if they're used by someone with a selfish heart, they'll be haunted by those they wronged until they make it right or something close to that."

He chewed over that for a moment. "Did you put them on?"

I shook my head. "No, Max did, and so did Perry, but Red Maple required a physical assessment of the package, so I did handle them. Briefly, to confirm they weren't damaged in any way."

He reached across the table, turned my white-knuckled fist over, and brushed his thumb back and forth over my fingers. "Breathe, babe."

Under his gentle touch, my fingers loosened, letting blood flow once more. "What if—"

"No." He cut me off, tangling his fingers with mine. "First, you didn't put them on. Second, I'm guessing the intent of the widow's curse in regard to the selfish-heart bit was to ensure whoever went looking for her husband's gold wouldn't get a chance to enjoy it, much less find it. And third, remember what Lena said? A curse's potency is based upon the caster's intent and target. If those glasses are hexed, it was done over a century ago, which means the intended targets are dust."

Okay, he has a point, but… "Lena also said it was possible to pick up residual effects from hexes, like catching a cold. What if my nightmares are that germ?"

He squeezed my hand and let go. "Then the Key she's hunting down should be able to remove it."

I'm glad one of us had that faith, but it was still unsettling as all get out to think I might be carting around a centuries-old curse. I thumbed my screen, checking my texts for any updates from Lena. Nothing.

Zev took my phone and set it facedown next to him. "Stop, Rory, you're just driving yourself nuts."

I sat back, folded my arms over my chest, and glared at him.

Unperturbed, he got us back on track. "Let's see if we can talk to Kent first, get his impressions of the others, see if he has any other names we should check out."

"Fine."

At my sullen response, amusement lit his dark eyes, but he shook his head and started texting Kent. On the table next to his elbow, my phone rattled.

I huffed out a put-upon breath and held out my hand, palm up, flicking my fingers in demand. "Give me."

He picked up my phone, glanced at the screen, frowned in puzzlement, then turned it toward me. "What's this?"

NINETEEN

I RECLAIMED MY PHONE. The text was from a blocked number, but the series of numbers in the text bubble had my pulse spiking in excitement. "It's an invite for a night race."

Zev finished his text, set his phone facedown on the table, and studied me. "Tonight?"

"Most likely." My fingers itched to hit the link, but I kept myself in check because there was something in Zev's tone that worried me.

He stared at my phone for a long, uncomfortable moment as he struggled with some unknown emotion.

"What?" I asked.

He shook his head and didn't answer. Before I could say anything else, our server, who was hovering nearby, made moves to come over.

Zev caught the motion and muttered, "We should go."

Okay, something was definitely up, but since I wasn't keen on hashing out whatever it was in public, I scooted out of the booth with my phone in hand and waited for Zev to join me. Whatever he was chewing on didn't stop him from curling an arm around my waist as he led me outside to his bike. He let me go and unlocked the helmets.

I caught his arm and stopped him. "Zev."

He turned, his jaw set, his gaze troubled, but didn't say anything.

"What's with the…" I used my phone and finger to circle my face then chose the polite description. "Grumpy face?"

He straightened then grabbed my hand, looking around. He spotted his intended target and started over, dragging me along in his wake. We got to a bench set off to the side of the restaurant that provided a modicum of privacy, and he motioned with his free hand. "Sit."

I let him go and took a seat.

He dropped down next to me, legs out, crossed at the ankles, arms crossed over his chest. His gaze was aimed at his boots. We sat there for a moment, then he looked up. "How often does this happen?"

I shifted on the bench's hard surface, bracing an arm on the back, and angled to face him. "What?"

He jerked his chin toward my phone.

"The race invite?"

He nodded.

"I don't know," I admitted cautiously, his strange vibe making me nervous. "Every few months or so, I guess." I fiddled with my phone, tapping it against my thigh, flipping it around, and doing it again and again. "You know there's no rhyme or reason to how these go down, not when night races are technically illegal. Someone decides to host, picks a spot and time, and sends out the notification. You either show, or you don't."

His gaze dropped to my restless movements, and his jaw clenched and unclenched.

It was unsettling to witness because clearly, he was struggling with something, I just had no idea what. "What's wrong?"

Instead of answering my question, he looked up and asked, "How do they determine who gets the coordinates?"

I shrugged, watching him closely. "I don't know all the ins and outs of their cloak-and-dagger routines, but it's not like they send this text to just anyone. Generally, they tag the drivers first, who share with their crew, who then share with friends."

He looked away, his gaze going out toward the parking lot, leaving me with his profile. He ran a hand through his hair then studied his feet. His hair fell forward, masking his expression. I studied his face, but there was nothing in it for me to read. Not like he was normally an open book or anything, but when it was just the two of us, his implacable mask disappeared, giving me a peek into the man beneath it. Right now, that mask was firmly in place.

"Zev," I started, but before I could finish, he turned to me, his eyes dark with some turbulent emotion.

"How long ago was the last one?" His question was abrupt, his voice low.

I didn't like the turn of our conversation or that I didn't know where it was going. It left me defensive. Not a good look for me. "I don't know. Maybe a couple months back. Why?"

"Did you go to that one?"

My temper woke, and I narrowed my eyes. *What is his deal?* Before I could snap back, a family of four walked by, heading to the restaurant. I waited until they were out of earshot before warning Zev, "This is starting to sound like an interrogation, and I don't like it."

Months of being with this man meant I had zero qualms about being honest. In the world he lived in, which happened to be the same one I was starting to find my place in, subterfuge was king. In the relationship we were trying to build, *subterfuge* was a synonym for *lying,* and no real, committed relationship could survive that. That was one thing we had both agreed to. Whatever this was, was starting to really piss me off.

"Do you have something against me racing?"

His body jerked at my question, as if he'd taken a hit of some kind. "No." A rush of color swept up his face, the red darkening his naturally tan skin as his gaze dropped away. "Shit, no. Rory, that's…" He wrapped a hand around the back of his neck and shook his head. He sucked in a breath, dropped his hand, and met my gaze. "No, I don't have anything against you racing."

Tension coiled around my spine as I settled back. My grip tightened on my phone, and it was my turn to do the folded arms of stubbornness. "Then care to explain the Spanish Inquisition happening here?"

He grimaced and covered my fisted hand with his, giving it a gentle squeeze. "I'm fucking this up."

Since I agreed, I held my tongue and raised my brows.

He opened his mouth, closed it, then shook his head. Finally, he blew out a hard breath. "Other than the race in June, have you been to any others since we've gotten together?"

"No," I answered slowly. Despite his assurance he had no qualms about me racing, a sour taste filled my mouth. "Why?"

He started brushing his thumb over my knuckles. "It's just we've been spending a lot of time together, and other than the race back in June, as far as I know, you haven't been to one since."

"That's because I haven't," I confirmed. "In fact, if we hadn't needed information, I probably would have skipped the one in June, considering all that was going on at the time."

The unsettling vibe grew stronger as he continued to study me with unnerving intensity. "Is that normal?"

Frustration underlaid with a hint of fear had me snapping, "Is what normal?"

"For you not to race for months on end." His thumb

stopped moving, and he shifted his hold, as if he were worried I might get up and leave.

Fat chance. I wanted answers, which I wouldn't get if I stormed off. "No, but the last few months haven't exactly been normal." I searched his face, hoping to find some kind of clue as to where the hell this was coming from. "What's going on here, Zev?"

His gaze drifted moodily over my face, and he brushed my hair behind my ear. "I'm being an ass."

The mix of resignation and remorse in his voice was clear, so I gentled my tone. "Yeah, I can see that, but can you tell me why?"

"Something someone said, I let it get under my skin." He looked down at our joined hands and shook his head. "I know better, but…"

Curiosity warred with frustrated confusion, and I demanded, "Spill, Zev."

His shoulders straightened, and his gaze, uncomfortable but unflinching, came back to mine. "Rumors are flying about you, through the Families. And I don't think I realized what that really meant, for either of us."

A knot formed in my stomach. I didn't like where this seemed to be going. I swallowed against the lump that had taken root in my throat. "And what *does* it mean?"

His eyes came to mine and sharpened. "It means that I underestimated my reaction to stupid rumors. Rumors I should've blown off—" He stopped short.

Zev wasn't easily fooled, so that sick roiling in my gut got worse. "What was it?"

He captured both my hands and held them tightly as his eyes met mine. "That you had someone on the race circuit and that our relationship was your way 'in.'"

I tugged against his hold, but he didn't let me go. "That's bullshit." I caught the flash of emotion before he could bury it, and it hit me. *Wait… is he jealous?* I pushed beyond my indignation to really look at him. Then I leaned in and got in his face. "You know that's bullshit, right?"

"Logically, yeah," he admitted reluctantly.

I tugged my hands free and cupped his face in my palms, forcing him to look at me. "No, not just logically. It just is."

For the first time, I witnessed the cracks in his mask, cracks made by insecurity. It was a shock to see, especially in someone as supremely confident and self-assured as Zev. *But, a voice whispered, maybe I shouldn't be surprised. Not after what happened recently with Imogen.*

His ex had not only turned to the dark side, but done so in such a way that had left even him stunned. And Zev was only human, and human hearts were notoriously fragile. How much had that betrayal rocked his sense of self? Eroded the foundation we had started to create? Trusting someone else was hard when he didn't trust himself.

I pressed my forehead against his without losing his gaze. I gave him the only thing I could. "I love you, Zev Aslanov. Just you. Not your connections. Not your reputation. Just you." Whether or not he believed me, that was up to him, but since he had yet to let me down, I had faith enough for both of us.

We sat there for a long moment, foreheads resting against each other, breaths mingling, before he finally broke and sank his hand into my hair, angling my head so he could kiss me. It was short but sweet.

When he pulled back, he brushed his thumb over my bottom lip. "I love you too, Rory."

Determined to take us out of the heavy, I managed a small grin and teased, "Then are we good?"

He pressed another quick kiss to my lips, grabbed my hand, and pulled me up as he stood, the earlier strangeness between us fading. "Yeah, we're good."

We headed toward his bike, his arm around my waist, our

hips bumping. "You know, it'd be easier if you weren't who you are?"

"What do you mean?"

"Well, considering how often our dates end in elevated heart rates and ripped clothes that have nothing to do with sexy fun times, dating a badass has its drawbacks."

His chuckle erased the last bit of tension. "You think dating a speed demon with a knack for finding trouble is any easier?"

I deliberately bumped his hip. "Aww, c'mon, you know you love it." This time, it was his laughter that rang out, and I grinned and waited until he was done to ask, "So you coming with me to the race tonight, then?"

He squeezed me. "Wouldn't miss it."

It was my turn to grin. "Good."

TWENTY

AS WE WERE PUTTING on our helmets, Zev got a return text from Kent, agreeing to meet at his home. The address took us to a mixed-use condo development called Camelback Village off Scottsdale Road at the southern edge of Scottsdale. It was a fairly new construction that spanned a couple of blocks. From the road, it was all boring square edges and glass, but once we walked into the landscaped courtyard, I let out a low whistle of appreciation.

Does no one recognize we live in the desert?

Lush landscaping and dramatic water features from waterfalls to reflective pools dominated the courtyard. Rooftop gardens shared space with green-draped private terraces, creating the illusion of strolling through a high-end resort turned into the depths of a rain forest, not a condo complex in the heart of Scottsdale. Even traffic noises and the expected dust appeared unable to breach the urban oasis.

"I do not want to think about the water bill for this place," I muttered under my breath as we walked past another alcove hidden behind trees and bushes.

"Forget the water bill," Zev said as we moved into the

shaded space where the elevators were located. "I bet the HOA fees are killer." He hit the call button.

I turned to look back to the verdant courtyard. "I don't know. If I didn't have to take care of all that but still got to look at it, might be worth it."

The melodious ding of the arriving elevator matched the serene surroundings. The doors slid open, and we stepped inside. Zev hit the button for the fourth floor. The doors closed, and soft flutes and bells drifted from speakers as we rode up. When the doors opened, we stepped out onto the walkway connecting the condos.

It was so quiet, it was almost disconcerting. Zev found Kent's condo and hit the buzzer. While we waited for him to answer, I turned to look out at the other units. All the condos faced in, but the boring lines from the exterior were not repeated here. Instead, private balconies and gardens broke up the lines, jutting out like mismatched stair steps. In fact, a small pool with lounge chairs, a couple occupied, sat below us. The sound of a lock being thrown and a door opening had me turning back around.

An exhausted-looking Kent stood in the doorway. Sometime between this morning and now, he had managed to change, because he was dressed in jeans and a T-shirt, but the circles under his eyes remained. "Zev." He looked to me. "Rory, welcome, come in." He stepped back and waved us through.

"Kent," Zev returned. He took off his sunglasses, hooked them on his collar and walked inside.

I gave Kent a nod as I followed.

"Please, make yourselves comfortable." Kent closed the door and threw the latch. "Can I get you two something to drink? Water? Tea?"

"Water's good." I followed Zev across the huge square tiles into Kent's living space.

"Same for me," Zev said.

The condo's layout was open, taking advantage of the abundant floor-to-ceiling tinted windows that flooded the space with light. The entry spilled into the kitchen and dining area. A short breakfast bar separated the kitchen from the living room. An outdoor balcony with a patio set stretched on the other side. Off to our left was a hall where I assumed the bedrooms and bathrooms were tucked away. Warm tones were everywhere, from the tile to the wall colors to the subtle cream furniture. It was gorgeous, but it was that *Architectural Digest*–type gorgeous that made me afraid to do much of anything except admire it.

Zev took a seat on the sofa, so I picked a spot on the chaise lounge at the end. Kent brought over two thick glass tumblers filled with ice and water. He handed me mine first, then Zev his.

Zev took it and asked, "How's Max?"

"No change." Kent took a seat on one of the stools at the breakfast bar. He hooked a bare foot over the bottom railing and left his other on the floor. "We finally got his parents to leave for a little bit, but I don't think they'll stay away long." He looked at a clock in the kitchen. "I'm heading back over at six."

"We won't take up much of your time," Zev reassured him.

Kent waved that away. "I'm assuming you met with the investigator?"

"We did, and she granted us access to Max's car," Zev confirmed.

"That's something," Kent muttered then cleared his throat. "And?"

Zev looked to me, handing off the conversational ball. I picked it up, drawing Kent's attention. "And they're still working through it, but it's going to take them time to go through what's left."

"Time?" Kent's voice carried a derisive edge that matched his lip curl. "Time to cover their asses maybe."

I leaned forward on the edge of the chaise lounge, braced my elbows on my knees, and cradled the glass between my hands, doing my best to get through his anger. "I..." After shooting a glance at Zev, I turned back to Kent. "We didn't get the impression that anyone has come to any solid conclusions on what caused the accident."

Kent sneered. "Because they think it was Max's—"

"Because the officers who notified you were working with the initial incident report," Zev cut in. "We were given a copy of that, as well. Along with access to the wreckage. To be honest with you, if you and Councilwoman Velasquez weren't so convinced otherwise, I'd come to the same initial conclusion, especially as there were no obvious signs of magical interference."

I thought Zev was stretching it a bit on that point, but I wasn't about to quibble in front of Max's friend.

Kent didn't miss much because he homed in on what Zev didn't say. "What about physical tampering?"

"Hard to tell," I answered. "What's left of the car is a mess, and they're going to need a skilled mech mage to go through it. But, again, that could take weeks."

Kent's mouth tightened as he folded his arms over his chest and dropped his glare to his feet. He took a few deep breaths, clearly struggling not to snap back but actually listen to us. When he was able to rein it in, he raised his head. "But you're here, asking questions, so does that mean you two no longer believe Max was at fault?"

"What we think and what we can prove are two different things." Zev neatly sidestepped answering outright.

Based on the dark frown that swept over Kent's face, he was not happy with Zev's response. "Since Christina doesn't tolerate fools, what exactly do you think happened?"

Zev and I exchanged a look, and when he dipped his chin,

I answered solemnly, "We think that if Max was not at fault, it means someone physically tampered with the car."

"Why?" Clearly agitated, Kent got up and began to pace. He ran a hand through his hair. "Or better yet, who?"

"That's the question we're hoping you can help us with," Zev said.

I watched the other man pace. "You're Max's best friend, right?"

"Yeah, we've known each other since middle school." Kent stopped, turned, and propped his hands on his hips. "I can't think of anyone who'd do something like this. I mean, for fuck's sake, Max is in a coma, and Devon's dead." His voice broke on the last word.

I gave it a moment then asked carefully, "What about the other guests at his engagement party?" When he turned and gave me a puzzled look, I elaborated. "The delivery I made, those glasses?"

Kent nodded.

"It's my understanding they were part of a treasure hunt Max was pursuing." I got another nod. Not wanting to reveal the facts Rebecca shared, I took a circuitous route, hoping he'd share something new. "It was easy to see that Max wasn't the only one excited about them; the whole room appeared to be interested in whether or not the glasses were real. In fact, the level of excitement felt like more than just simple curiosity. Did I read that wrong?"

He studied me for a moment. "You couldn't have been there more than fifteen, twenty minutes, and you got all that?"

There was a skeptical note in his question that got my back up, but I refrained from snapping back and simply shrugged. "I'm observant that way."

"The glasses," Zev cut in before Kent could stick his foot farther into his mouth, "had to cost a pretty penny or two." He waited until Kent's attention turned to him before elaborating. "It's a guess on my part since we haven't had a chance to check with Red Maple about it, but even I've heard about Max's treasure hunts, how expensive his hobby can be."

Kent headed back to the stool at the bar, muttering, "Hobby, yeah, guess you could call it that." He sat, his shoulders slumped, his hands dangling between his knees. "If I didn't love the jackass so much, I'd have slapped some sense into him. But every time he found another rainbow to chase, he would get so damn caught up in the idea, there was no talking to him. This time…"

When he didn't say anything else, I prompted, "This time?"

Kent sighed. "Max was beyond excited and so certain it really existed, it was easy to get caught up in his enthusiasm." He looked up, his face drawn. "So a bunch of us agreed to chip in, even knowing it was a long shot. We figured it was Vegas odds. Either we got lucky, or we didn't."

"Who all chipped in?" Zev asked.

"Me, Rebecca, Perry, Barb, Devon, and Max, of course." He frowned. "There was another investor that came on board just recently, but I don't know who it was. Max never said, or if he did, I don't remember."

"I hate to ask," I said. "But how much did you all give?"

Kent blinked and managed a shrug. "I don't know about the others, but I put in twenty K. I think Rebecca and Perry did too, or close to it. Barb probably more; her pockets are deeper, and she was always generous to Max. The most recent investor, I have no clue."

Twenty grand on Vegas odds? My brain stumbled, trying to reconcile the kind of attitude that considered a serious chunk of change pocket money.

"Anyone try to back out?" Zev asked.

Kent shook his head. "Unless the glasses turned out to be

fake, there was no reason to. Even if someone had wanted to back out, Max would've let them."

I set my glass on a nearby side table. "Has that happened before?"

"Yeah, a few times. People get excited by the idea, chip in, then get home, sleep on it, and decide it's too risky. It never bothered Max. He got it. It's not like it was the end of the world. He could always get his hands on cash if he needed it. It's not like he was hurting financially."

"Tell us about the others," Zev said.

"You mean Perry, Barb, and Rebecca?" When Kent got Zev's nod, he sat back and rubbed his hands up and down his thighs. "Well, Barb is a friend of Max's mom. She's kind of like an honorary aunt."

"Barbara Warren, correct?" Zev asked.

Kent nodded. "She spends most of her time working with businesses to promote 'inter-community relations.'" He used finger quotes. "Which is a fancy way of saying she manages mergers between various businesses that can't see eye to eye."

I had no idea what he was talking about, but Zev didn't seem to have the same problem. "By 'various businesses,' you mean Traditionalist and Arcane-backed organizations?"

"And a few of the First Nation ones, as well," Kent said. "She has a knack for being able to get them to the same table on a project without creating a pissing contest."

"Impressive," Zev said.

"It is," Kent agreed. "Which is why she's highly respected. I sincerely doubt she's behind any of this. She adores Max, loves Devon, and considers their families hers."

Zev set his empty glass aside and asked, "Was she the one that got Max and Jayson Guzman together?"

The question threw Kent, who looked confused for a moment. "How did you…" His confusion cleared, replaced by a hint of disgust. "I'm guessing you ran into Jayson at the hospital?"

Zev cocked his head. "As we were leaving, yes."

"I don't know why he bothered stopping by," Kent said. "He could have just sent flowers, like everyone else."

"You don't like him." I made it a statement.

Kent snorted. "Not really, but then that's not a secret. He's a narrow-minded, self-centered asshole as far as I'm concerned. His father's views on an Arcane Registry are bad enough, but at least he's honest about his opinions. Jayson, on the other hand, is sneaky as shit and can't be trusted an inch. I told Max he shouldn't deal with him, but he explained that the initial deal with Watershed was drafted with the senior Guzman and the support of the other investors. If Jayson tries to screw anyone on this project, he'll lose any and all business in the valley."

Zev studied Kent. "You sound as if you think that's exactly what he'll do."

"Because I do."

When it looked as if Kent wasn't going to say more, Zev asked, "Why?"

"Jayson went to high school with Max and me. He was a year younger than us, but somehow, he got it in his head that he and Max were in competition for everything—girls, awards, grades, you name it. It was annoying as hell, but you know how it is. We thought it was all about the Arcane-versus-Traditionalist thing. We graduated, left the idiot behind, and didn't give him a second thought. Unfortunately, the last five years or so, Watershed Investments has gotten more and more involved with economic development, which means more and more interactions with Guzman and Sons. Max was working with Jayson's father, but when the senior Guzman stepped down a few months back due to health reasons, Jayson took his place. It wasn't long before Max realized that Jayson's attitude from high school hadn't changed. He just got better at hiding it." Kent paused and narrowed his eyes. "If I thought Jayson had the balls for it, I'd tell you to put him at the top of your list. He might talk shit behind your back and throw you under a bus, but there's no way he'd risk the fallout of going after Max physically."

I didn't know about Zev, but I was definitely penning Jayson's name on the list. "What kind of fallout?"

"The kind that would ruin his father's business, not to mention their family's reputation." Kent scratched his chin. "Jayson's all about his image, and if rumors are true about his wife leaving him for another man—and not just any man, but a mage—he's got more than enough trouble on his hands."

Based on the brief conversation with Jayson at the hospital, those rumors wouldn't be rumors for long. The fact his wife left him for someone so diametrically opposed to his worldviews had to be difficult, and I felt a pinch of pity for the guy.

"All right, let's go back to the others." Zev redirected the conversation. "What about Perry and Rebecca? Do either of them have a bone to pick with Max?"

Kent shook his head. "Not that I'm aware of. I mean, we've been tight since college. Perry is one of Max's groomsmen, and Rebecca is..." He winced, and his voice softened. "She was Devon's maid of honor. There's no way either one would want to hurt Max."

"What about Devon?" Zev's quiet question hit like a silent bomb.

Kent shot out of the seat, his face paling and his mouth falling open. When he found his voice, he sputtered, "Wait, are you... What..." He stopped and visibly regathered his composure. "You think someone was targeting Devon? Not Max?"

Unmoved, Zev watched him. "We don't know if anyone was targeted, but until that possibility can be ruled out, everything needs to be considered."

Kent dropped his head and wrapped a hand over the back of his neck. "I just can't… I don't understand." He dropped his hand and pressed both palms to his eyes for a few moments. Zev and I stayed silent while Kent battled his emotions. When he finally dropped his hands, his eyes were red and watery. He took a deep breath and blew it out. "Devon never met anyone she didn't like. She was outgoing, friendly to a fault, and could relate to anyone. There's no one I can think of that she didn't get along with."

No one was ever that good. Humans didn't work that way. I could think of one type of person who could find a reason to be upset. "What about exes?"

For the first time, Kent looked uncomfortable. "Exes?" He asked it like the question was beyond comprehension.

Interesting reaction there. "Previous relationships? Someone she was with before Max, maybe?"

Kent turned and fussed with the barstool, keeping his back to us. "There were a couple of guys, nothing serious."

Zev and I exchanged a look, then when Kent finally retook his seat, Zev leaned forward. "We'll still need names, if you have them."

Kent's jaw clenched and unclenched. "Look, total transparency here. Devon and I dated back in college, years ago. In fact, I'm the one that introduced them initially." His shoulders rose and fell in an uncomfortable shrug, and his lips curved into a tight line as his jaw gained a belligerent jut. "You know how it is in college. Friends get together, fall apart, and come back together in different pairings. Romance gets replaced by friendship and vice versa. It all makes for a tangled group."

Glad I missed that part of my twenties. That made me grateful for growing up in the Guild. No weird college drama for me. Besides, the idea of dating someone who dated Lena… I shuddered. *No thank you.* I cleared my throat. "So you and Devon?"

A hint of color stole through his face, and based on the irritated light in his eyes, I was betting Kent really wanted to avoid answering. Unfortunately for him, he had no way to dodge. His tone was abrupt when he said, "We dated for a few months then realized we were better off as friends. She dated on and off casually for years before she and Max hooked up. I didn't exactly sit around and pine for her."

I wasn't sure I believed that, but then again, I wasn't Little Miss Social either. Because I was focused on getting clear of the Guild and its training debts, my dates had been few and far between before Zev.

Zev didn't seem to share my skepticism. "No persistent hopefuls? Guys that maybe wished for more than she was willing to give?"

Kent shook his head. "Like I said, I didn't monitor Devon's social calendar after we split. Didn't have time, honestly. She didn't bring anyone around to the group that sticks out, but you might want to check with Rebecca. I'd bet she'd be more in the know than me on stuff like that."

Zev took out his phone. "Do you have a number for Rebecca and Perry? We'd like to set up a time to talk with them, as well." He stood, and I followed suit.

"Yeah, let me share the contacts with you." Kent went over to a console table where a phone and tablet were charging. He picked up his phone and pulled up the information. "They were both at the hospital today. I think they plan to be back tomorrow since it's Sunday."

"We'll touch base and see what works for them," Zev said as we both started for the door. A beep sounded as the contacts hit his phone. "Thank you."

Kent took the lead, unlocked his door, and pulled it open, his hand gripping the door's edge. "You'll share updates? Let us know what's going on?" he asked as we stepped over the threshold.

"I've got Christina's number," Zev assured him, holding his gaze.

Kent frowned but dipped his chin in acknowledgement.

"Thank you," I murmured into the taut silence. "We understand how hard it is, but we appreciate your help."

"I just want..." His gaze went beyond us, his throat working. When his eyes came back to us, they were filled with a mix of grief and rage that was painful to witness. "Just get us some answers."

Zev and I nodded and left to do just that.

TWENTY-ONE

"SHE WON'T BE able to make it back until tomorrow morning," Lena explained through my speakers.

"That's fine. I should be home by three or four." The headlights of my custom rebuilt 1968 Mustang Fastback swept over the gates guarding the drive to the Cordova Family home.

"Can I just say one more time? I have concerns with your plans for the evening."

"You just did, babe, but I'm still going." I stopped, rolled down my window, smiled at the camera, and punched in the code Zev gave me. "I'm picking up Zev now. He'll have my back. I'll be fine." I rolled the window back up as the wrought-iron gates rolled back.

"Uh-huh." Disbelief was clear in her voice. "Is he going to be in the passenger seat when you race?"

"You know I don't do ride-alongs." I braced for the press of active wards and drove through the gates. After a heartbeat, then two, the magic recognized me as friendly and let me through. I continued up the long, sweeping drive to where the stunning mix of stone and stucco was illuminated in strategically placed lights intended for dramatic effect. It worked. Add in the warm glow that spilled from the arched openings stretched along the second-floor verandas and joined those from the windows below, and the front of the villa was well lit. "It messes with my mojo."

"And having a latent hex kick in at the worst possible time wouldn't."

Sarcasm, thy name is Lena. I fought not to roll my eyes. "Okay, look, Calamity Jane, you said it yourself—everything looked fine this morning."

"There were a couple of bumps," she reminded me unnecessarily.

"Which is why we're bringing this Beverly chick in to double-check things." I passed the four-car garage and brought my ride to a stop near the wide stone steps that led to the front entryway. "Look, I'm here, and I need to grab Zev, so I'm going to let you go. I promise I'll be careful."

"Fine," she said begrudgingly. "Text me after you win, so I know you survived."

A spurt of amusement had my lips curving. "I will. *Ciao, chica.*"

"Later." Then she disconnected.

I pushed open my door and got out. I was rounding the hood when the front door swung open.

"Hey," Zev called as he stood backlit in the doorway. He started toward me.

"Hey back."

We met at the top of the steps, and when we got close, he pulled me into a hug. I wrapped my arms around his neck. He bent and brushed his lips over mine. When he lifted his head, I leaned in and buried my nose in his neck, enjoying his spicy sandalwood scent.

He chuckled and gave me a squeeze.

Without releasing him, I leaned back, taking in his features from up close. Dressed in jeans and thick-soled boots, paired with a long-sleeve thermal covered by a canvas jacket, his dark, shoulder-length hair was pulled back with his habitual leather tie and was matched by his close-cropped beard and matching goatee. The entire image created an unmistakable rough and sexy vibe to an already-dangerous allure.

And he's all mine.

That thought never got old, and I hoped that wouldn't change anytime soon. "Were you able to get the stuff done you wanted to get done?"

We'd parted ways after leaving Kent's and sending Rebecca and Perry texts inviting them to meet with us. Zev had a couple things he needed to take care of, and I wanted a chance to make sure my baby was ready for my nocturnal activities.

He cupped my cheek, his thumb brushing along my skin and leaving chills in its wake. "Yeah, had a couple things I had to run down for 'Milio, and afterward, I worked with Jeremy on some defensive skills."

Jeremy was Emilio's orphaned nephew, and Zev, while technically the Arbiter for the Cordova Family and Emilio's first cousin, played favorite uncle to the kid. As the heir apparent to the Cordova Family, the eleven-year-old was being trained by both men to ensure he could not only survive, but also thrive in the brutal Arcane world. Unlike his unfortunate parents.

"How's he doing?"

"Jeremy?"

I nodded.

"Good, settling in finally." Zev let me go and repositioned so his arm was curved around my hips.

I followed him to the door—an art piece of alder wood, wrought iron, and glass. "Nice to hear." And it was, especially since my first meeting with Jeremy, and by extension Zev, had occurred during the boy's kidnapping. The details around that were convoluted, at best, and involved seriously twisted corporate espionage and a sketchy magic-altering serum.

Fun times. Not.

We hit the threshold, and Zev let me go so he could step inside and call out, "'Milio, I'm out. I'll be back later."

"Got it" came the return call. "Have fun!"

I snorted at Emilio's drag on parental greetings for wayward teens.

Zev turned back to me, nudged me back out, and pulled the door closed behind us. We walked back to my car, holding hands.

"Did you hear anything back from Rebecca or Perry?"

"Just Rebecca," he said, letting me go so I could round the hood to the driver's side.

I got to my door and opened it as he did the same on his side. I looked at him over the Mustang's roof. "And?"

He paused, one arm on the roof, the other on the edge of the open door. "She said she couldn't meet tomorrow but would be happy to see us on Monday morning around nine or ten. I didn't confirm, because I wasn't sure what your schedule looks like."

I thought about my upcoming week. "I think I'm clear, but let me check."

We both got in and closed our doors. I started up my baby then pulled up my calendar on my phone. "I've got a couple of runs at seven, but I should be free for a few hours after that."

"So, ten?"

"Yeah, that works."

He dug his phone out of the inside jacket pocket and sent a quick text to Rebecca while I added the time to my calendar. He buckled up as I entered the race's GPS into my phone and set up a music playlist. Then I put the Mustang in gear, and off we went.

Our conversation flowed as I followed the GPS

coordinates that took us north of Phoenix then west, until we were somewhere between Wickenburg and Lake Pleasant. The tension that had set up shop in my neck and shoulders over the last few days slowly bled away as I found my happy place behind the wheel.

There was something soothing about running the ribbon of asphalt with five hundred fifty-one horses under your hood. There was no denying I was in love with my sweet ride. One of my best memories was winning it off another speed freak, because no way could I have afforded her otherwise. At the time, I was buried under the Guild training debts, so their cut of my jobs left its mark. With a limited income, I focused on enhancing what already existed without selling my soul. Now, debt free and earning wider profit margins, I was starting to look around for another acquisition. Maybe a bike so I could race Zev.

Being protective of my baby also meant that if a race took place on a dirt track, I refused to risk damaging her by doing something stupid, like racing on a craptastic course and bottoming out. That left me to either play spectator or sub for another driver. That wasn't unheard of, especially when someone needed a skilled heel-toe driver. Downshifting was an art form, especially in older cars since most modern automatic transmissions made manual shifting a lost art. Luckily, I rocked that shit. Depending on how things landed tonight, my baby and I were ready and willing.

The farther out we got, the darker it became as there were no streetlights this far out in the desert. Traffic was nonexistent this late, which worked for me as I was exceeding the posted speed limit with impunity.

Zev squeezed my hand resting on my gearshift. "Got to know—am I still going with the Felix story?"

"Depends on you," I said. "If you're okay being you, we drop it. If not…" I shrugged.

The Felix story was a cover we'd created when Zev

accompanied me to the race in June. We'd needed gossip, and the racing crowd wouldn't talk if they knew someone like Zev, with serious connections to the Families, was listening in. Instead, we explained his presence as an out-of-town Guild Hunter. It wasn't unusual to spot the Guild retrieval specialists at races since their targets tended to hang with the less-than-legal types. Race crowds had a plethora of those, including me in my younger years.

"Will it cause issues if we drop Felix?"

It was a valid question. The illegal race world was a tight society where the main players were known, and being able to identify their hangers-on was key to getting in good with them. Because I was one of those main players, my career with the Guild was common knowledge. Now that I was an independent, it wouldn't be a stretch to believe my connections were branching out.

Which is exactly what those damn rumors prey upon.

That made me wonder which of the Arcane Families had racers in their closets. They might not only have recognized Zev back in June, but also gone out of their way to make sure their whispers got to the right ears to cause problems.

I opened my mouth to share then thought better of it when I realized it might just be my paranoia rearing its ugly head. Instead, I shifted verbal gears. "I think it's best to put Felix to bed."

"Are you going to catch any flack for lying about who I am?"

"Maybe from one or two, but I'll handle it." I checked the route and noted we were coming up on our turn. I eased off the gas, not wanting to miss it. "What about you?"

"What about me?"

I shot him a look. "You going to get tied up if it's known you're hanging out at illegal gatherings?"

"Seriously?" he drawled. "I don't think anyone's going to

give me shit. Besides, the only way they know I'm there is because they're eyewitnesses."

Too true. My headlights illuminated a pitted sign that had been used for target practice and now leaned against a rusted metal gate that was guarding what appeared to be nothing. Whoever had picked tonight's location seemed to have chosen well. I recognized the name on the sign. It belonged to an abandoned auto-testing track.

"Yes," I muttered under my breath.

Catching it, Zev asked, "What?"

I flashed him a wide grin. "Paved track means I get to race tonight."

"Wasn't that the plan all along?"

"Yeah, but I don't like taking my baby out on dirt tracks. Too risky." I drove carefully down the weed-choked road.

He shifted in his seat. "So, if it had been dirt?"

I shrugged, feeling the weight of his attention. "I'd have volunteered to drive for someone else."

"Adrenaline junky," he muttered in an amused tone.

I shot him a raised-brow look. "Pot, meet kettle."

He chuckled because I was not wrong.

Eventually, the inky shadows were broken by other headlights and portable flood lamps, some powered by generators, others by wards, depending on who they belonged to. Figures milled about in the haze and shadows. Some were gathered around fifty-gallon drums filled with flames licking at the night.

I rolled down my window and slowed even more as I edged around the makeshift lot. Excitement and music rode along the night breeze, interspersed with barks of laughter, occasional shouts, and the revving of engines. Edgy anticipation crawled through my veins and set my pulse on fire. I couldn't stop my grin from growing full blown.

Gods, I love race nights.

I found a spot between the collection of souped-up

muscled classics and tricked-out, sleek-lined racers and pulled in. Heads turned our way, noting our arrival, but after a few seconds, they went back to their original positions, mouths moving as they shot the shit.

I shut down the engine, undid my belt, and popped my door open. On the other side, Zev did the same. I sent Lena a quick "made it" text then leaned over the console to grab my gloves from the box. With phone and gloves in hand, I straightened and went to leave the car.

Zev, ever the gentleman, stood there, hand out. "You ready?"

"Yep." I took it and let him help me out.

He waited as I pulled my gloves on and tucked my phone into a pocket. I moved away from the door, and he threw it closed behind me. "Where to first?" He came up behind me and set his hand low on my hip.

"Check in."

I led the way as we moved through the crowd. We didn't go unnoticed. My name came at me from different directions, and I returned the greetings but didn't stop. Bass-heavy music vied with engine growls and exhaust pipe snarls, adding a feral intensity to the cool night air. Natural firelight and magic-fueled lamplight danced over the crowd. People ran the gamut from barely drinking age to gray-haired gearheads, all out to do one thing—celebrate speed.

And tonight looked especially promising.

Night races could take various forms, depending on the location and the organizer's preference. There were the straightaways that catered to drag races and burns, the makeshift tracks that mimicked the accepted time races and drifts, and the extremely dangerous and illegal street challenges. I didn't mind watching the first, and now that I had more wisdom than hormones, I stayed far away from the last. But the second? I was all about the timed speed and drifting, which was perfect since tonight's track was the traditional oval.

Yay!

We rounded a group giving each other shit about their chosen rides, when a flash out of the corner of my eye caught my attention. A niggle of unease brushed over my senses as I stopped and turned to see what it was.

Next to me, Zev asked, "What?"

I couldn't see anything unusual, and that weird sensation drifted away, so I shrugged it off. "Nothing." I turned back as the knot of people ahead of us veered off, giving me a clear shot to the area close to the track. I spotted my goal sitting on the lowered gate of a truck and picked up my pace. "Em!"

A heavily tattooed woman sitting with one leg braced on the gate, knee bent, the other dangling, the toe of her boot scraping the dirt, looked up. When her gaze landed on me, her white teeth flashed in her tanned face. "Rory, long time no see, woman!" Her attention shifted to Zev, lingered, then returned to me, noting the gloves on my hands. "You racing tonight?"

"Hope to," I said as I stopped in front of her. "What are we looking at?"

She braced an arm on her raised knee. "Timed races only. Track's shit for drifting."

"Nice." I dug out my cash.

"So you know," she went on, "we're switching it up tonight, going formal. Ten heats, then the final. You in?"

Sounded like the organizer wanted to maximize their betting options. "So in." I handed over the entry fee.

Em took it and dropped it into the glowing can at her hip. The wards that kept that money safe from sticky fingers nipped at my Prism in warning. Not that it was necessary. I had no intention of risking any of my digits to its bite.

A sharp whistle pierced my eardrums, and Em looked up at someone behind me and raised her hand in acknowledgement. She turned back to me. "You know the drill. You got about thirty minutes before they blow." Then she looked to Zev. "And you?"

He held a folded bill between two fingers. "A hundred on Rory."

That earned him a bark of laughter. "Smart man." She took his money and gave him a blue poker chip, which was his betting slip. "Don't lose that, handsome."

Zev gave her a grin, touched the chip to his forehead, then tucked it away.

She made a very feminine hum as she picked up the bottle of beer at her hip. "Mmm, I like your sidepiece, girl."

I bumped Zev's hip with mine, my lips curving in a grin. "So do I." I half turned to check out those gathered a bit away. "Looks like I better get over there." I turned back to the official race bookie. "I'll be back, Em."

"I'm sure you will." She lifted her bottle and sent us off with "Steady hands, fast feet."

TWENTY-TWO

ZEV and I left Em behind and wandered through the crowd as we retraced our way back to where I'd left my Mustang. I got stopped a few times by familiar faces. A couple confirmed I was driving then wandered back toward Em's spot.

"I'm guessing you're a favorite," Zev said after we stopped so I could nab a water from a hawker.

"Yep," I said without any false modesty. Not that I needed it. I was damn good and knew it. "But I'm not the only favorite here tonight." I turned, looking over the crowd until I spotted the man standing next to a Dodge Hellraiser with a distinctive fluorescent-orange paint job. I used my water bottle to draw Zev's attention to him. "That's Wheelz, and he'll be the one to beat."

Zev studied my competition for a moment. "I remember him. He's the one you bet on last time we were here, isn't he?"

I nodded and took a drink.

"Is he a Transporter?"

For a second, I considered taking offense at Zev's unspoken insinuation, but studying his face, I realized I was reading too much into his comment, and he was simply curious. So I tempered my tone to sardonic instead of viciously sarcastic. "No, he's like me—just that good because we know our shit and have spent years honing our skills."

"Damn." Zev winced, catching his faux pas. "Sorry, that came out wrong."

"You're not the only one who's made that assumption, and you won't be the last." I started walking.

He fell into step beside me. "I can see that, seeing how it lends itself to giving you an edge over other drivers."

It was an old argument that had been tossed around for so long, it was like a ratty pair of well-worn socks, complete with holes in the heels. "I can't deny it helps, but it's not the only magical ability that creates an edge in racing. You've got animal mages who have off-the-chart eyesight, combat mages with hand-eye coordination and reaction times that are hard to beat, then there are the mech mages that can modify their rides like no one's business, not counting—"

He caught my hand and, with a tug, pulled me around to stumble against his chest. Then he cut me off with a kiss. When he raised his head, his eyes were dancing with laughter. "You made your point, babe. You've got skills."

"Mad skills," I corrected with a grin.

We resumed our trek and were almost back where we started when I heard my name.

"Rory!"

I turned as Zev stopped at my side. Then it was all I could do to brace as a wiry-framed blond with a manic grin caught me up in a tight hug. My "oof" was muffled against his narrow shoulder, but when he finally pulled back enough that I could breathe, I managed, "Hey, Gunnar."

"Hey, yourself." He let me go and stepped back, his attention shifting from me to Zev and back. "Long time, no see, chica."

"You know how it goes," I said. "Been busy."

"Right." Gunnar drew the word out as his gaze shifted to the man at my back. "California, right?"

Dammit. Of course he would remember.

Zev reached around me and held out his hand. "Good memory."

Gunnar shook it. "You make an impression, dude."

"Good to know," Zev said, his hand dropping back to my hip.

"Hey." I regained Gunnar's attention. "You racing tonight?"

"Oh, hell yeah, chica." Excitement had him bouncing on his toes. "Maiden run."

How time flies. I'd last seen Gunner in June, when he was in the midst of reupholstering a 1968 Chevy Impala, his current passion project. "It's done?"

He nodded. "Gorgeous as shit, runs sweet and tight. Gonna put her through her paces tonight."

I leaned back into Zev, enjoying his heat against my back. "You planning on adding her to your garage?"

Gunnar bounced his head from side to side. "Not sure. You know how it is. Maybe someone will make me an offer worth considering." He stilled momentarily, his gaze sharpening as he studied me. "Why? You interested?"

I laughed. "I don't have pockets deep enough to even think about it."

His frenetic movements restarted, and he grinned. "Wanna make a bet, then?"

"No." I shot that suggestion right down. "I have no intention of losing my baby to some shiny new pretty. Even if it is one of yours."

It was his turn to laugh. "Right, well, got to get ready."

"Me too."

"See you at the starting line, chica." We exchanged high-fives, then he lifted his chin to Zev with a "Later" and loped away.

Zev watched Gunnar make his way through the spectators. "Surprised he remembered me."

I tagged his hand and started off. We didn't get far before I had to do a quick jig to avoid being bumped by a pair of giggling women who were finding it hard to walk in their spiked heels because they were so busy eyeing Zev. He caught my hips and pulled me close, keeping me between him and the drunken duo.

Pressed against his front, I tipped my head back so I could see his face. "I'm not. Gunnar might act like he's buzzing, but the man is scary sharp. He can remember specs from cars he's worked on years ago."

"Good to know." He waited until the two women had moved away, then he nudged my hip to start walking. "Things are getting a little crowded."

"Because the race is about to start." That meant I needed to get a move on. Luckily, I could see my Mustang's roof nearby.

"And you need to get to things."

"I do, yeah." There was a hint of regret in my voice because as much as I enjoyed having him with me, I needed some me time. "But you can ride with me to the starting line."

We made it the last few yards to the Mustang unmolested. We got in, and I drove the short distance to where the other drivers were gathering. After I stopped, Zev got out and came around to my side. I left the engine idling and stood in the open driver's door.

Zev crowded me and brushed a quick kiss against my lips. "For luck." When he lifted his head, he looked behind me. "Where do you want me?"

I turned to check out the situation. "There should be room for you to hang over there." I pointed to a small group milling around near the starting point. "Anyone gives you grief, just let them know you're with me." Not that I thought anyone would.

Zev stepped back, letting me go. "Leave 'em in the dust, babe."

"Going to do my best." I watched him walk away with that long-legged, confident-as-hell walk. Shaking my head free of the Zev haze, I got focused.

It was time to ride.

⋯⋯⋯⋯⋯⋯⋯⋯⋯⋯⋯

My mind was crystal clear, my breathing steady, and my heart beat in time with the rumble of my Mustang's engine. I was on the sixth heat and in the third position, having worked my way in from seventh. I had an eye on the pole position, but the two drivers ahead of me, one of which was Wheelz, were proving to be a challenge.

I didn't mind. It made for a better race.

Like most mages, a Transporter utilized both magic and inherent skill to do what we did. It was a strange symbiotic relationship with vehicles that was hard to explain. When I got behind a wheel, the innate power that made me a Transporter slid into place as simply as breathing. My world shifted until I could anticipate, at an unexplainable level, the changes necessary to get what I needed from the mechanical beast at my command. Minute adjustments in speed, mechanics, navigation, and reaction times all came together in a metaphysical relationship that gave me that edge Zev had asked about.

But all that magic was limited to the car's performance and the driver's expertise, which was why Transporters weren't blacklisted from racing. Put a Transporter in a beater, and they might make a tricked-out banger work for their win, but nine times out of ten, that souped-up racer would win if the driver's experience was deeper than the Transporter's.

I flexed my fingers against the steering wheel and blew

out a breath as I waited for the signal. The world around me narrowed to my baby, the track, and me.

Three... two... one!

The air horn blared through the night, and I hit the gas. My baby shot forward, and we raced down the first leg, keeping pace with our two main rivals. Engines revving, we slid into the first curve. Keeping that momentum going, I used my toe on the accelerator and my heel on the brake and downshifted smoothly. I shot out of the first turn without a hitch and picked up speed, adding space between me and the one nipping at my heels. Inch by inch, I increased that lead and crawled up to the second car as we headed into the second turn. After another dance of heel-toe, we came out of that turn neck and neck for second place.

A buzz of warning hit as the other driver made a quick correction, his back end starting to drift, but I was already gone, over-steering to gain the necessary inches to avoid getting clipped. We jockeyed for position as we approached the third turn. I kicked the clutch, worked the wheel, and felt the tires claw the track, but I got my nose out ahead of him. Adrenaline filled my veins until every nerve ending vibrated in sync with the horses hauling my 'Stang. The speedometer ticked upward as we shot down that final stretch and pulled away from the one chasing us and gained on the orange blur that was Wheelz.

Now it was a matter of speed. My baby and I reached deep. Tires chewed up the track as we pulled on the outside of the Hellraiser. I had one shot at taking the lead from Wheelz and a fraction of a second to make it work.

I got close, racing alongside, pulling far enough ahead to dump air from my rear quarter panel to spill alongside his passenger side and into his spoiler, dropping his speed. The second he started to slow, I veered out and broke the side draft to shoot ahead. I cleared the finish line with a victorious whoop. Riding the high of my win, I continued around the track and let my girl drop her pace at her leisure.

I was down in the double digits, with Wheelz behind me, when something darted out into the track. In that heartbeat of time, my breath stopped. My mind split. One part tried to make sense of the split-second visual while the other ran through calculations like lightning strikes, sparking scenario after scenario. It was the second part of my mind that took the driver's seat, merging instinct, skill, and magic into one fluid motion as I worked the wheel, clutch, and brake to avoid impact. The shrill scream and acrid scent of tires painting the track with rubber came first. Then the body slam of an invisible punch as I straightened out the front end to offset the rear's wild swing. My bones jostled, and my vision danced as I bumped off the track. I had a fleeting wince for the shocks and undercarriage. Then my tires regained traction, and I came to a rocking stop.

I sat there for a long moment as the engine grumbled and my harsh breathing filled the interior. Finally, I found my voice and my anger as my brain slid into gear and started to put everything together. "What the actual fuck?"

I peeled my fingers off the wheel, and blood rushed back in, making them tingle. I fumbled with my belt until finally, the straps released, and I threw open my door. Faint shouts pierced the dull rush of my thundering pulse. I got out and stood, a little shocked to find my legs felt watery. To not drop to my ass, I held on to the top of the doorframe and braced my other arm on the roof as I looked back toward the track.

I tried to see. I don't know what—mostly likely something that would clue me in to who or what was dumb enough to risk life and limb to cross a racetrack. But the night shadows and sporadic light made it hard to make out much. It didn't look like anything was there, but I knew that was bullshit. And not just because of the freaked-out voice in my head that kept trying to insist a dead man had just made me crash.

"Rory!" a deep voice yelled.

I forced my gaze away from the empty track ahead and looked toward the stretch behind me. Wheelz's Hellraiser was there, angled across the inside lanes, along with a couple of other cars haphazardly parked behind him, like some kid's abandoned Hot Wheels. Figures rushed toward me, the night hiding their features, but as they got closer, I recognized Wheelz's bald head and thick shoulders in the lead, followed by Gunnar's lanky form a step or two behind him. Another shout had me turning to the sidelines to see Zev running toward me.

I lifted a hand in the universal sign that I was okay, but none of them slowed.

"Rory, are you okay?" Wheelz stopped in front of me, his gaze worried, his normally brown skin a bit pale. He grabbed my elbow and started to lead me away from the car. "What the fuck happened?"

"Wait." I tried to pull free to go back and shut off the ignition, but Wheelz wasn't having it. "I need to turn—"

"Rory"—Gunnar slid to a stop next to Wheelz—"you okay?"

"Get her keys, man." Wheelz jerked his chin toward my car as he led me off to the side. Gunnar rushed off to do his bidding. Wheelz, still holding my elbow, finally stopped and pressed gently on my shoulder. "Sit your ass down before you fall."

I gave in and sank to the ground. Zev joined our party and crouched in front of me. "Are you okay?" He cupped my face with his hands as he studied me.

The heat of his touch against my chill skin was startling. I shivered but managed to nod as I absently noted the sound of my engine had disappeared. The dull thunk of a car door closing followed.

"I'm good." My voice came out rough.

Zev didn't say anything, but his mouth was tight, his eyes

dark as he studied me. He must have found what he was looking for because he let my face go.

Gunnar rushed up and dropped to his knees beside me. "Here." He held out my keys and waited until I lifted my hand to drop them into my palm.

Both of us ignored the visible tremor as I clutched the metal keys, feeling the teeth bite into my palm. "Thanks."

Wheelz moved up to Zev's side and crouched, dropping to my eye level. Now both men were facing me with identical looks of concern.

"I'm okay, guys. I just need a minute." *Or three.*

"What the hell happened?" Wheelz rumbled.

My brain shifted back into gear, and I realized sharing what I'd actually seen would be a bad idea. I needed an easy out. My mind spun and landed on "There was something on the track, a jackrabbit, I think. Came out of nowhere."

All three turned back to the track, and if I hadn't been so shaken, I might have laughed at their unintended synchronization. One by one, they turned back to me, each one wearing some variation of a frown. Wheelz and Gunnar exchanged a look, while Zev stayed quiet and watched me.

"Are you shittin' me?" Wheelz muttered.

Gunnar's voice was careful, but not careful enough to mask his skeptical tone. "You about killed yourself for a rabbit?"

Wheelz snorted and snapped, "Never pegged you as a bunny hugger."

I winced, knowing exactly how stupid it sounded, but that was better than having them question my sanity. "I get it—trust me—but I caught movement and reacted. That's all."

"Shit, Rory." Wheelz shook his head, slapped his beefy hands against his thighs, and straightened. "You're damn lucky you didn't flip your girl."

"I know." I looked at Gunnar. "You think you can do a once-over, make sure I didn't crack anything?"

"Sure." The mech mage looked back at my car. "It's going to have to be quick and dirty though. They need the track for the next race." He loped toward the car.

Zev, who had remained strangely quiet up to that point, stood and offered me his hand. I took it and let him help me to my feet. He squeezed my fingers, and I met his gaze. Concern and knowledge stared back. He knew my rabbit story was shit. Instead of confronting me, he asked, "You good?"

I held tightly to his hand and managed a jerky nod. We started to follow Gunnar, Wheelz falling in beside us.

"Dammit, Rory," he grumped. "Why'd you have to flinch? We had a good thing going tonight."

"Next race night," I promised. "We'll do a rematch." I looked over to the track. The other cars were clearing the track. I stopped, both men stopping with me. "You better get back before they decide to start without you."

"Not fuckin' likely." He grinned and started walking backward toward his ride. "Guess I owe you a thank-you, since I'll be taking the pot home tonight."

"Don't worry. I'll get it back next time."

"Maybe I'll bring a bunny or two," he teased. "Just to even the odds."

I flipped him off, and he laughed. He raised his hand and turned to jog back to the track.

Zev waited until we were alone. "Rabbit?"

"Later," I promised, my voice low. "For now"—I handed him my keys—"you're driving."

TWENTY-THREE

ON THE RIDE HOME, I shared the truth with Zev—that the ghostly image of Bryan, not Peter Cottontail, had sent me four-wheeling my Mustang. The resulting atmosphere in the car was dark with frustrated anger mingled with worry. Sitting in the passenger seat wasn't easy. It gave me plenty of time to mentally explore some very dark rabbit holes. Not my favorite pastime, but it beat risking another potential crash. I was lucky the first one hadn't damaged my girl, but my faith that such luck would hold was dim.

Zev didn't say much, but his hands kept flexing on the wheel, the leather creaking under his grip. Thankfully, he knew how to drive a stick.

Shortly before we hit the city limits, I got a text from Lena. After I read it, relief washed through me, and I blew out a shaky breath. "Thank you, baby Jesus." Before he could ask, I shared, "Lena's at the condo with her contact."

He frowned. "Thought she wasn't going to be back until morning."

I checked the time on my phone. "Technically, it is morning." My response rode the edge of sarcasm.

He shot me a look then turned back to the road. "That wasn't a complaint."

I opened my mouth, only to shut it before an acerbic response could escape. *What the hell am I doing?* I didn't need to cut into him just because I was freaking the hell out. Instead of trying to claw back some false sense of control, I reined in my emotional mess and settled for staying quiet.

Minutes turned into miles before Zev asked, "You okay?"

I stared unseeingly at the windshield and answered honestly, "Not even a little bit."

He reached over and squeezed my hand as it gripped my phone against my thigh. "Not much longer, and hopefully we'll have some answers."

Emotions rose, making it hard to swallow, and my eyes burned. I gritted my teeth and breathed away the useless reaction. Zev let me go so he could downshift as we exited the freeway. When I thought I could speak without sounding like I was gargling glass, I said, "I hate this on so many levels."

Thankfully, Zev didn't rush in with empty platitudes. Instead, his non-answer conveyed his agreement.

Fifteen minutes later, he was pulling up to the gate that led to my condo's parking garage. Living in downtown Phoenix proper brought a lot of benefits, like easy access to restaurants, bars, and other delightful distractions. It also meant parking was at a premium. Thankfully, Lena and I lived in one of the newer high-rise condos, and our mortgage payment included assigned spaces in the secured parking garage. The gate arm lifted, and Zev wound his way to my space, then we were heading to the elevators.

We rode up to the lobby, where the elevator stopped to pick up a couple who reeked of smoke and perfume, clearly coming in from an enjoyable late-night romp. After the couple got off on the fifth floor, we made it to the eighth floor and stepped out into the quiet hallway. I led Zev to my door, keyed the code for the lock and security ward, and pushed it open.

"Lena, we're home," I called and followed the lights into the kitchen.

Lena, sitting on a barstool at the island, twisted around toward me and hopped off. Her gaze darted to the clock above the stove, and she turned back to me with a frown. "What happened? You're normally out later than this." She looked beyond me as Zev came up behind me and tossed my keys into the bowl on the entryway table. "And why does he have your keys?"

Her outraged tone almost made me smile. Almost. "Hello to you too." I skirted the island and headed straight to the refrigerator. I caught sight of an older woman sitting on the other barstool. *Must be Bev.* I managed to lift a hand in acknowledgment. It was all I had in me for the moment. I stayed on course to the fridge, yanked open the door, grabbed a soda, and lifted it in silent query to Zev, who nodded. I handed it over. He took it then settled in to lean back against the counter so he could watch the drama unfold.

I grabbed a second can, closed the fridge, and turned back to my glaring roomie. I raised my eyebrows and pointedly tilted my head to our visitor. "Want to introduce me?"

Hands propped on her hips, Lena kept rocking her snit, completed with a barefoot toe-tap, but she did say, "Bev, Rory. Rory, Bev." She dropped her hands and sat back down. "Now, what happened? And why do you both have that look?" She waved her hand in my direction.

I moved to the island until I was standing across from Bev. I set down my soda and held out my hand to the honey-haired woman watching us all with barely concealed amusement. "Bev, nice to meet you."

She took it, her grip firm. "And you, as well." She let me go and settled back. "Lena didn't get into the nitty-gritty, but I hear you're worried you picked up something nasty."

Before I could reply, Lena pinned Zev with a hard stare. "Since she's avoiding my question, it's your turn, so spill."

Zev lifted his soda and took a long drink, all without looking away from Lena. What he didn't do was answer her.

Lena's imperious demand got an amused snort and a "Babe, cool it" from Evan, who didn't bother looking up from the couch behind Bev as he played a game filled with frantic movement and bursts of color on the TV in the living room. As she often did, Lena ignored Evan's reprimand and continued to stare at Zev in silent demand.

He lowered his can and set it aside on the counter next to him. Then he braced his hands on the counter's edge and stared back.

I turned away from the battle of the wills and spoke to Bev. "I don't know what all Lena told you, but after tonight, I'm pretty sure I picked up something."

Her amusement faded, and her brown eyes sharpened. "Are you okay sharing what happened?" It was a carefully phrased question, typical of a mage trying to be circumspect of another.

I appreciated the approach. "You know I'm a Transporter?" I waited for her nod. "I was behind the wheel when I thought I saw a ghost." Ignoring Lena's sharp, shocked inhale, I continued. "If it had been anyone else driving, they wouldn't have walked away."

Bev frowned as she studied me. "A ghost?"

I nodded. Behind her, Evan paused his game and turned to tune in to our conversation.

Bev thought it over for a moment. "Lena mentioned you were concerned someone managed to access your dreams, but she came up empty when she checked the wards. She was hoping I could double-check she didn't miss anything."

I cocked my head. "You specialize in latent hexes, right?"

She nodded. "Keys, like most mages, come in different specialties, but those skills fall under one of two distinctions,

Agile and Static. Lena's what is considered an Agile Key because she deals with active hexes. I'm Static. Sometimes it helps to bring in opposing Keys, because we can pick out nuances the other misses."

Learn something new every day. "That actually makes sense."

The basics of magic theory and classification were taught in most schools. The Guild went a bit deeper in its education since it was the main supplier of highly skilled magic workers, a fact reflected in their contract rates. Years of training went into creating a specialized mage worthy of the Guild distinction. A Guild mage needed to not only understand the variations that existed in their specific Arcane classification, but also know how their magic stacked up against others of the same ilk. Only after a mage had that down did the Guild expand to pit their magic against other types, with a focus on defense and offense capabilities. Unfortunately, that meant I had vast knowledge of Transporters, but when it came to other mages, like Keys or illusion mages, I was constantly discovering new, unexpected facets. I tucked away those tidbits because I never knew when that small bit of information would come in handy.

Lena reclaimed her seat next to Bev. "I had Bev check the security wards before you got home."

"And?" I felt Zev come up behind me. "Did you find something?"

"Nothing serious," Bev said, shifting her attention to Zev.

I caught the hint of nerves she tried to hide. Clearly, she recognized him. I looked to Lena. "What about those bumps you mentioned?"

"Taken care of," she said.

Heat hit my back, and Zev's arm wrapped around my waist, tucking me in close. It was like being wrapped in a human blanket. "What were they?"

The last bit of tension, which I hadn't been aware of, bled away. I relaxed against him.

Bev and Lena exchanged a look, then Bev answered, "Think of them like scratches."

"Scratches? Like someone tried to magically pick our locks?"

"Close enough," Lena said. "Except it happened a while ago, probably before I reinforced them." She got a pained look on her face. "I don't know how I missed it, but I did."

Bev patted her arm. "It's easy enough to overlook, especially since they didn't get far."

"Yeah, well, I won't make that mistake again."

"Cut yourself some slack, Lenabee," Evan said as he got up and joined us at the island. "They didn't breach your wards, so it's all good." He got to Lena and nudged her stool around until she was facing him. He moved in close, caught her face in his hands, and leaned in until their foreheads touched. "Remember, perfect is overrated." The last was a gentle admonishment.

Knowing how fast Lena could fall into a self-recrimination hole, I redirected the conversation. "So how do we find out if something's playing with me?"

"Well," Bev said, "I told Lena I had a cast that I can do that will scan your magical signature for any magical germs, for lack of a better term."

"How deep does this scan go?"

"Since we're looking for latent magic, it's just surface." Her gaze darted between me and Zev, and when it came back to me, it was wary. "Since you're a Transporter, it should be fairly easy to pick out any anomalies."

Zev's arm at my waist tightened. "Rory, can I talk to you for a second?"

Caught off guard, I twisted to look back at him and saw his jaw was tense. "Um, yeah?" I turned back to Bev. "Excuse us for a second?"

She nodded.

Zev guided me out of the kitchen, and I heard Lena murmur something behind me. Zev took me into my bedroom, and Lena slipped in before he closed the door. He stood with his back against the door and kept his voice low as he glared at Lena. "How much do you trust this woman?"

Lena studied him. "Enough to allow her to check out Rory."

Not following their conversation, I broke in. "Excuse me. Someone want to clue me in here?" They both turned their attention to me. "What's wrong?"

"Allowing someone to scan your magic isn't smart," Zev growled. "It's like inviting a stranger into your bedroom. You blink, and you may find yourself fucked. And not in a good way."

Okay, that was a bit… blunt.

"Like I'd leave her unprotected," Lena shot back. She got in Zev's face, her tone quiet but unmistakably pissed. "Rory is my best friend. I would never, ever leave her ass hanging, and I really don't like you insinuating otherwise."

Before things could explode into a hell of an argument, I squeezed between them, my back to Zev, my front to Lena, my hands lifted in the universal "calm down" position. "He knows that, Lena, but he's just as protective." I turned just my head and shot Zev a warning glare. "Right?"

His dark eyes dropped to mine, and amusement crept into his thunderous expression. His lips tightened, but he did incline his head.

I turned back to Lena and caught her gaze. "This cast Bev's talking about, explain it to me."

"It's pretty standard for a Key. One of the first things we do when evaluating a client's potential for a hex is to check out their magical aura." Her gaze shot to Zev. "It's surface level only."

"Give me more," I demanded, because I couldn't see why that would upset Zev, or her.

She turned to me, and whatever she saw on my face made her sigh. "Okay, give me a minute to figure out how to explain this."

My eyebrows rose, but I gave her time as she paced in the space between my dresser and bed. On her second trip back, she finally stopped.

"Okay, think of your magical signature like a coat. You wear it everywhere, everyone has one, and there's nothing unusual about it. Mages wear their magic in similar fashion, their specialties coming across in the fit and style. Keys use this to determine if there's something not right hidden in that fabric. Like a rip or a stain, maybe even a loose thread here or there. Damage to the magical coat generally indicates exposure to a hex."

"But she's going to be looking for latent magic," Zev cut in. "It's my understanding that requires a deeper level of scrutiny."

Logic clicked for me. "You're worried she'll find out I'm a Prism."

Zev folded his arms and held my gaze. "There's no maybe about it. That level of a scan guarantees she'll figure it out."

I got his concern, but the thing was I had already outed myself to the Council and various high-ranking Families. It wasn't like I could stuff that genie back into its bottle. If Bev learned that one of the magics I held was a power most believed had been wiped out years ago, that might come back to bite me, but it was a risk I was willing to take to make sure I wasn't losing my damn mind. "So she finds out. You and Lena will be right there. She tries anything, you two stop her."

"And if she decides to share that information?" he pressed.

"She won't," Lena answered before I could.

"How can you guarantee that?" he asked her.

"Because her contract includes a level-four covenant, ensuring she can't violate client-Key confidentiality."

The way Lena said that made it sound much more serious than a simple I-will-sue-you contract breach. So did the fact that Zev's intensity level eased back. I'd also heard something similar when Emilio made a deal with a Seer to examine Zev's memories after he'd been cursed. "Covenant?"

"It's a magical agreement that ensures breaking it results in a world of hurt," Zev said.

"Good to know," I muttered under my breath before saying, "Right, if you two are done, can we get to this?"

Zev stepped back and opened the door. "After you." He waved me through.

Shaking my head, I headed back to the kitchen, with Lena and Zev trailing behind. I got back to the kitchen, where Bev and Evan were chatting. They both looked up when I entered.

"Everything okay?" Evan asked.

"Yeah." I looked at Bev. "Just a heads-up—I'm a dual-level mage."

She blinked, a hint of confusion in her face. "Okay. So Transporter and…"

"Prism."

Her jaw dropped.

TWENTY-FOUR

BEV'S EYES WIDENED. "Prism? But they don't…" Her mouth snapped shut, and color rose under her cheeks as her brain caught up to the situation. "Sorry."

I waved off her apology as I went over to the couch. "I get it, but I also figured you needed to know before we got underway."

"Um, yes, that…" She shook off her shock and regathered her composure. "Let me start again." She drew in a breath, blew it out, and eyed me with an unsettling mix of excitement and curiosity. "I don't mean to be rude, but from what little I know about Prisms, it's my understanding that your magic is reactive, correct?"

I folded my arms over my chest and leaned against the back edge of couch. "If by reactive, you mean defensive, then yes."

Her brow furrowed. "That might be a problem." She shifted uncomfortably on the stool. "Theoretically, a magical scan, like the one I'll be doing, runs a chance of being seen as an 'attack'"—she used finger quotes—"which can trigger instinctive defensive reactions."

Like a Prism snapping into place to repel any active

magic. What Bev didn't know was that Prisms could turn an offensive magical strike back on its user. But that particular quirk had been kept quiet, even when Prisms were more common, so I simply said, "You're worried it may nullify your cast?"

Her gaze darted to Zev then back to me. "Yes?"

I wanted to smile at her hesitant uncertainty but didn't. It couldn't be easy to rein in her avid curiosity while maintaining a professional cool. Instead, I did my best to reassure her. "Thank you for the heads-up, but I don't think that will be problem."

She considered me for a long moment, then whatever she figured out must have reassured her, because her misgivings were replaced by her previous competent composure. "Right, then. Well, shall we get to it?"

I dropped my arms and straightened. "What do you need?"

Bev got up, pushed in her stool, then turned to where Lena and I had put our pub-style dining set. "If we move that off to the side, that should be enough room for a circle."

The next few minutes were filled with movement as we followed Bev's directions and cleared a workable space in the dining area. We shoved the table and chairs against the wall and moved the couch back a couple of feet. Lena did a fast sweep of the floor so nothing would mar Bev's chalk lines while Evan turned off the TV and grabbed a couple of thick candles from one of the cabinets. Bev drew a circle then added a series of runes and sigils as Lena handed Zev a feather and me a small yellow bundle that carried hints of orange and ginger.

The bitter scent made my nose itch, and I held it out a bit so I wouldn't sneeze. "What is this?"

"Turmeric," Bev answered without looking up from what she was doing. "It goes there." She motioned to the circle's point closest to the kitchen then waved to my left. "The feather goes there."

Zev set the feather down on the far side. Lena walked around me and set a small clear bowl of water to my right. Evan, standing at the circle's opposite point from me, lit a candle and placed it on the floor.

"Hold up," I said, making everyone freeze in place. "Evan, you need something under that candle." The chalk wasn't a worry—that was easily cleaned—but hardened wax could scar our wooden floors.

"I got it." Lena grabbed a stone coaster from the living room and took it to Evan.

Floors safe from harm, we stood off to the side while Bev completed her intricate markings. When she was done, she motioned me over. "I need you over here." She pointed to the top-right quadrant, where there was just enough room for me to sit.

I stepped carefully over the markings and took a seat on the floor, folding my legs tailor-fashion.

Bev settled in at the bottom-right section, facing me. She gave me a reassuring smile. "This shouldn't take very long, but I'll need you to stay still the entire time."

That shouldn't be a problem, but holding my Prism's reaction in check might be a different story. I tightened my metaphysical hold on my magic and braced. "Got it."

"Okay, ready?" She waited for my nod then touched one of the sigils closest to her.

Magic spilled into the markings, running like a lit fuse along the circle's lines and leaving behind a soft, diffused green glow in its wake. My Prism bucked against my hold, fighting to get free. I tightened my mental grip as Bev's magic nipped over my skin. The stinging sensation grew in intensity until it was a dull ache.

I really didn't like this. I glanced at Lena, who was watching us both intently from where she stood between Zev and Evan. When she caught my gaze, she mouthed, "Hang in there." Obviously, I wasn't hiding how uncomfortable I was. I looked at Zev. He was frowning, his arms crossed over his chest as he glowered. Our eyes met, and for some reason, the frustrated worry in his made the discomfort easier to bear.

I needed to focus on something other than the dull ache of holding my Prism in check, so I watched Bev work. Not that there was much to see. She sat there, lined in a soft-green glow that was a tad darker than the circle's surrounding illumination. Her eyes remained closed as the mossy-green light pulsed from bright to soft and back as she did her magical scan. An edge of tension rode the air, but I wasn't sure if that was just my nerves or the combination of mine and my friends'. Bev looked completely Zen.

As the moments passed and her magic did nothing more than nip at me, my Prism finally settled into a watchful stillness. It was weird, but most of the time, I viewed the ability that made me a Prism as a separate entity, mainly because it sometimes acted on its own. I had considered asking Zev if that was normal, or at least as normal as Arcane magic could be, but I hadn't yet found the courage. I had enough things to set me apart. I wasn't looking for more.

Coming out as a Prism had never been on my agenda. Not until I had no choice. I'd managed to avoid the Arcane Families for years, until I got caught up in Jeremy's kidnapping and dragged into an elaborate conspiracy. Since the only way forward was through, I'd stumbled clear of that mess only to discover I was well and firmly entrenched in the messy pit of Family drama with no way out. Then I'd learned that the powerful matriarch of one of the oldest Families was Sabella Rossi-Giordano, my great-aunt. It soon became clear that my continued survival meant embracing everything that I was.

Hiding my Prism had been easy when I was growing up, mainly because it wasn't until I was attacked by a young fire mage at one of the shelters that I realized I had a built-in shield against magical attacks. I'd managed to walk away unscathed, but he'd ended up in the hospital with third-degree burns. I'd thought it was a fluke until I heard the term *Prism* from an old, homeless schizophrenic and started digging.

Prisms had become urban myths in Arcane society, and the details of what their magic entailed was shrouded in secrecy. There were a few stories of personal shields who served powerful Arcane Families, keeping them alive during their endless feuds scattered throughout history. But around the second World War, when the world banded together to fight a delusional dictator, they'd started to disappear—mainly because they were being killed off in record numbers. The war ended, but for known Prisms, the nightmare kept going. They were favored targets of assassins because to wipe them out meant getting a clear shot at whichever Family member was in their crosshairs. When the Families finally acknowledged that they had all but extinguished an entire Arcane group, they erased Prisms by rewriting history.

With no training and nonexistent history, I was left to figure out what I could and couldn't do. Only recently had I discovered that there was much more to being a Prism than simply having a shield. Like any power, it could be used defensively and offensively. I was still learning the extent of my offensive abilities, but with both Sabella's and Zev's help, I was gaining experience at a rapid rate.

Bev's lashes rose, and her gaze met mine. I sucked in a sharp breath at the unnaturally bright green glow that had taken over her brown eyes. Those disturbing orbs drifted down until they were focused on my hands resting on my knees. "Well now."

I looked down, but everything looked normal to me. "What?"

"It seems you've recently been in contact with something

very, very nasty." Her tone matched the seriousness in her expression. "It's almost gone, which tells me you are not the intended target."

Everything in me stilled, and my grip on my power slipped. *How in the hell could I pick up anything? I'm a Prism.*

Bev sucked in a breath, and her eyes narrowed. "That's interesting."

I reclaimed my magical grip, yanking my Prism back in line. "What is?"

Before she could answer, Zev stepped in behind Bev, careful not to breach the chalked lines of the circle. "Can you tell when she picked it up?"

Her attention went back to my hands, and she frowned. "If I was to go by how faded it is, I'd say within the month, but based off that little blip you just had, it's probably closer to a week." Her gaze came to mine. "I'd bet your magic has been keeping the worst of it off of you."

If she was right, I didn't want to know what a full-on infection entailed. "Can you remove it?"

She went back to studying whatever it was she could see. "Yes."

"Wait," Lena said as she dropped to a crouch outside the circle. "I want to unravel it with you."

Bev nodded, picked up the chalk sitting next to her hip, and leaned over to draw a second, smaller circle that remained linked to the main one. Then she handed the chalk to Lena, who quickly drew out a series of interlocking runes inside the smaller circle then sat down, creating the last point of a triangle.

A burst of gold flecked with red surrounded Lena, and the moment it touched Bev's green lines, an invisible punch of air rocked me back. My power bucked in response, but I held it in check. Magic poured into the circle until the pressure was almost smothering. Then something shifted, and the pressure took a huge leap back. It didn't disappear, because although I couldn't see anything, I could feel it, like blunt fingernails being dragged down my arms then twisting around my wrists and hands.

An "ow" escaped on a hiss. I caught Zev's sharp look but shook my head. It was uncomfortable but bearable.

Lena's attention dropped to my hands, so now both women were staring intently at the same area. "Oh wow, I never would've seen that." She sounded impressed.

Bev made a soft hum, and after a long moment, the scratching sensation eased. "There now, we should be able to—"

"Stop!" Lena raised her hand, palm forward, and leaned in. "See that?" She pointed at something only the two of them could see.

Bev's gaze went to whatever Lena was pointing out. "Is that a signature?"

"Damn skippy, it is," Lena muttered. Her eyes narrowed. "Hang on. I think I've seen this before." She looked to Bev. "Can you hold this for me? Just for a minute?"

"Sure, but work quick. It's starting to dissipate."

"Evan, can you get me a piece of paper and something to write with?"

He grabbed an envelope and pen off the counter and handed both to Lena. She quickly drew something. "Okay, got it, Bev." She handed it back to Evan, who looked at it and frowned. "Right, let's get this off of her."

Together, the two women fell quiet, but I could feel magic shifting between them and then around me. They exchanged a few cryptic comments, but eventually, Lena sat back. "Okay, I think that should do it. What do you think?"

Bev's head tilted as she studied whatever hex they were working on. "I think we're good." She fell quiet for what felt like forever, then finally, the invisible presence curled around my wrists fell away. Bev looked up and smiled at me. "All clear."

I shook out my hands as the power that swam through the interlocked circles slowly receded. Bev's eyes resumed their normal brown color while the reddish gold of Lena's power faded to nothing. Bev brushed one of the chalk lines, breaking the circle. As the magical energy dissolved, the air in the condo lightened.

After Bev stood up, stretched, then stepped outside those lines, I finally relaxed my hold on my Prism. Like a disgruntled child, it slid into place and sulked. *Yep, definitely has its own annoying personality.*

Zev offered me a hand. I took it and let him help me to my feet. My movements were stiff, as if I'd been sitting for hours. I checked the clock. The whole thing had taken less than half an hour.

Lena stood with Evan, their heads bent over the sketch on the envelope. Bev joined them, and Lena shifted the paper so the other woman could see it. "Does this look familiar to you?"

Bev took the paper. "I'm surprised you got any of it, it was so faded." She studied the sketch and went to shake her head, but then she stopped and frowned. "Wait." She looked at Lena, her eyes wide with worry. "That part there"—she traced over it—"is that what I think it is?"

"I don't know, but if it is, it's bad news." Lena's tone was grim.

Zev headed over, and I hobbled along. He held out his hand to Bev. "May I?"

She handed over the sketch. I got closer so I could see what the fuss was about, not that I would be much help.

"What is that?" The lines on the paper didn't look like any sigils I'd ever seen.

"It's a personalized rune," Lena said. "Most casts utilize certain sigils in specific patterns. That"—she pointed at the paper—"is part of a magical signature that adds a unique glyph to a rune." She dropped her hand. "At least I think it is."

"And?"

"And…" Lena leaned into Evan, who held her close. "If it's who I think it is, it would explain how you managed to get tagged by a curse when you normally wouldn't." She looked at Bev. "Would you agree?"

Bev looked a little pale around the edges, and her voice held a slight tremor. "If it's him, then yes, that would explain it."

Considering how freaked the two women looked, that might not be the good news it sounded like. "Do you want to share with the class?"

It wasn't Lena who answered. It was Zev. "The Heretic Key."

I turned to him, totally lost. "Who is the Heretic Key?"

"That's the million-dollar question," Evan joined in. "No one knows for sure, but rumors abound. He's a high-level Key who sells his services through the dark web."

"He's been tied to a number of deaths, most connected to prominent Families." Zev handed the envelope back to Lena. "If Rory got tagged with his work, how is it you two managed to break it so easily?"

Lena and Bev exchanged a long look, then Bev offered, "Truthfully, I don't know. Maybe it was because Rory wasn't the intended target?"

"More like it was just because she's Rory," Lena said. "Her Prism would've kicked in, keeping the worst of it off of her."

That made sense to me, but it didn't stop the quiver of unease that ran through me. I inched closer to Zev, who looked down at me. I managed a half-hearted shrug. "That tracks."

A cellphone trilled somewhere. Bev moved to her bag on the island, while everyone else automatically reached for their pockets.

"It's mine!" Bev held her phone aloft like she'd won a prize, then blushed when we all looked at her. "Sorry." She dropped her hand, swiped her screen, then looked up. "Apologies, but I have to go. One of my other clients is in a bit of a bind."

"Of course," I said. "Thank you for coming by at the last minute."

Lena joined me, and together, we walked Bev to the door.

"Like I told Lena, I was happy to help." Bev's smile was a little wan, probably because she wanted to get clear of whatever mess we were tangled in.

Not that I could blame her.

"And we appreciate it," Lena added. She unlocked our door and held it open. "Again, if you ever need a return favor, please call me."

Bev nodded, her smile tight as she dashed out the door. Behind us I heard the guys dragging our dining table back into place. Lena and I watched as she waited for the elevator, then we gave her a wave when it arrived, and she stepped inside. Only when she was safely on her way down did we go back in and close the door.

Zev and Evan were at the table, the envelope lying between them.

Lena and I headed over to join them. "Anyone have any idea how we track down the Heretic person?"

Lena put her elbows on the table, propped her chin in her hands, and gave Evan wide eyes.

"Don't look at me, woman," Evan said. "This dick nozzle has managed to evade Council Hunters for years. Not sure what makes you think I can find him if they can't."

Lena opened her mouth to respond, but Zev got there first. "Because this time, he left someone alive."

For a moment, I didn't get it, then I did. "Max." Zev inclined his head, but when Evan and Lena still looked confused, I added, "If the Heretic person works off the dark web, that means there has to be some sort of communication, right? Like an email or a contract or something?"

Evan sat back, his arms crossed over his chest, and his brow furrowed. "It's not like ordering DoorDash, Rory."

"But there will be something, right?" I asked. "We know the curse was aimed at Max—"

"Or Devon," Zev said.

"Or Devon," I added. "It had to be tied to those damn glasses. So we have the object, a window of opportunity, and potential targets. Shouldn't that get you something?"

Evan looked at Lena, who tilted her head. He stared down at his feet without saying anything for a long moment. Then he shook his head and rubbed his face. When he dropped his hands, he leaned forward and, in a cautious tone, warned, "All right. I'll see what I can do, but no promises."

TWENTY-FIVE

ZEV and I had finally fallen into bed somewhere after three o'clock, both of us taking advantage of a now-quiet Sunday before we officially kicked off our work week. Thankfully, whatever Lena and Bev had done had worked beautifully, because I managed to get a solid eight hours of uninterrupted sleep. After lunch, Zev and I played board games with Lena and Evan until Zev had to take off around seven. All in all, it was just what the doctor ordered—a quiet day without any wise-guy rodents, vengeful ghosts, or killer curses. When my alarm went off bright and early Monday morning, I was ready for my work week.

Lena and I bustled around the kitchen as we poured to-go mugs and gathered keys, phones, and other necessities before heading out the door. We rode the elevator down to the garage, where we stood by our cars, comparing calendars.

"Call me if Evan comes up with anything this morning," Lena said as she juggled her drink, phone, and keys with practiced dexterity. "I can always shift my afternoon around if I need to."

"Why?"

"You're seriously asking me that?"

"Um, yeah?"

She dropped her chin so she could look at me over the top of her sunglasses. "Because you on your own is just asking for trouble."

I rolled my eyes behind my lenses, opened my door, ducked down, and set my drink in the modified console. "Whatever."

"Not 'whatever,'" she shot back. "Need I remind you that every time you go poking around by yourself, things get dicey?"

Okay, she might have a teensy-weensy point there. I backed out and turned to her. "Fine, if Evan finds something, I'll tag you." I held up my hand as she opened her mouth. "And if you're tied up, I'll ask Zev."

She considered me for a moment before giving in with a huff. "Fine." She opened her door. "No going solo, Rory. Promise."

My intentions were good when I made an X mark over my heart. "Promise."

"Good." She got one leg into her car before she added, "Watch yourself, girl."

"Always."

With that, we got into our cars and headed out to earn our respective paychecks.

⁙⁙⁙⁙⁙⁙⁙⁙⁙⁙⁙⁙⁙⁙⁙⁙⁙⁙⁙⁙

It was a quarter past nine when I finally pulled into the loading zone at Dueñas Park to pick up Zev from his office. That my dark and deadly boyfriend had an actual office tended to make my brain hurt, but even I had to admit, for a workspace, it was the shit. He had a leather couch, a big-ass TV screen that doubled as a monitor, and a killer coffee setup. I'd discovered it when we were stuck spending hours watching surveillance recordings while chasing down a demented scientist.

Fun times.

Since I was running a little behind, I had texted him my ETA. So now, idling in a spot guaranteed to piss someone off, I followed up with a quick *I'm here.* Hopefully, Zev would get to me before enforcement did. The last thing I needed was a parking ticket. Thankfully, it was only a minute or so before I saw him push through the glass doors and jog over to where I was parked.

He pulled open the door and dropped into the passenger seat. After he did a few contortions to get his legs in, he closed the door and dragged his seatbelt on. "Next time, we're taking my SUV."

I checked my mirrors and pulled out. "Just shift the seat back."

There was some rustling. "It's all the way back, and I still feel like my knees are up by my ears. This car was made for midgets."

"This car is a classic," I said but couldn't help my smirk. "Not all of us can be lean, mean fighting machines, babe."

He snorted. "Well, us lean, mean fighting machines do not appreciate being twisted into pretzels."

"I'm sure you'll survive." I stopped at a red light and angled my phone toward him. "Can you put Rebecca's address in for me?"

"Did you get your runs done this morning?" he asked as he typed in the address.

"Yep, a nice uncomplicated pickup and drop-off." The GPS piped up, and I hit my blinker for the upcoming left. "Unfortunately, there was a four-car accident on the freeway. Backed traffic up for miles. I had to take surface streets, which is why I was running late."

"Five minutes isn't late," he teased.

"You say toe-ma-toe, I say toe-may-toe," I sang and caught his grin out of the corner of my eye.

The GPS took us out of downtown Phoenix and out toward Rebecca's place. We chit-chatted for a few minutes before he finally asked, "Anything from Evan?"

"Not yet, but I know he started searching last night after he left our place, because Lena said he was texting her until she shut down at midnight." I paused then asked, "Do you really think he's going to be able to find something?" Even with all his skills, which were impressively vast, digging through the dark web couldn't be easy, not even for an electro mage.

Zev took a second before answering, and when he did, he picked his words carefully. "I think, if the Heretic is behind this, then he fucked up with Max."

"It's not like Max is in any shape to identify him," I pointed out.

"But he's still breathing," he said. I must not have looked convinced, because he continued. "Typically, a contract requires at least half the payment up front, the other half when the contract is completed. The fact that Max is breathing means the contract should still be open."

"So what? The Heretic will try again?"

"My guess, yeah, especially if it means taking Max out underneath the nose of a Council member."

"That's why you called Christina at four in the morning."

"That's why," he agreed. "If Evan can find the contract, we might get lucky and take out both the Heretic and whoever hired him."

The intensity in Zev's voice made me pause. "What's your deal with this guy?"

A mix of anger and contempt heated the air between us. "He's an arrogant parasite that needs to be eradicated."

I slid Zev a look. "You've hunted him."

"Yeah, but he's a slippery little shit and a pain in my ass," he bit out. "Got close last time, but somehow, he slithered away."

And clearly, Zev took it as a personal affront. "Well, maybe we'll get lucky." It was lame, but it was the best I could up with.

He didn't say anything, and I left him to brood. It wasn't like I could offer much comfort. Zev was a hell of a hunter. He had to be to hold his position with the Cordova Family. Unfortunately, no matter how good anyone was at something, there was always someone else out there with a bit more skill or luck.

It took a bit, but he finally managed to shake off his dark mood by the time I turned in to Rebecca's subdivision. Situated between the Salt River and South Mountain Park, it was a modest neighborhood built in what had once been farmland. While a few fields remained, over the last ten-plus years, most had been replaced by planned developments. What it wasn't was what I'd expected from someone who ran with Max and Devon's moneyed crowd.

"Is this the right address?" I asked as I pulled up in front of a single-level, two-car-garage home done in white stucco with dark-tan trim. A sleek silver Acura was parked in the drive, but nothing shared that this was the home of a woman who could afford to throw mad money around, say like twenty grand, at Max's pipe dream.

"So it says," Zev said.

I parked on the street in front, and we got out and headed up the short walk to the door. Zev hit the doorbell, and the resulting chime brought the sound of movement.

The door opened, and a barefoot but exhausted-looking Rebecca stood in the doorway. Her gaze hit Zev first, and she managed a polite yet wan smile. "Mr. Aslanov?" Her reddened eyes ringed by dark circles fell on me, and her smile turned a little more real. "Rory, nice to see you again."

"And you," I answered. "Sorry about the circumstances."

She managed a jerky nod that almost dislodged the messy knot of her hair. "Um, yeah. So, thanks for making the trip out here." Dressed in lounge pants and a flowy shirt, she shifted out of the doorway, still holding the door. "Sorry, come in, come in."

Zev stood to the side, letting me enter first, then followed me in. We moved through the tiled entryway as Rebecca closed the door and trailed behind us. "We can sit in here." She stepped around us and motioned to the couch and two plush side chairs that sat in the front room. "Can I get you something to drink? Water? Coffee?"

We both demurred and took a seat on the sofa. Hostess that she was, Rebecca took one of the chairs and tucked her feet up under her.

Zev sat back, a silent prompt for me to take the lead.

"We appreciate you making time to talk to us, and we'll try not to take up too much of your morning. We're so sorry about Devon."

"Thank you," Rebecca choked out, tears swimming in her dark eyes. "I'm still trying to make sense of it."

I didn't bother sharing that was likely to be a futile endeavor. Somewhere under her grief, she already knew it.

She looked away and pressed her fist against her mouth, struggling for composure. When she found it, she dropped her fist to her lap and twisted her fingers together. The knuckles pressed white against her skin. She looked at Zev. "Kent said Max's aunt asked you to look into what happened." Her gaze slid to me. "That you wanted to ask some questions about Devon and Max."

I nodded. "We're trying to get a handle on who might have a grudge against either of them."

"Is Kent right?" A hard light hit her grief-stricken eyes. "It wasn't an accident? Someone targeted Max?"

Zev leaned forward and braced his arms on his knees. "It's starting to look that way. Do you—"

A door opened somewhere in the house, and a male voice called, "Sweetheart, do you want a warm-up?"

I frowned. There was something familiar about that voice.

Rebecca twisted in her seat, her gaze toward the kitchen.

The man kept speaking, getting closer. "I can get a…" The rest of what he planned to say petered out when Perry hit the opening between the front room and the kitchen and stopped. "Oh, hey," he greeted, running a hand through his wet hair. "You're already here."

"I left my mug on the counter," Rebecca said. "Can you grab it for me?"

"Yeah, sure." He turned back to the kitchen, disappeared, and reappeared less than a minute later, coffee in hand. He carried it over and handed it to her. "Here you go."

"Thanks," she murmured.

Perry bent down, brushed his lips over hers, and murmured something too low for me to make out.

Zev and I exchanged a look, but we quickly turned back to the unexpected couple.

Perry moved around Rebecca's chair and took a seat on the floor in front of her. He looked at both of us, and his lips twisted into a wry curve. "I'm guessing Kent didn't share that Becca and I are dating."

"Um, no," I started, my voice awkward. "It didn't come up."

There was no sign of the sneer that had seemed to be permanently etched on his face the night of the engagement party. Instead, lines of grief and exhaustion had replaced it. "Not surprised," Perry muttered. "He's had a bit of a time adjusting to it."

Even though I knew it wasn't why we were there, I couldn't help but ask, "Why's that?"

Rebecca answered, "Because Kent feels like the odd man out in our group."

"More like, he's jealous as shit," Perry said.

"Perry," Rebecca chided softly.

He tilted his head back. "You know I'm right." He turned back to us. "Kent and Devon were a couple before Devon hooked up with Max."

"So he said." Zev shifted back, relaxing into the couch. "In fact, he mentioned he was the one that introduced them."

"Huh, I didn't expect him to admit that." Perry bent one leg and rested his arm on his knee. "It was rough there for a bit, what with everyone tiptoeing around each other." He shook his head. "When he finally realized that Devon and Max's relationship would go the distance, he pulled his head out of his ass and stopped moping around. Unfortunately, the whole experience left its mark."

That fit with the impression I got when Kent talked about Devon. "How so?"

Perry shrugged. "He and Max took a while to find their groove afterward."

That, however, did not. "Oh?"

Obviously in the mood to share, Perry said, "Yeah, Max is pretty easygoing for the most part, but Kent was driving him batty there for a bit, acting like a jealous ex, even though Kent and Devon had never been anything but casual. Kent was an ass, especially when Max and Devon were just starting out. He kept taking verbal shots at the two of them."

"He knew it was just hurt feelings," Rebecca spoke up, and when I looked at her, she explained. "Max did, I mean. He's known Kent for, like, forever, and he knew Kent doesn't handle rejection well. But Max knew it was only a matter of time before Kent would come back around."

"What about Devon?" Zev asked. "Was she able to brush it off?"

"It took her longer." Rebecca danced her fingers absently on the side of her mug. "Mainly because of the guilt of being the one to break it off with Kent. She knew it was bad form to go from one friend to the other, but she said when she saw

Max, she just knew. It helped that she and Kent had only been going out a few weeks, so she told me it wasn't like Kent's heart was overly involved."

"More like his ego," Perry muttered.

"Perry," she chided with a look at the man at her feet.

He tilted his head back, resting it against her leg. "You and I both know Kent's first love is his career."

With the hand not holding her coffee, Rebecca brushed her fingers through his hair and softly admitted, "Yeah, she did find it hard to compete with a mistress like that." There was a hint of bitter knowledge in her voice.

"Sounds like the voice of experience."

She looked up, and her smile was wistful. "Some, not with Kent, but previous boyfriends."

"Luckily for me, I prefer something warmer than cash." Perry caught her hand and pressed a kiss to her knuckles as she blushed.

"Speaking of cash…" Zev switched subjects. "Kent mentioned that you both invested in Max's latest treasure hunt."

The couple exchanged glances then turned back to us. "Yeah, we both did," Perry admitted cautiously.

"Kent said he put in twenty," Zev pressed. "Did you do the same?"

Perry grimaced. "I only put in ten. Things have been a little lean lately. Plus, last time I threw in, things didn't pan out. Wasn't hyped up to repeat that mistake."

Zev looked to Rebecca.

"Ten," she admitted. "My investments have had a rough ride with the market lately. It was all I was willing to risk without impacting my long-term goals." She hefted her mug and motioned to the house. "This is a long-term investment. I've got plans to retire while I have time to enjoy my life."

I felt that. It also explained the modest lifestyle. "Do you happen to know who the latest investor was?"

Perry frowned and let go of Rebecca's hand so he could rub his chin. "You're not talking about Barb, are you?"

I shook my head. "No, Kent mentioned there was a last-minute investor who shelled out a hefty amount, but he didn't have much else by way of details."

Lines furrowed across his brow as he thought. "I don't know who it could be, but that at least explains why Max's been so wired these last few weeks." He looked at Rebecca. "And here I thought it was because he had to deal with that dick Guzman."

I shot Zev a look, and he asked with deceptive casualness, "As in Jayson Guzman?"

Distaste laced Perry's voice, and Rebecca gave a small shiver. "The one and only." The sneer from the engagement party made a comeback. "That asshole thinks he's better than everyone, and he had no trouble shoving shit Max's way. Especially after the dick took his old man's place at the contract table. Max came close to telling the Watershed powers that be that he'd hand off the Guzman contracts to someone else, but the pissant changed his attitude." Perry shook his head. "Actually, if you ask me, I'd bet good money Jayson's father told him to check his shit because Guzman and Sons needs the contracts, especially since Guzman Senior had to step down after his heart attack."

"And you know all of this, how?"

"I've listened to Max bitch, rightly so, for the last few weeks. I couldn't offer much advice, just a sympathetic ear. Which is normally Kent's role, but he's been tied up with some big project that's kept him MIA lately. Hell, I was surprised he showed up to the engagement party."

"Not me," Rebecca cut in. "Kent promised Max he'd be there." She turned her attention to us. "But if you're looking for names, you might want to put Jayson's at the top."

"Do you think he's capable of doing something like this to Max and Devon?"

"Capable?" She shrugged. "I don't know. But I do know that Jayson's spent his whole life being overshadowed by people like us, and the resentment that sowed is obvious."

"How so?"

"You know his family are Traditionalists, right?" She waited for our nods. "Then it shouldn't come as a shock that they've sunk quite a bit of money and political support into the proposed Arcane Registry movement. They resent those that have magic, and they really, really resent the power and influence wielded by the Families."

"Not enough to walk away from a lucrative development project," Perry pointed out.

"No, but that's about money, which spends no matter if it comes from magic hands or not," Rebecca shot back with cynical wryness. "However, every time Jayson's and Max's lives brush against each other, Jayson will try to minimize Max's successes, saying they're only achievable because of Max's Family ties, that if Max wasn't part of the Arcane elite, then he'd be no better than Jayson."

"That is such bullshit," Perry muttered.

"Not to Jayson," Rebecca said, not unkindly. "I got to admit, I feel for him."

"Seriously?" Perry scowled.

"Yeah, seriously," she shot back with undeniable heat. "I can't imagine being magic-less when that's the one thing our society values most. Traditionalists have to fight twice as hard and twice as long to get the same things we tend to earn."

Before the two could get into an ethical argument about Arcane society, I cut in. "Would Jayson gain anything by targeting Max?"

Perry and Rebecca both gave my question serious consideration. Perry was the first to answer. "I don't think so. Max's condition might delay contract negotiations by a couple of weeks, but in the scheme of things, Watershed will just bring in another representative to work with the

Guzmans' contract. From what Max told me, the contract was pretty much done."

"Jayson might not like Max, and he might want to see him fail publicly, but this?" She shook her head. "It doesn't make sense. Jayson is the type that wouldn't hesitate to take credit for humiliating Max, especially if it made it appear as if he one-upped the son of an Arcane Family. But risking the wrath of a Family and possibly being hunted down for taking one of them out? That takes the kind of guts he doesn't have."

In that, at least Max and Devon's three closest friends agreed, which left us with one last name. "The final investor," I said. "You two mentioned you don't know who it is, but do you know who would?"

Perry looked at Rebecca. "Barb, maybe?"

"Maybe," she agreed hesitantly. "If not her, she might be able to get you on the right path."

That would be good, because as far as I could tell, unless Evan got lucky, we were pretty much at a dead end.

TWENTY-SIX

ZEV and I left Rebecca's, and I wasn't sure if it was a wasted trip or not. It wasn't like we learned anything new. Well, other than the fact that Devon broke Kent's heart at one point, and that Perry and Rebecca were a thing. But it was the couple's take on Jayson, on top of what Kent shared about him, that made me wonder.

"You think he's behind all this?" I asked Zev as I headed back into Phoenix.

He didn't look up from his phone. "Who? Jayson?"

Guess I wasn't the only one wandering down that particular path. "Yep."

"It's possible." He finished typing out something and sat back. "But as the two back there pointed out, there's no real gain to be had from taking Max out."

"Still," I said, thinking how people did seriously twisted shit over much less than imagined slights and childish resentments.

"Still," he agreed. "But based on what little information we have, there's no way to say one way or the other. The thing is anyone can hire off the dark web, so long as you have the pockets for it."

He wasn't wrong. "Okay, so if not Jayson, what about Kent? Maybe he wasn't as copacetic as he said he was about Devon."

"So he takes out his best friend and his ex?"

Not missing his world of sarcasm, I risked a glance his way. "Do you not listen to true crime? That's, like, the basis for every other murder."

"You might want to cut back on your bingeing, babe." Feigned amusement colored his voice, then he turned serious. "It's not that it's not possible, but it makes no sense that he'd risk Devon being caught in the fallout. So no, I don't think it was Kent."

I didn't either, but it was something that had to be considered. Didn't it? "Okay, so what about this mysterious investor?"

"Now, that avenue does intrigue me." There was a predatory anticipation in his response.

"That mean you're going to call Barb and see if she'll share?" I felt the weight of his gaze and snuck a look to find him studying me.

"Why is it me who has to call?" He drummed his fingers absently against his phone, which lay facedown on his thigh.

"Because your name is the one she'll recognize," I pointed out.

He snorted. "You do realize most of my work goes down behind the scenes?"

"I do," I said. "But your reputation and connections open more doors than mine." I hoped to change that, but it would take time.

"You keep going the way you've been, that won't always be the case." There was a wry mix of prophetic warning and admonishment in his voice.

"You make that sound like a bad thing."

He picked up his phone. "I just think you should be

careful what you wish for." He swiped over the screen, hit a number, and put the phone to his ear. "Christina, Zev. I apologize if I'm interrupting your business." A pause. "How is he? Any change?" Sympathy infused his voice when he said, "I'm sorry to hear that. I won't keep you long. I was hoping you had a number for Barbara Warren?" He paused, listening. "She is? Can I speak to her for a moment? Thanks." Another pause, this one a little longer. "Ms. Warren, my name is Zev Aslanov. I don't know if Christina ex—" He fell quiet and listened. "Yes, we are, which is why I wanted to talk to you for a moment. We've spoken with Perry, Kent, and Rebecca, and they mentioned Max took on a last-minute investor for his treasure hunt. Do you happen to know who that was?"

The air in the car went wired as Zev froze in his seat. "Are you sure?" His empty hand fisted for a moment then relaxed. "No, ma'am, that's not my intention. It's just a surprise." Another pause, longer again.

I continued to head back toward downtown, straining my ears, but I couldn't make anything out. I risked a look at Zev. Whatever Barbara was telling him left his expression dark and forbidding.

"No, I wasn't aware, but I appreciate you filling me in. Thank you, though. We appreciate your help. Of course, you too. Good-bye."

I waited until he clicked off before demanding, "What?"

"The last-minute investor was Jayson Guzman." He dropped the bomb without looking up from his phone's screen.

Shock rolled through me. That was the last name I would have ever imagined coming out of Zev's mouth. "Are you shitting me?"

"Nope." His finger flew over his phone as he kept talking. "According to Barbara, Jayson approached Max a few weeks ago, asking if he could invest in the latest treasure hunt. Max agreed."

"Just like that?" I knew I sounded incredulous, but seriously, if the two men had such bad blood between them and Max knew Jayson was a dick, why in the hell would he do that?

"Just like that," Zev said, sounding disgusted. "Barbara speculates that Max was so focused on getting those glasses, he'd take money from the devil if it was offered."

"I'd think, in this instance, Jayson would qualify." I shook my head. "Okay, so Max was desperate. What was Jayson's excuse? Why would he give his money to a man he resented?"

"When Barbara asked Max the same thing, he told her Jayson wanted to shift his money out of his accounts before his soon-to-be ex-wife cleaned him out. He needed it to go somewhere her lawyers wouldn't look, so they came to an agreement. Jayson would give Max the money as an anonymous investor, which allowed Max to get the glasses. Then, at a later date, when the divorce was finalized, Max would return that same amount to Jayson, using the funds provided by the other investors."

I tried to untangle that logic. "Sounds a lot like a shell game to me."

"Me too," Zev agreed as he typed out a number into his phone. "But Max justified it to Barbara as a temporary loan of sorts. Either way, both men got what they wanted."

"I'm not sure Devon would agree." There was something to be said about Max's obsession, and I wasn't sure it was anything good. "We need to talk to Jayson."

Instead of answering, Zev brought his phone up to his ear, and I could hear the line ringing. Someone picked up, and Zev said, "Can I speak to Jayson Guzman, please?" A pause. "Do you know where I can find him?" Zev leaned forward and angled my phone holder toward him. "And the address?" He typed it in. "Thank you." He hung up then turned the phone back to me as the GPS piped up with an ETA.

Stopped at a light, I tagged the destination. "Metro Center? Isn't that scheduled to be torn down?"

"It is," Zev confirmed. "But Jayson is on his way to meet with the developer to finalize plans on planned apartments. According to his admin, the meeting is scheduled for one."

It was just past noon now, and so long as construction didn't interfere, we should make it with five minutes to spare. "Let's go the mall."

Located just off I-17, the Metro Center was a piece of the valley's history. Once home to over a hundred and seventy-five stores, it was the largest mall in Arizona, and now it was being torn apart to make way for a mixture of high-rise apartments and multi-story retail space. Finding Jayson wasn't going to be easy, not when the site spanned sixty-eight acres.

I followed the chain-link fence that circled the empty parking lots. It was clear that demolition was well underway —portions were nothing but piles of rubble. There was activity on the south end, where bulldozers emptied their loads into huge containers while figures stood around in hard hats and yellow striped vests. Signs strung along the fence warned off trespassers and proclaimed the site was under surveillance.

I finally found the entrance over on the far west side, where the fence had been pulled back to leave a wide gap. No one was monitoring the entrance, so I drove on through. Parked in front of what used to be one of the big-name anchor stores was a collection of work trucks and dust-covered sedans. Off to the side was a portable trailer, likely being used as onsite office space. I pulled into a spot on the far side of a beat-up Mazda.

Zev and I got out and started for the trailer. Off in the distance, I could hear the crash bangs of rubble being dumped and the faint shouts of the crew. I let Zev climb the metal steps to the trailer door while I waited at the bottom. He knocked, and the door shuddered under his knuckles. I looked around as we waited for someone to answer. When no one came, Zev tried again.

We waited some more, then I said, "They must be somewhere inside."

"Must be." Zev came back down. "Come on."

We circled around the trailer and headed toward the building. Like many older malls, big stores stretched out around a central hub like spokes on a wheel. We picked our way over cracked sidewalks until we found an entrance of sorts. Where the glass doors had once stood were sheets of plywood marked in orange paint, but one was shoved back, leaving an opening. We ducked inside.

My boots crunched over grimy tiles as we skirted around empty display counters. We made it out to the main space that connected all the shops. Light spilled through dirty panes above. Walking through the dead mall was as eerie as shit. The escalators were still, and some of the stairs were nothing but twisted metal. Abandoned kiosks were scattered throughout, and the glass elevator sat stuck between the first and second floors.

"Maybe we should've asked for Jayson's number," I whispered to Zev, unwilling to disturb the weird silence.

"I doubt they would've given it out," he said just as quietly.

We came to the center part of the mall, where we could

choose left, right, or straight ahead. I looked to Zev. "Which way do—"

Something clanged somewhere to our left, followed by the sound of voices. Zev and I shared a look then started off in that direction. We were about halfway down the wide corridor when something scampered off to my right. I caught a glimpse of something small and furry scurrying away into the shadows.

"Was that a—?"

"Rat, I think," Zev said.

"Yuck."

He just shook his head.

We came around the end of the corridor as it opened up into the old food court. There, gathered around a couple of tables pushed together, was a group of men. They turned at our entrance.

An older man, his hair silvered, his face deeply tanned, frowned. "Who are you? You're not supposed to be in here."

Zev lifted a hand. "We're looking for Jayson Guzman. His office said he'd be here."

The men exchanged looks, and a couple of them shook their heads. "Haven't seen him yet," said the older man, who was clearly the speaker for the group.

"He'll probably show in another ten or so," another man, a bit younger, said. "If you want to catch him, you'll need to wait out by the trailer."

"Of course, thank you. We'll do that."

The older man shot the younger man a look. He sighed and moved toward us. "Here, I'll escort you back."

We waited for him then followed him back through the mall and back out the opening we'd come in from, exchanging meaningless pleasantries as we did so. Once outside, he walked us toward the trailer, his gaze roaming over the collection of parked cars in front of the trailer. He pulled up short with a soft "Huh."

I stopped a few steps ahead and turned back to ask, "What?"

He angled his chin toward a newer white Ford F-150 that hadn't been there when we arrived. "That's Jayson's truck." He looked around then shook his head. "Must have missed him." He turned back to us. "Might be best if you call his office and make an appointment. I don't think you'll catch him today."

I made a mental note of Jayson's license plate as I started walking again.

"Thanks," Zev said, pulling out his phone. "We'll do that."

Zev and I headed toward my car as the younger guy watched. I skirted a pile of wood and boxes and caught movement out of the corner of my eye. I turned to see a pair of black eyes watching me intently, a bushy tail standing at attention. The chipmunk bared its teeth and hissed in warning.

Yeah, right back at'cha, bud.

I held that beady gaze as I yanked open my door. It wasn't until Zev called my name in a low voice that I broke the stare-down with the furry little enforcer. I looked across my roof.

Zev stood in the opening of the passenger door with his phone pressed to his ear, his face to me, and his back to our watcher. "Tell me when he leaves."

I gave a tiny nod and dropped into the driver's seat. I looked to where the chipmunk had been, but it was gone. As Zev pretended to talk to Jayson's office, I watched our human escort turn around and jog back the way we'd come.

I waited until he disappeared before I said, "He's gone."

Zev bent down so I could see him. "We need to find Jayson. If we don't corner him now, I have a feeling he'll rabbit."

Of that, I had no doubt, and considering how big Metro Center was, it wouldn't take much for Jayson to avoid us while his associates kept us off the site. We needed eyes on our target, eyes that wouldn't be noticed. "Get in. I've got an idea."

I started up my baby as Zev went through his origami routine and pulled his door closed after him. I waited until I reversed and was heading back toward the gap in the fence before I shared. "I'm going to need you to have a sit-down with a furry informant."

TWENTY-SEVEN

"DO YOU AGREE?" Zev, his arm braced on an overhead branch of a tree in the hotel parking lot, gave the brown-and-white chipmunk a hard stare as they faced off.

Beady black eyes held steady as its tail quivered and its clawed hands folded and unfolded. Finally, the little brown head dipped in a nod.

"Be back when the shadows start to grow."

That earned a spate of irritated chittering, then with a dismissive hiss, the chipmunk scurried down the trunk and took off.

We stood on the far side of the Doubletree Hotel that sat on the north end of the construction site in one of the small grassy patches that tried to fool visitors into believing they weren't in the desert. The blinds were pulled on the nearby windows, but I wasn't overly concerned with being seen. Not only was the parking lot all but empty, but two people talking under a tree wasn't cause for alarm. "Is making a deal with the chipmunk mafia going to cause you problems?"

Zev pushed off the tree and started back toward the car. "First, they aren't chipmunks. They're squirrels."

I rolled my eyes as I followed him. I didn't care which

name they went by. They were all small, furry pains in my ass.

"Second, what kind of problems do you think they could actually cause?"

I shrugged as we stopped at the car and leaned against the hood. "I don't know. Maybe you'll wake up to find a decapitated cricket in your bed or something."

His lips twitched as he stretched out his legs and folded his arms. "They're not exactly the underworld threat you seem to imagine."

Maybe not the one we just talked to, but those others… "Yeah, well, the ones after Mr. Nutter weren't quite as fluffy as this little guy."

"From what you told me, I'm betting those were magicked informants set up with a specific purpose. This one is exactly what he appears to be—a squirrel."

"Lucky for us, you speak squirrel." I pulled out my phone. "But just in case our little spy strikes out, I'm going to ask Evan to hack and track Jayson's GPS. If we can't corner him here, maybe we can run him down afterward." I typed out a quick request and included the truck's plate number. Then something struck me. "Wait. How does our furry friend know what Jayson looks like?"

Zev turned his phone toward me, and Jayson's headshot from his professional page stared back.

"Guess that works." From where we stood, we could see the chain-link fence that blocked off the construction site. "How long are we waiting for a report back?"

Zev's shoulders rose and fell. "Half hour, give or take."

With nothing more to do at the moment than wait, my brain jumped from thought to thought and landed on a question. "If Jayson did hire the Heretic to take out Max, how's that going to go?"

Zev dropped his arms and propped his hands behind him

as he looked at me over the top edge of his sunglasses. "How's what going to go?"

I laid out the worries crowding my head. "Jayson's an avid Traditionalist. Christina's an Arcane council member. There's no way Max's family or Devon's are going to be satisfied with turning Jayson over to law enforcement. Jayson's family will fight tooth and nail to keep him out of the Council's clutches. So who gets dibs? Because any way this goes down, it's going to cause issues."

"That's not our problem," Zev said.

I opened my mouth to protest, because yeah, it was, since we would be the ones handing him over.

Zev cut me off. "We were tasked by Christina to find out the cause of Max's accident. Not only is she a representative of the injured party's family, but for all intents and purposes, she speaks for the Arcane Council. As agents of the Council, we are required to bring the results of our investigation to them. They will render judgement, and their judgement stands, regardless of the affiliations of those involved." His voice was hard, his expression even harder.

And it struck me in a flash of insight why Traditionalists were so resentful of the Arcane Families, and pity welled for Jayson's family. In the power games played by society's big hitters, Traditionalists ranked dead last. Without the magical clout of the Arcane Families or the First Nations, the Traditionalists were left with only one weapon in their arsenal —political influence. And that wouldn't count for shit if Jayson was named as the reason Devon was dead and Max nearly so. Even worse, his family would have no recourse for whatever judgement the Council decided to pass.

My phone vibrated, and I checked the screen to see Evan's name. I picked it up, put it to my ear, and kept my gaze on my boots. "Hey, Evan."

"Hey back. Got your text. I'm working on it now."

"Thanks."

"Got something else for you."

I lifted my head and met Zev's gaze. "Hang on. I'll put you on speaker so Zev can hear." I lowered the phone and switched it to speaker. "Okay, go ahead, Evan."

"Right, so it took some doing, but I managed to piece together a trail on the glasses. Long story short, it looks like Max was the target, not Devon. I can't be a hundred percent certain it's the right one, but if it is, it appears that the initial outreach came from an e-café downtown. I'm going to send you the address and a couple of still shots I snagged from their surveillance video at roughly the same time as the message was sent out. The quality's shit, but it's better than nothing."

"Anyone stand out?" Zev asked, frowning down at the phone.

"Not to me," Evan said. "But you two might see it differently." Before I could thank him, he added, "Lena said to tell you she's tied up until about four, but she wants you to keep her looped in."

"Got it." I looked at Zev as I told Evan, "We'll be here a bit longer. We're just following up on something. As soon as we're done, we'll head over to the café and poke around. Let me know once you've got Jayson's truck tagged."

"You'll be the second to know." He hung up before I could say anything more.

Zev and I waited for Evan to send over the photos, neither of us saying anything. The phone shimmied in my hand, and I pulled up the text and the attached photos. Zev got closer, and the two of us studied the images.

Zev read Evan's text out loud. "'Check out the third computer from the left.'"

"He wasn't wrong. These are shitty," I murmured. The black-and-white images were okay, but the angle was bad, and as I zoomed in, the fuzziness got worse. Still, we studied the area around the computer Evan had identified. The café was buzzing, likely because university classes were in full swing.

Despite the crowd, the camera caught a figure sitting hunched at the terminal. It was a partial side view, most of which was hidden behind the bodies of other patrons. The person was wearing a hoodie with the hood pulled up, obscuring most of the profile, but I was able to see a bit of chin and a tip of a nose.

"I can't tell if they're male or female," I said, exasperated.

Zev took my phone and used his fingers to zoom in. "I think male. Look at the watch."

I took it back and peered down. The watch was a heavy circle with a wide band, but it fit the wrist. "I think you're right."

Zev leaned in close until his head brushed mine, both of us peering down at the screen. "Hang on," Zev murmured, then he shifted the image a bit and zoomed in closer on the wrist and the watch. "Motherfuck," he hissed.

"What?"

"See that mark?"

"Where?"

"There." He pointed to a mark that was partially hidden by the watch band. "Look familiar?"

"Is that…" I angled the phone, trying to make it out. "That looks like a brand of some sort."

"Or maybe the top of an old-fashioned key?" Zev straightened, a fierce light in his dark eyes. "Like the one used by the Heretic?"

"Holy shit," I breathed and looked up. "That's him."

"That's what I'm thinking."

"I'll see if I can get Evan to clean that up." I wasn't sure it would do us any good, but right now, even a faint trail was better than none. I zoomed the picture back out and started to check out the other patrons. A fine-boned face with wire-rimmed glasses caught my eye. Excitement shot along my nerve endings, and I zoomed in. "No way."

"What?" Zev leaned in so close, I could feel his breath along my neck.

I angled the phone and started to answer, only to be stopped by a familiar chitter. We both looked up to find our furry spy had returned and was perched on a branch.

"I'll tell you after," I assured Zev. "Go talk to our friend."

Zev nodded, pushed off the car, and strolled over to the tree. Magic nipped at my skin as he talked with the squirrel. All I could make out was a few chirps and hisses and Zev's low-voiced responses. While he was busy chatting up our chipmunk… squirrel, whatever… I shot Evan a request then sat back to wait. I wasn't sure if it was good news or bad that Zev returned within minutes, and the squirrel darted off.

When he got close, I asked, "Well?"

He sighed. "He made it inside, but the meeting was breaking up, and he didn't see Jayson."

"Great, guess we wait for Evan to hack his GPS then. In the meantime, I might have another lead for us."

"Oh?"

I nodded, thumbed back to the surveillance photo, and zoomed in on the fine-boned face. I got in close to Zev so he could see the screen. "This is Cass. She was bartending the night of the engagement party. I asked Evan to track down the catering company and find her address."

He took my phone and studied the image with a frown. "You think she might have seen Jayson there?"

"If not Jayson, maybe someone else?"

He handed back my phone. "It was a party, babe. I'm thinking there were a lot of 'someone else's there."

Yes, sarcasm could be a love language, but I still rolled my eyes. "Bartenders see things others don't." Remember the disconcerting familiarity Cass had displayed with me, I added, "Plus, there's something about her..." I trailed off, not quite sure how to phrase it.

Zev's gaze sharpened. "What do you mean?"

I shrugged. "Don't ask me to explain. Just believe me when I tell you, if someone was there that shouldn't have been, I'm betting she'll know." My phone went off, and I checked my text. "Sweet." I straightened from the hood and headed for the driver's side. "Evan got an address on Cass. Let's roll."

Zev went to the passenger door, and I pulled mine open. "Did he get into Jayson's ride?"

"Hang on. I'll check." I dropped into the seat and sent the text. Then I started putting Cass's address into the GPS, even though I was pretty sure I recognized it. Sure enough, the address popped up with the name of a familiar bar in the downtown business district. Evan's response hit my screen as I turned the ignition over. I read it and frowned. "Huh."

"What?" Zev snapped his belt into place.

"Evan says Jayson's truck hasn't moved." We exchanged a look, neither of us having to voice how very not good that was. I ignored the muttered curse from Zev and backed out. "You think he's still at the site?"

"Doubt it. I bet he caught a ride with someone else," Zev said.

Yeah, that's what I was afraid of. I threw my baby in gear and headed back to the defunct mall. I drove along the chain-link fence, keeping my pace casual as we came up on the entrance. It was still open, and as we passed, we saw the white Ford hadn't moved from its spot. "Do we go in?"

"No," Zev said. "Head around and park in the lot by the restaurant over there." He motioned ahead of us.

Minutes later, I was sliding into another parking spot in a lot that was much closer to full and still gave me a line of sight to the mall. "Now what?"

Zev unbuckled his belt, shoved open his door, and started

to get out. "Sit tight." He got out, closed the door, and rounded the Mustang. I twisted in my seat to see what he was doing. It wasn't exciting, because he settled in ass to my trunk and just stood there.

Magic crawled over me as the minutes ticked by, each feeling longer than the last. The tension and discomfort went on forever until I wanted to crawl out of my skin. I was just about to storm out and demand Zev share whatever it was he was doing that was driving me nuts, when the scrape of magic disappeared. I dropped my forehead to the steering wheel as a whispered litany of curses escaped, and my body shuddered in relief.

Zev's shadow darkened the passenger-side window, cutting my rant short. I lifted my head as he opened his door and dropped back into the seat. I studied his face and caught the lingering glow in his eyes. "What did you do?"

"Had a friend do a flyover."

When he stopped there, I prompted, "And?"

"And nothing." He shifted in his seat, yanking his belt over his shoulder and clicking it into place. "No sign of Jayson anywhere."

I turned over the ignition and hit Go on the GPS. "Well, at least he isn't dead."

"Not yet," he muttered.

I snorted as I made a left out of the restaurant's lot and headed for the freeway. "Aren't you the cheery one."

"Nope, just pragmatic," he said as he sent off a text. "I don't think we're the only ones looking for him."

Unfortunately, I was starting to think the same.

TWENTY-EIGHT

RUSH HOUR STARTED EARLY in the valley, and unfortunately, it doubled my drive time. To add insult to injury, it took another ten to find a damn parking spot.

"Shouldn't this be a thing for you?" Zev asked on my fourth round of the hunt.

"What thing?" I bit out, eyes peeled for an empty space.

"Getting a parking spot."

"I'm a Transporter, Zev, not a freakin' miracle worker." A flash of red caught my attention. "Yes!" I pulled up close enough to ensure no one could sneak in, and waited for the van to back out. They inched out, doing their best not to back into oncoming traffic. Downtown Phoenix was made of narrow roads, some even daring to be one way, all of them making travel by vehicle a pain in the ass.

Finally, the van got out and started to roll away. Before the late-afternoon shadows could resettle, I zipped in and took the spot. We got out, and I made a quick stop at the meter to use my company sigil to pay for parking.

"You know this place?" Zev asked.

"Yep," I said as we headed down the sidewalk toward Cass's day job at a bar called Wonderland. "Been in a few times, actually." That made my initial unease at Cass's recognition seem silly. Clearly, just because I didn't remember seeing her around, didn't mean she didn't recognize me from my previous visits.

"This your neighborhood bar?"

I laughed. "Kind of?" When he looked at me, I shrugged. "Lena and I've done happy hour, a couple of live shows, and even a storytelling night here. She dragged Evan in once when they had a free game night at the arcade."

Zev looked around, taking in the limited options for something of that size. "Seriously?"

"Seriously," I answered. "Just wait. You'll see."

We turned into an alley, where a door sat in the brick wall of a building from the late 1940s and a dumpster was tucked in at the far end by a gray cement-block wall. Cracked pavement mixed with packed dirt sat out front. An abandoned bike, the pedal kind, wrapped in a rusted chain was left forgotten on a nearby utility pole. There was no sign, no neon lights, nothing to indicate anything worthwhile existed here.

The only thing that stuck out was the dark-haired man leaning in the propped-open doorway. Black cargo pants, tight black T-shirt, and sunglasses, he wasn't someone anyone wanted to start something with. He watched us get closer, his arms crossed over his chest, and a polite smile on his otherwise hard face. "Afternoon."

I flashed him a smile, and even though it was closing on five o'clock, I answered, "Afternoon. I was wondering if Cass was around?"

He studied us for a moment, and with his sunglasses firmly in place, it was hard to tell what he thought, but we must have passed muster, because he straightened and ducked inside the doorway. A ruffle of magic washed over me, followed by the indistinct murmur of his voice. Clearly, he was giving Cass the heads-up. Sure enough, he reappeared and said, "Go on down. Just watch your step, yeah?"

"Thanks!" It never hurt to be polite. I slipped past him with Zev on my heels, and we made our way down a narrow set of stairs shrouded in dim lights and matched by an equally thin metal railing so patrons wouldn't slip and fall.

Stepping off the last step, I moved into a three-piece eclectic mix of music hall that included the requisite bar, fairground-type arcade, and hole-in-the-wall restaurant. Exposed pipes ran overhead, a legacy from its former incarnation as storage space, and the brick walls were unmarred by windows. Instead, a huge set of double metal doors covered in spray-painted tags and sigils guarded an emergency exit. I knew from previous visits that they opened to a sloping loading ramp that led up to the street. Hanging metal art threw silhouettes over the interior and danced over the faux living room set up tucked under the stairs. On the bar's far end, patrons could shoot Skee-Ball, foosball, and pool for anyone who wasn't inclined to battle digital foes from twenty-some-odd years ago. Altogether, it was funky as hell, artistic without trying, and one of the coolest dives around.

It was also surprisingly busy for being a well-guarded valley secret, but then again, it was an hour into happy hour for the corporate crowd. Voices buzzed under the music, glasses clinked, and a couple of servers wove between seats, delivering drinks and food of the hot dog and taco type. I led Zev back to the bar, where bottles lined wooden shelves backed by a silver-laced mirror that would've fit into the 1800s. The lighting was brighter back here, probably so customers could watch the bartender work. I stood at the end, out of the way, waiting for Cass to spot me.

Sure enough, within minutes, she was headed our way, lips curved in a welcoming smile and her eyes partially hidden behind the purple lenses of her wire-frame glasses.

Her hair, a startling mix of browns, reds, blacks, and golds that couldn't possibly be natural, was in a messy topknot that matched the bohemian-slash-rock-chick vibe of her multi-hued peasant blouse and black leather pants.

I questioned her choice of pants because leather and Phoenix weren't always a good mix, but the rest of her outfit worked. Based on the number of appreciative looks coming from the males, and a few females, gathered nearby, it worked on multiple levels.

She stopped in front of Zev and me, braced her hands wide on the bar top, and leaned in to pitch her voice above the din. "Ms. Rory Costas, lovely to see you again."

"Cass," I returned. "I'm sorry I didn't recognize you earlier." When she gave me a quizzical look, I explained, "At the party in Sedona."

Amusement washed through her face, and she waved off my apology. "No worries. Can I get you two something to drink?"

Since we were taking up her time, and I didn't want to be rude, I ordered an Arnold Palmer, and Zev asked for the same. I waited until she served our drinks, then asked, "Do you have a minute or two to talk?"

She cocked her head. "The party the other night, right?"

That wasn't quite the reaction I expected, but I went with it. "Um, yeah."

"The cops swung by a few days ago, told me what happened." Sympathy swept through her face, softening her smile into something wistful. "I feel bad for him and his family." She shook her head and straightened. "Life sucks sometimes, you know?"

That about summed it up. "Yeah."

She looked down the bar, judged her patrons, then turned back. "We've probably got three minutes, tops, but I'm happy to help if I can."

I nudged Zev, who handed me his phone. I turned it

around so Cass could see the screen filled with Jayson's face. "I was wondering if you saw this guy there the other night?"

She took the phone and studied it intently, her brow furrowed. Finally, she shook it slowly and handed the phone back. "Not at the party, but he's been in here a couple of times during the last month."

Excitement fizzled in my veins, but I kept it in check. "Was he alone when he came in?"

"No." Her gaze drifted past me and went unfocused.

I turned to follow her gaze, but nothing stood out. Just tables filled with worker bees determined to wind down. When I turned back, her brow was no longer lined, and her attention was back. Even her tinted lenses couldn't hide the sharp edge of curiosity.

She angled her chin toward the far corner. "He sat over there with another guy, same one both times."

"You're sure?" Zev asked.

Cass gave him a saucy grin. "He was a bland rum and Coke, his buddy was a Corpse Reviver, so yeah, I'm sure. Tricky drinks are my specialty, and folks like to try and stump me."

I almost asked what a Corpse Reviver was, but I decided to ask next time Lena and I came in. "Were they friendly?" When she cocked an eyebrow, I clarified, "The two guys. Did they seem like friends or..."

Catching my drift, she finished, "Acquaintances, definitely. And last go-around, things got a bit tense between the two. Not that I could hear anything, but your rum and Coke was all up in Corpse Reviver's face. Not that it did him much good. Reviver kept his cool and didn't back down until your guy gave in. I remember thinking Reviver best watch his ass, because Rum Boy all but lit the place on fire with his glare when his buddy took off."

"You ever see either one of them before the two showed up together?" Zev asked.

She shook her head. Down the bar, someone called her name and held up an empty glass. "Excuse me," she said then strolled down to take care of her customer.

I looked at Zev. "You think Corpse Drinker is the Heretic?"

Zev stared after Cass, his expression considering. "Probably." He turned and leaned back against the bar, his gaze drifting over the space. "I wonder if they have cameras in here?"

I cradled my drink between my hands, spinning it slowly on the bar top. "If they do, it will take time to get the footage, and that's if it hasn't been deleted." I leaned in a little more, going on tiptoe to see over the edge. I spotted what I was looking for and dropped back down. "They've got an Astra Security sticker near their register. I'll see if Evan can work his magic." I sucked down some more lemonade and tea then sent another text to Evan. At this rate, I was going to end up with cramps in my fingers.

My drink was almost gone by the time Cass returned. "Sorry about that."

I waved off her apology. "We won't keep you long, Cass. Just one more question—could you describe the Corpse Reviver guy?"

She drummed her fingers against the bar and frowned. "I'm not sure how helpful I'll be. I'm better with drinks than faces," she said apologetically. "Unless you've got another photo for me?"

I shook my head.

"All right. Let's see… brown hair, average height. Didn't see his eyes, but he was clean shaven and dressed like most of the students that come down here. In fact, he had a backpack, if that helps."

She was right—the drink preference *was* more descriptive.

"And you're sure you haven't seen anywhere else around here?" Zev nudged. "Like a coffee shop or e-café?"

Her frown returned, and she shook her head slowly. "No, sorry. Just the meets with your boy."

"Thanks, Cass," I said. "We appreciate the help."

Zev echoed my thanks and tucked a hefty tip between our glasses. We said our good-byes and made our way out. Zev and I discussed our next steps, not that we really had any until we heard back from Evan. We'd started throwing ideas around about grabbing something to eat when my phone vibrated with an incoming text. Since we were only a few feet away from my car, I waited until we were inside, doors closed, engine on, air conditioner blowing, before I pulled it up and read it with equal parts exasperation and exhilaration. "Of freakin' course."

"What?"

"Evan's got movement on Jayson's truck." And we were a good thirty minutes out from its location near the construction site. It was times like this that Phoenix's sprawl was a pain in my ass and my gas tank. Giving my texting digits a rest, I hit Evan's number, and the sound of the line ringing filled my speakers.

"He's heading south and east," Evan said without bothering with a greeting. "I tagged Lena with the route since she was closer. She said if he stops, she'd wait for you before approaching."

"Send me the route. We'll head over now."

"Where are you?"

I let Zev fill him in while I concentrated on getting us out of the maze of downtown.

"How fast can you get ahold of the bar footage?" Zev asked.

"If Wonderland is like most of Astra's clientele, their recordings are backed up to a cloud service. Navigating their firewalls will take some doing, especially since I've got to stay invisible. I can't risk Astra thinking the Guild is poking around, because they won't hesitate to bitch about privacy violations to the director."

And no one wanted the Guild Director on their ass. "Just be careful, Evan."

"No shit, Sherlock," he shot back. "I like my job and my head as they are. Pissing Sylvia off is not my agenda."

Even knowing it was a stretch, I still asked, "Anything new on the glasses or money?"

"You do realize I'm navigating in a cesspool blind, right?" he snapped.

"And here I thought you were the undisputed king of all things electronic," I teased.

"You want answers faster, stop asking me for shit," he shot back. "Go bug Lena and leave me alone." With that, he hung up.

My lips twitched at Zev's sigh.

"Feel better?" he asked as he pulled up the GPS and the route Evan had sent us.

"Yep." It was so easy to ruffle Evan's feathers, which was why I could never resist. "Much."

TWENTY-NINE

"THE TRUCK STOPPED MOVING in that neighborhood," Lena said as we stood in an office-complex parking lot between my car and hers. The sun was starting to drop, and evening was setting up shop, muting colors and cooling temperatures. "I don't know what he's up to, but he circled through like three times. Since I didn't want to spook him, I parked here and figured I'd wait him out."

I couldn't fault her logic.

"We're not that far from Metro Center," Zev pointed out, zooming out on the map until I could see the mall and the blue dot of Jayson's truck.

The two-story office complex sat right between the two. The parking lot was about half full, likely because so was the building if the "space for rent" signs were anything to go by. Someone hadn't considered location when they built it. Not only was it tucked in an older residential area behind the mall, but across the street was a sprawling apartment complex. Jayson's GPS placed him well inside the collection of cinder-block homes.

Lena turned in the direction of the dot. "I asked Evan to

see if Jayson had any obvious connections to a home around here, but nothing came back."

I gave her a once-over, knowing her additional request coming on the heels of mine had likely set off the electro mage's infamous temper.

She caught my look. "What?"

"Just checking for singe marks."

She rolled her eyes.

"I don't like this," Zev said.

Yeah, neither did I. I could think of two reasons for Jayson's strange ride—either he was holed up somewhere, knowing his ass was being followed, or it wasn't Jayson in the truck at all. I wasn't sure which one I was hoping for.

"Did you get a look at the driver?" I asked my friend.

She shook her head. "Not enough to be sure it was him behind the wheel. I had to stay back, and with the tinted windows…"

I turned to the one who hunted on the daily. "How do you want to do this?"

Zev studied the map for a moment. "Recon first." He handed back my phone and strode away. He came to a stop under the trees offering sporadic shade in the lot.

Magic brushed against me, and I shivered. "Come on," I muttered to Lena, then we both headed over to Zev.

As we drew close, there was movement in the branches, then a brown body with blue-gray wings and a long tail burst from the tree and flew off. We came up to Zev, who had one hand on the tree's trunk, the other holding a feather down by his thigh, and his head angled back and up.

This close to him, the itch of his power was inescapable, and to combat the urge to rake my skin raw, I thickened my Prism until it became only a minor irritant. Lena and I waited in silence while Zev and his avian eyes did their thing.

It was always strange to watch him work with animals, and

this time was no different. His movements became distinctly animalistic as his head twitched in small ticks. When his gaze hit mine, I repressed a flinch. Nothing human stared back, just an unearthly blue glow that emanated deep in his dark eyes.

"Truck's empty." So was Zev's voice. It was so detached, it was unnerving. "There's no movement in the house."

"Don't get too close," Lena warned. "If Jayson's making deals with the Heretic Key, there's no telling what kind of traps they may have left behind."

Zev shifted his weight then stilled. We waited as the minutes ticked by. Then, with stilted movements, Zev brought the feather up and snapped it in half with an audible crack. Magic winked out, and my Prism eased back in response. Zev shook himself like a dog shedding water. He dropped the broken feather to the ground. "I think someone dumped the truck."

"Only one way to find out." I turned toward the cars, leaving the other two to follow.

"We'll take mine," Lena said.

I didn't argue. It wasn't like my Mustang had much by way of a back seat.

We made our way through the neighborhood of single-story homes that dated back at least three decades. Each had a garage to one side, doors and two large windows to the other, and small front yards in either gravel or grass. Some of the short drives held cars, most family oriented and older, while others were parked out on the street, two tires up on the sidewalk to stay out of the way.

The white Ford truck sat in a dirt side yard of a corner house. It was actually a smart place to dump it since the side yard was accessible from the street and the block fence sat far enough back for a car to fit. Even better, there were no windows on that side of the house.

Lena pulled over in front of a house just down from the corner, then we all got out.

Lena took the lead. "Give me a minute to make sure we're clear."

Zev and I hung back and let her do her thing. Magic pulsed in the air as she walked slowly around the truck, occasionally crouching down. Finally, she waved us over. "A few faint whispers of magic, but no trace of a hex."

A Traditionalist didn't do magic, so who did? "Right, then my turn." I tried the driver's door handle, unsurprised to find it unlocked. I had a feeling whoever had ditched it was really hoping someone else would come along and take it for a joyride or simply steal it. I studied the interior. An insulated mug sat in the cupholder, and a charging cord dangled from the wide console, but nothing electronic was attached. I leaned in, noting the electronic push start and the papers in the passenger seat. I pulled back and looked at Zev. "There's papers in the passenger seat."

He went around to the other side, opened the door, and started to thumb through them. "Documents relating to the Metro construction," he said, putting them back.

I eyed the driver's seat. "How tall would you say Jayson is, Zev?"

"I don't know. About an inch shorter than me?"

That would make Jayson just over six feet tall. "Whoever drove last was shorter." I reached up, grasped the chicken handle, and hauled my butt into the driver's seat. I stretched out my feet and grabbed the wheel. "My guess, they're under six."

Zev eyed the passenger side. "No signs of blood." He backed out and opened the back passenger door. "Nothing back here either."

I flipped open the top of the console and found more charging cords, a battered baseball hat, and crumpled-up napkins. I closed it then leaned forward to feel around the floorboard.

Nothing. Hmm.

I hit the electronic starter as Zev reappeared on the passenger side, and the engine turned over.

Lena moved into the open space next to me. "You found a key?"

I shook my head.

"Stolen?" she pressed.

I nodded. "I'm betting whoever moved it used a relay method."

"Relay method?"

"Typically, it's a device that can capture the key's signal and mimic it," I explained. "But it's not limited to tech. A good electro or mech mage could create a charm or sigil that does the same thing." I turned to Zev, who was listening in. "You didn't find a remote or anything in the back?"

He shook his head.

"Then I'm betting they used a spell, which is why it's still working."

"Explains the magical traces," Lena added.

"Also adds weight to it not being Jayson who was driving," Zev pointed out. "He's a Traditionalist. He can't wield magic."

"Which is why he would hire someone like the Heretic in the first place," I said, restating the obvious. As frustrating as it was, I felt like we were stuck running in circles.

"Yeah, but to create a magical copy of the key's signal, they would still need access to his key at some point," Lena said.

"Which could've happened at any time." I shut down the engine, swung my legs out, and waited for Lena to back up before hopping out. "Which means we're still stuck with nothing."

Zev closed the passenger-side doors and came around the hood to join us. "We need to go back to the construction site, because whatever happened, happened there."

"What do you mean?" Lena asked.

"He ghosted his one-o'clock meeting," I explained. "And then his truck didn't move until—what? Five thirty? Five forty, right?"

She nodded.

I looked at Zev. "That's a hell of a long shot. We're looking at a window of close to four hours where something went down."

"It's all we really have until Evan pulls something useful," Zev shot back. "If you've got another idea, I'm all ears."

Unfortunately, I was all out of inspiration. I shoved the driver's door closed. "Fine, let's go back to the mall and poke around."

•••••••••••••••••••••••••••••••••••••

We left Lena's car in the Doubletree's lot then beat feet to the chain-link fence that stood as the lone barrier on the mall's north end. Zev used a charmed blade to cut through the metal links while Lena and I stood on either side, keeping an eye out. There were no lights or signs of life on this side of the site, likely because all that remained of the mall was a pile of rubble. We would have to circle our way around to the west side, where Jayson had done his initial disappearing act. Thankfully, the encroaching evening provided us cover.

Zev straightened then yanked on the fence, bending it back to create an opening. "Go!"

I ducked in first, then Lena and Zev followed. There was another metallic protest, not quite as loud, as he shoved the cut section back. It wouldn't stand up to a close inspection, but it was good enough for now. Zev put away his knife and held out what appeared to be two small stones. "Ready?"

Lena took one, and I took the other, noting the rasp of the pitted surface under my touch. *Not stone, bone.* The bead warmed as Zev's magic spilled out in a wave, raising every hair on my arms. I gritted my teeth at the uncomfortable sensation, knowing the cloaking spell was a necessary evil. I dropped the bone into my pocket. None of us wanted to spend our night in lockup. Zev's magic slunk around me, nipping here and there, before finally settling in like a mohair suit—itchy as hell but bearable.

"Remember, stick to the shadows as much as possible." He turned and headed west at a quick pace.

It took a good ten minutes to make it to the still-standing portion, which was plenty of time for me to get ready for my part in tonight's adventure.

In the hotel parking lot, we'd discussed the best option for tracking Jayson. I'd offered up my ability to visually follow magical signatures, arguing that if the Heretic was involved, his trail would be there. They'd agreed that was worth a shot, but pointed out that Jayson's lack of magic might be easier to trace considering there were bound to be various levels of mages working on the construction site and we had no real idea of what the Heretic signature would look like. She and Zev exchanged ideas on how best to track the lack of magic, and Lena won the honor of playing leader when she told Zev she had a spell at the ready. I got the part of keeping an eye on any magical echoes. Between all of us, there had to be something here to track.

We stopped behind a huge dumpster with a line of sight to the office trailer. The three of us dropped to our haunches and huddled close.

Zev looked to me. "Go."

I closed my eyes, and as I inhaled, I thinned the natural barrier between me and my magic. I exhaled and opened my eyes to see a soft network of faded colors threaded through the night. "Ready."

"You're up," Zev told Lena in a low voice.

She pulled out a deep-green crystal the size of a finger and the color of an antique bottle and brushed the rune etched on it. Power flashed then settled into a hum.

I inched back and rubbed my arms at the additional weight of magic. *Ugh, this sucks.*

Lena flattened her palm and held the now-glowing stone over it. After another pulse of power, she released the stone. It hovered over her palm for a long moment then slowly started to spin, like a compass needle. Her eyes now lit by a matching green, she stared toward the mall. She straightened, keeping her hand under her magical compass. "I think I've got it, but it's hard as hell to hold on to."

She took the lead, and we followed her to the office trailer. Not an unexpected stop, but then instead of heading into the abandoned mall, she took us around the trailer and back toward the mall's center. Navigating the rubble wasn't easy, but I used a hand on Zev's belt a couple of times to keep my footing. Magical traces flickered here and there, brighter where mages had put their abilities to work during demolition and muted where time had passed since the use of active power.

It was a disconcerting way to see the world, and I couldn't keep it up for long without earning serious physical repercussions like blinding headaches and nose or ear bleeds. It'd only taken enduring those fun times once or twice to learn my lesson. I'd been working on strengthening my magical muscles, but like most training, it took time to master, and I wasn't quite there yet.

We slipped around rubble and half-standing walls until we came across what had probably served as the loading area, based on the various concrete ramps. Here, the echoes of magic were a jumbled mix of colors, some clear and bright, some faded around the edges. The brighter flashes were triggering a warning ache, so I knew I would have to shut it down soon.

Until then…

"I think they're currently working this area," I warned the others. "Lots of magical activity here."

We wove through the remains until Lena stopped abruptly, her compass swinging back and forth. She oriented herself and her charmed locator until she stood in front of a still-standing section blocked off with plywood and heavy chain.

I came up to her side and sucked in a sharp breath. The green crystal's magic pulsed with eagerness. "There's something in there."

Zev moved up to the padlocked chain and wrapped his fist around the lock. A burst of deep sapphire erupted, swallowing the green traces of Lena's tracking spell. Under Zev's magical grip, the lock released its hold with a dull thud.

The ache in my head started to spread, setting up a deep throb behind my eyes. I was running out of time. Concerned about what or who waited for us beyond the makeshift door, I tightened my visual hold and dug deep.

Using as much care as he could so the heavy links wouldn't rattle, Zev unthreaded the chain, but the sound still felt overly loud in the quiet evening. He carefully let the chain dangle from its anchor then wedged his fingers in the narrow opening so he could grip the edge of the plywood sheet. He looked to me and Lena, a silent signal to be ready.

Lena nodded, but something in my expression must have given me away, because I got a heavy frown. I gave a small shake of my head, mutely requesting he let it go. I moved in front of Lena, since I was the best one to take a direct hit and still walk away. In position, Prism at the ready, I dipped my chin.

Zev yanked the plywood free.

THIRTY

THE ONLY THING that rushed out of the dark opening was air, but the trails of magic wound deeper into the inky interior.

"Okay, that was a bit anticlimactic," I muttered, earning a snort from Lena and a brief glare from Zev.

Lena edged out from behind me and moved closer.

"Hold up." I grabbed her arm, keeping her from going inside. "Let me go first. Something in there is emanating magic."

I brought a small orb of light into being and set it just above my left shoulder, keeping my hands free. Then, ignoring the age-old wisdom of all horror flicks, I headed into the darkness. Even with Zev and Lena at my side, it was nerve-wracking as hell moving through the distorted interior shrouded in misshapen shadows.

Magic clouded the air. Zev's was coiled to strike at any threat. Lena's hovered at the ready. Mine was locked around the three of us to hold off a direct attack. The muddied echoes of earlier activity lingered, adding to the jumbled colors. Trying to follow the right trail while stumbling through the obstacle course of plaster piles, broken boards, and junked objects was a challenge. The third time my shin slammed into something solid, I stopped cursing and bit my tongue. I would be black and blue tomorrow, but so long as there was a tomorrow, I was good.

I squeezed around a jammed security door and stepped out into a wide hallway that was oddly undisturbed. Motioning my light higher, I realized we were in what had been the back-office hallway. Red-and-yellow arrows with markings like NO/MCI or MF 4" IHP marred the dingy walls, clearly notes of some kind for the demolition crew. A couple of doorways broke up the space, one with a door still intact, the other with the door propped drunkenly in its frame.

Magical trails wove back and forth down the hall. I moved off to the side, studying the mishmash of magical echoes as Lena and Zev joined me. Once Zev stood at my side, his hair streaked with dust, I kept my voice low and said, "The strongest trail leads to the door on the right, but it's already fading."

"We still need to watch our step," Zev reminded me unnecessarily.

Nerves stretched to a breaking point, I couldn't stop my sarcastic "Wasn't planning on charging in."

Lena waded in. "If it's fading, it means whatever happened, happened, right?"

I nodded.

"Then let's do this."

Once more in the lead, I ignored my racing heart as we got closer to our target. Nerves, trepidation, and the rising press of Zev's and Lena's power left my knees watery, but there was no way I would let either of them be unprotected. I stopped a few feet out from the door and braced.

A brush of fingers over my hand had me turning to see Zev step forward, and a ribbon of power ripped the wonky door out of the doorway and slammed it up against the far wall. Using the cover of the explosion of sound and movement, I slid around the doorjamb, ready for anything.

Or maybe not. "Holy shit!" I breathed, frozen in place by shock.

A sharp inhalation from Lena and a harsh curse from Zev weren't too far behind.

Eyes wide with panic, mouth opened in a silent scream, and his body bowed in an unnatural arc, Jayson Guzman hung in midair in the center of the room. Ugly brown cords of magic flecked with smoldering orange wove in and out of his body like a macabre loom, all of it anchored in a peculiar pattern.

"What the hell?" I breathed as we stood just inside what had clearly been someone's office.

"Tell me what you're seeing." Lena's demand snapped through my horror.

"Um…" I tore my gaze away from Jayson's agonized face and studied the magic holding him captive. "Thick ropes of magic, brown with orange embers, but they're stitched into his skin." I was having trouble putting the image into words, not only because of how disturbing it was, but because the longer I studied it, the more intense the throbbing became in my head. "I can't see a starting or end point. It's almost as if he's been woven into the spell itself."

Lena moved to my right and inched closer to Jayson.

"Careful," I warned her as she got scarily close to one of the thick bands.

She stopped, and Zev moved out from my left. He stayed close to the walls, which kept him out of reach of the magic. When he got to the far side opposite me, his gaze hit mine, and he frowned. "Rory, stop. Pull back. You've got a nosebleed."

I reached up and brushed at my nose. Sure enough, when I looked at my fingers, they were stained with blood. "Dammit." I didn't want to stop. Something warned me we needed to watch the spell, but I also didn't want to liquefy my brain. Reluctantly, I let my second sight go. Instantly, the throbbing in my head eased off, and I shuddered in relief.

Assured I wasn't going to kill myself, Zev turned back to his task, studying the walls then crouching to study the floor.

"What are you doing?"

"Searching for a sigil or a rune," he answered. "Something that would anchor the spell."

An invisible wind kicked up, and I turned to see Lena, eyes glowing, trace a symbol in the air. Under Jayson, power ignited and raced over the space where he hung. It spiraled into a figure eight that wrapped around him without touching the walls or the floor. Green sparked and flickered before fading slowly, but the afterimage lingered a few seconds longer.

"It can't be that easy," she murmured.

Feeling a little useless in this mess, I moved closer to her and did my best to block out Jayson's silently pleading gaze as he twisted and turned in the invisible net. Every couple of seconds, his body flinched with sharp, jerking movements, and his mouth moved in another silent scream. "What can't be that easy?"

"This is a Torturer's Dream cast," she said. "It's designed to break a prisoner without leaving behind any physical marks."

I dug through my memory and pulled up a dusty piece of information. "Because you can feel everything like it's really happening, but it's all in your mind, right?"

"Yeah, in this case"—she cast an analytical eye at Jayson—"I'm betting he thinks his bones are breaking one by one."

"He's not going to last much longer." Zev's voice was hard and cold. "If we don't get him out of that, his heart will give out."

A little voice wondered if that wouldn't be more merciful than turning him over to the Council.

"I can get him out of this easily enough," Lena said, talking with Zev as if a man weren't hanging between them, going through excruciating pain. Not that what was happening around him could penetrate the unrelenting agony he was enduring. "But if we are dealing with the Heretic, there's no way there's not something in here to make sure it won't be interrupted before it finishes its job."

Finally, something I can help with. "Actually, there is." When Zev opened his mouth, I held up my hand. "Don't. You know there's no way I'd let Lena risk shit if I can keep her, and you, safe. And since Christina wants him alive, we really don't have a choice."

He relented but not happily. "Fine."

I turned to Lena. "Tell me what I need to watch for."

She grimaced. "I can't tell you exactly, but you remember the symbol we showed you? The one the Heretic uses?"

I nodded, recalling the curlicues that made up the sigil.

"Look for that—"

"Or for something new to pop up," Zev chimed in.

"Right," Lena agreed. "Or for some new sigil or cast to pop up with no notice." She held my gaze, hers deadly serious. "You have to be fast, Rory, because every second counts in countering a hex."

"Got it." But to be doubly certain, I reinforced my Prism, curling it around Zev and Lena like a protective cloak, ready to yank it closed with a moment's notice. I thought the two could handle themselves, but… I calmed my mind, knowing any distraction could be fatal when I was juggling so many details.

I blinked, and the network of magic flickered into life. I studied every line, searching for the unique sigil or anything that struck me as off. Finally, I said, "Go."

Lena's power flared up in a burst of red and green. Her power was so fierce, it was hard to keep an eye on the brown cords. Her magic snaked through the brown cords without touching it or Jayson. When it overlapped the entire cast, Lena said, "Now."

The green ribbons snapped down and wrapped around the brown cords, tightening and squeezing, thinning out the initial cast. Jayson thrashed. Ugly sounds escaped from his throat, and his eyes rolled back in his head. Lena didn't relent, tearing apart the spell piece by piece, yanking the ugly lines from Jayson's writhing body. When she tore the final cord, his body dropped to the floor, and two things happened at once. A flash of dull yellow came from the far corner, near Zev, and the Heretic's sigil erupted from Jayson's chest toward Lena.

I yelled a wordless warning and pointed while I jumped in front of Lena.

Magic, dark and grasping, hit my shield like a sledgehammer, spreading like diseased oil as it searched for an opening. It hurt. It raked sharply against my Prism, followed by agonizing spikes of unrelenting pressure as it tried to claw its way to me.

"Hurry," I urged Lena through gritted teeth.

"Tell me," she demanded from behind me.

"Heretic sigil, black, oily, trying to rip me to pieces. Yellow something over by Zev." I couldn't even see Zev. The attack spell determined to get to me blocked my view. But I could hear a disconcerting hum that was growing louder. I held the spell back, barely. It was like holding a maddened tiger at bay with only my hands. "It's humming. I don't think that's good."

Lena didn't say anything else, but red flames erupted from the edges of the magic attached to my Prism. For a moment, nothing else happened, then those flames roared to a blinding height and swept over the oily spell like a wildfire. The black magic curled under Lena's attack but couldn't escape the hungry flames. The viscous magic withered to ash, and I stumbled back as the pressure disappeared.

Lena caught me before I fell on my ass. "You okay?"

I managed a nod as my muscles quivered in protest, then the hum from earlier was back, but it was growing louder. I looked to Zev and found him wreathed in a blue-white power as a black cloud poured through the air vent near the ceiling, the humming now a deafening buzz. Horrified, I flinched back as I realized it wasn't a cloud but a swarm.

Fear stole my breath, and I squeezed out a thin scream, even as I pushed my Prism toward him. "Zev!" I was going to be too late.

A coil of blue rushed the swarm, and the two entities collided. At first, it appeared as if the swarm had swallowed the blue coil, but then azure streaks flickered in the mass, picking up speed and brightness. I had a heartbeat to think, *Oh shit*, then the room filled with an explosion of searing blue-white light.

I shut my eyes, turned my head, and lifted a hand uselessly in front of me. Blind, all I could do was listen and flinch as small objects hit my body like a demented hail. It took long moments to blink my vision clear, but when I was finally able to see, I could make out the twisted insectoid bodies that littered the floor at my feet.

"Eww." I stumbled back, unable to look away from the disgusting mix of cockroach and spider. "What the hell are those?"

"Demonic swarm." Zev shook out his hair, and dead bugs rained down.

I flinched as shudders wracked me. Multi-legged creatures and I did not get along. Unable to watch as he brushed more of those carcasses off his shirt and jeans, I turned to Lena. "You okay?"

She was batting at her hair, her face twisted in a grimace. "Yeah, I'm good, but I call dibs on the shower." She looked behind me. "Let's go see if he survived."

Together, we went to where Jayson lay crumpled on the

ground, and Zev joined us. We spent a few minutes brushing more of the dead swarm off Jayson's body before Zev put his fingers to the man's neck then wiped his finger against his thigh. "He's breathing."

"I doubt he'll wake anytime soon," Lena said. "Actually, I'm not sure if he'll wake at all."

Zev straightened. "Probably for the best since we're going to have to haul him out."

Feeling sore and battered and knowing the other two had to be experiencing the same, I said, "Hang tight. Let's see if there's something we can use to move him."

Lena rose and stretched. "Sheesh, Zev, I'd think a hunter like you would carry a levitation spell."

His eyebrows rose, and his tone was dry when he said, "Kind of a waste when there's not much to haul back."

Lena snorted in dark amusement.

I left the office and crossed the hall to the other room, hoping to find maybe a chair or something. The second office was cluttered with broken furniture, but I found a dented aluminum hand cart under a pile of display shelves.

"Found something," I called out, yanking it free. I dragged it over to the doorway. "It's not much, but it might help."

Lena looked over and laughed. "Oh, this'll be fun."

Even Zev was shaking his head, but he still crouched and grabbed Jayson under his arms. "Help me?" he asked Lena.

She grabbed Jayson's feet, and together, they brought him out into the hall. Then the three of us cursed and huffed until we had him in place. Zev used a binding spell to strap his limp body to the handcart's frame. So long as we kept it angled back, we shouldn't lose him. I hoped.

THIRTY-ONE

"THIS WON'T MAKE it back the way we came," I pointed out. Once we were clear of this area, there was too much rubble and debris cluttering the floor.

Lena studied the hall then pointed back beyond where we'd come in. "Over there is an emergency exit. Let's see where it leads."

Zev took control of the handcart, and I walked beside him, just in case Jayson started to slip. Lena stayed ahead of us and was using her shoulder against the heavy exit door.

"Hold him for a second," Zev said.

We switched places. Not that it was easy to keep the handcart steady. Jayson was dead weight.

Zev nudged Lena out of the way. "I've got this."

She gave him space, and he put his hands on the door. There was a surge of magic, then the door flew back as if punched by an invisible fist. Cool air swept in as Zev angled his head and shoulders through the doorway. When he pulled back, he said, "Looks like we're on the far end, but we should be able to take him out through the parking lot."

Zev reclaimed the hand cart, then together, we hauled an unconscious Jayson through the mall parking lot. We did our best to stay in the shadows, which wasn't hard since the construction was on the opposite side. By the time we hit the hotel parking lot, I was ready to drop, and Lena didn't look much better. Even Zev looked exhausted. Thankfully, Jayson didn't stir.

Although we'd parked on the back side of the hotel, where we should be safe from prying eyes, we weren't taking chances. Zev kept his cloaking spell in place as we got Jayson's limp body into Lena's backseat. I got in too, leaving Zev and Lena the front. I slumped in the backseat as the last press of magic slipped away, leaving me drowning in exhaustion, physical and mental.

Zev pulled out his phone and hit a number. "It's Aslanov. I'm bringing someone in." Whoever was on the other end must not have needed much more, because that was the extent of the conversation. Then he was dialing another number. This time, the conversation was a bit longer.

"Hey, Locke, can you meet me at the Guild? I've got a delivery for the Council." He paused. "Yeah? Good. No, that's okay. Tell him I'll fill him in tonight. Right, yeah, later." This time when he hung up, he sat back and rubbed his face.

I found enough energy to lean forward. "Not to be a pain, but I'm not leaving my car up here." No way did I want to come back to find my baby stripped.

"Don't worry," Lena said as she turned out of the hotel and onto the street. "We'll swing by so you can grab it."

"You can follow us to the Guild," Zev added.

Instead of whining, I murmured, "Got it." I looked over at Jayson. He was still out and slumped in the seat. I didn't envy what lay in store for him. No one ever aspired to being questioned by the Council, and if Christina confirmed he was the reason Devon was dead and Max was in a coma? I couldn't squash the thought that he would have been better off to have died under the Heretic's spell.

Which reminds me. "Zev, won't the Heretic come after him now? Especially since Jayson can identify him?"

"Only if he wakes." Zev twisted in his seat so he could see me. "And I hope he does."

I studied the grim cast to his face, and I knew. "You're going to hunt him, aren't you?"

Zev held my gaze without blinking, answering without saying a word.

We got my car, and I followed Lena and Zev to the Guild, where Zev's friend and coworker, Locke, was waiting for us, along with Councilwoman Christina Velasquez and the Guild Director. The two women watched Zev and Locke drag Jayson from Lena's car and into the Guild. Lena and I then spent the next couple of hours answering Christina's questions. Once she'd gotten all she could from us, she turned her attention to Jayson. Zev insisted on being part of the man's interrogation. I didn't feel the need to join them, and neither did Lena. So Zev escorted us out of the Guild offices. At my car, he gave me a kiss and told me he would be in touch.

Four days later, I finally got a text asking if I was free for the evening. I explained it was game night and invited Zev to join us.

Now, Zev was sprawled on my couch, his fingers playing with my hair while I sat on the floor next to him, thumbing through a car magazine. Lena and Evan were curled up in the loveseat, and a single thin slice of pizza was the lone survivor of our game-night feast. On the coffee table was the in-progress board game that we planned to return to after eating. The TV droned in the background.

Lena groaned. "I'm so stuffed."

"Shouldn't have had that last piece," I said without

looking up from an article discussing the new injector prototypes.

A throw pillow smacked my head. I snatched it up and sent it back.

"So, Zev," Lena said, "I heard Jayson finally woke up. So you going to share what happened with him?"

I froze but didn't look up. It was the same question I'd been dying to ask, but I hadn't found a chance.

The fingers in my hair stilled then tugged gently. I let my head fall back until I was staring up into Zev's face. His dark gaze drifted over my upturned face, and humor lightened his eyes. "She win the coin toss?"

"Nope, just got there before I did."

He let me go, so I set my magazine aside then turned, putting my arm on the couch cushion, and watched him.

"The Council is holding him for trial next month, on murder one and attempted murder," he said. "Christina wanted it sooner, but Max's condition has remained critical, and the other Council members advised she wait."

"Charges could be amended," Evan pointed out.

"Yeah, they can, but in this case, moving quickly will cause more problems than being patient."

"Jayson's family," Lena said, and Zev nodded.

That made sense. As staunch Traditionalists, the Guzmans could cry foul and rile the public about the highhanded nature of the Arcane Council. "I'm surprised it hasn't been all over the news."

"I don't think that will remain the case for long," Zev said. "The Council plans on making a statement next week, but the end result is a given. Jayson conspired with a known outcast mage to kill one or more members of a prominent Family. He's not going anywhere anytime soon."

"They get an ID on the Heretic?" Evan asked.

"Basics that are easily changed—hair color, eye color, that

kind of thing," Zev said. "If he stays true to form, he'll go back underground."

"What does that mean for you and your hunt?"

He shrugged, but it didn't disguise his frustration. "Makes it harder, but Christina is insistent that he be found and brought to the Council."

And what the Council wanted, it got, one way or the other. That did not bode well for me since it meant Zev's responsibilities would cut into our time together. That was an unfortunate reality, but hey, that was life, right? I would make do with what I could get. "Did you find out why Jayson went after Max and Devon?"

"Just Max, actually," Zev said. "Turned out, Devon was collateral damage. You know the rumors about Jayson and his wife separating?"

I nodded.

"They were true. Including the fact she was leaving him for another man, who just happened to be a mage."

I winced. "Ouch. That definitely stings."

"Oh yeah. In fact, to add insult to injury, the board for Guzman and Sons was threatening to vote him out based on his poor financial decisions. Guess who was the suggested replacement?"

"Who?" Lena asked before I could.

"The same guy his ex-wife hooked up with."

My mouth dropped open, but it was Lena who said, "Wow, that's... that's..."

"So wrong," I finished.

"Yep." Zev popped the *p*. "It was the proverbial straw that broke the camel's back. Jayson blamed Max for losing the respect of the board, and the fact that Max was part of an Arcane Family and a mage just made it even easier to make him the epitome of everything that was wrong in Jayson's life."

"So he goes out, invests in Max's treasure hunt, and hires a black-market mage to kill him?" It was hard to believe.

"Jayson needed an in, and Max's weak spot was his passion for treasure hunting. It was easy enough to convince Max he wanted to invest, it was just money, nothing personal. Max wasn't one to turn down extra funds for his hobby, so he went with it." Shadows drifted over Zev's face. "Hiring the Heretic was Jayson's way of throwing off suspicion."

"Because no one would think of him if magic was involved in Max's death," Evan said.

"Right," Zev agreed.

"That's pretty twisted." Maybe I shouldn't be so surprised, but man, people continued to shock me. Of course, mixing greed and resentment created a very toxic brew. "Poor Max," I murmured. "I think if he had a choice, he'd rather have Devon than a treasure."

We all fell quiet for a moment, then Lena broke it. "You said Max was still critical?" When Zev nodded, she asked, "What do the doctors say?"

"They're cautiously hopeful," Zev said. "Each day he pulls through is another win."

I wasn't sure if Max would feel the same when he woke, considering the news that waited for him. "I hope he makes it."

A murmur of agreement came back.

On one of the side tables, my phone vibrated. I crawled over and checked the screen to find an unexpected text. "Hey, looks like Sabella's heading back into town next week." I sent back a reply.

Lena frowned. "I thought she wasn't flying in until the end of the month?"

"That's what she said." I watched the three dots rotate on my screen.

"She and Christina are friends," Zev pointed out. "I bet she knows about Max."

The three dots disappeared, replaced by Sabella's message.

"You'd win that bet. Looks like she decided to cut her visit short." I told her to send me her flight information so I could be there when she got in.

"So back to business as usual?" Lena asked.

I shot Zev a look. "For some of us, yeah."

"Well, if you need my help, Zev," Evan said, "ask."

"I might take you up on that," he said.

"Good." Zev wasn't the only one frustrated by the Heretic's disappearing act.

As the conversation turned to more mundane things and our unfinished game, I couldn't help but be relieved I was out of the mess. It sucked that Zev was still in it knee-deep, but then again, that was his job. Was I worried? Hell yes. Going up against an outcast Key was a serious cause for concern, but then again, the nature of his job wasn't exactly good for my nerves. Still, it was an integral part of who he was, and being in a relationship with him meant letting him be free to be who he was. It was only fair since he did his best to return the favor.

At least with Sabella coming back to town, she would keep me busy and unable to obsess over Zev's safety. Sometimes, it sucked being in love, but it wasn't like my skills would help him catch the Heretic. I just had to have faith he could keep his ass covered.

But it wouldn't hurt to stick close just in case, and I knew just who to ask to ensure I wasn't completely cut out. There were benefits to being the niece of one of the most powerful Arcane Family matriarchs, and it was time to cash in.

THIRTY-TWO
FOUR DAYS LATER

HE WAS HOLED up in a shitty hotel room in the middle of nowhere, watching as the white-toothed, overly tanned broadcaster tried to pull off a believable facsimile of compassion while sharing the grim news of the death of Maximiliano Vasquez, nephew to Arcane Councilwoman Christina Velasquez. The camera shifted to the grief-stricken faces of Max's parents, who stood at the entrance to a Phoenix hospital as Christina addressed the press.

He ignored the "blah, blah, blah" part and focused on the faces standing behind the family, off to the side. He recognized Sabella Rossi-Giordano's patrician features and the stoic face of Emilio Cordova, but it was the shadowed features of the dark-haired man that held his attention. He got off the bed and got close to the TV, leaning in to study the image. *Was that… It was!*

Zev Aslanov, the Cordova Arbiter and current pain in his ass, stood behind Emilio, next to a shorter, younger woman.

If that fucker Jayson hadn't been such a pussy, he wouldn't have been stuck in this dump and checking over his shoulder. Instead, he was out half his fee and on the fucking run from that dick of an Arbiter. And that was not good for business.

First thing first, make an example out of Jayson on why it wasn't smart to fuck with the Heretic. Then… Well, then it was Aslanov's turn.

*Brace for impact as Rory and Zev take on a Council contract, an obscure relic, and a lethal vendetta in **BLIND SPOT**.*
Now available at your favorite bookseller!

ARCANE TRANSPORTER

Go back to the beginning with Rory and Zev in this thrilling urban fantasy series!

Meet Rory Costas, Arcane Transporter, and strap in for a spellbinding ride through the Arcane world, where powerful magical families make the mafia look like choirboys and connections are everything.

GRAVE CARGO

When a questionable, but lucrative delivery job takes an unexpected turn, will Rory survive the collision or crash and burn?

RISKY GOODS

A dead mage, a missing friend, and an unpredictable alliance merge into a volatile package sending Rory careening through the Arcane elite's deadly secrets.

LETHAL CONTENTS

A failed assassination, a kidnapped ally, and a treasonous scheme pit Rory and Zev against a devious enemy determined to watch Arcane society crash and burn.

COLLSION COURSE

A last-minute Guild delivery, a cursed treasure, and a nefarious revenge scheme sets Rory on a collision course with one of Arcane's most wanted mages.

BLIND SPOT

A council contract, an obscure relic, and a lethal vendetta blindside Rory with dodgy ramifications and pitch her into a slippery tailspin.

TERMINAL DRIFT

Seething Family hostilities, a stunning classic car, and a last-minute trip to Sin City send Rory barreling towards a pivotal crossroad that will either put her in the driver's seat or hurtle her into oblivion.

ABOUT THE AUTHOR

"This story is an emotional roller coaster, from betrayal, anger, fear, love…" —InD'tale Magazine

Jami Gray is the coffee addicted, music junkie, Queen Nerd of her personal Geek Squad, Alpha Mom of the Fur Minxes, who writes to soothe the voices crammed in her head. Her series combine high-stakes urban fantasy and edgy paranormal romantic suspense into books you don't want to put down. Buckle up and get ready for a wild ride through the fascinating worlds of the Arcane, the Kyn, the PSY-IV Teams, and the Collapse.

Come visit Jami's website at **https://www.jamigray.com** and stay up to date on what kind of trouble she's getting into and when you can expect to join in.

amazon.com/author/jamigray

instagram.com/jamigrayauthor

facebook.com/JamiGrayWriter

threads.com/@jamigrayauthor

goodreads.com/JamiGray

bookbub.com/authors/jami-gray